enjoya

Happy reading!

Philip Cox
July 2014

Philip Cox is married with two children, and lives near London. He pursued a career in banking until 2009, when he took a break from financial services to be a stay-at-home father. Between changing diapers, Philip wrote *After the Rain*, which was published in 2011. *Dark Eyes of London* followed early in 2012. *She's Not Coming Home* is his third novel.

Also by Philip Cox

After the Rain
Dark Eyes of London
Last Man's Head

SHE'S NOT COMING HOME

PHILIP COX

Front cover image by sameliaz8

Back cover image (paperback version) by
soelin/flickr

www.philipcox.moonfruit.com

ACKNOWLEDGEMENTS

All I did was write the book! Other people helped during the process. I'd like to thank Nicole Allen of the Boston Police Department, Chetan Parmar and Sagar Chauhan for their help with the cover titles, Anne Poole for help with the text, and finally the managements of the *Rochester Democrat and Chronicle* and of the New York Downtown Hospital, New York City.

Plus of course, all those who have read *After the Rain* and *Dark Eyes of London* and have spread the word.

Chapter One

IT WAS THE Day Before It Happened.

The third Tuesday in January.

The day after Martin Luther King Jr day, so to all intents and purposes it was the beginning of the working week.

'Do you want eggs?' Matthew Gibbons called out, his voice competing with the sound of Daffy Duck and Bugs Bunny on the television and the first batch of eggs cooking on the stove.

No answer. Matt shrugged and continued stirring the eggs.

'More Coco Snaps, Daddy,' called out a voice from the table behind him.

'Hold on a second,' said Matt, quickly turning some eggs over.

'I'll get them, Daddy,' came the reply.

'No, wait. I'll -' Matt moved the pan off the stove and turned round, just in time to see his five year old son lean over and knock the cereal box on the floor, spilling its contents everywhere.

'Oh, Nathan, no,' Matt wailed as he knelt down to pick up the box.

'Sorry, Daddy,' said Nathan quietly.

Leaning over, Matt reached under the sink and pulled out a small dustpan and brush. He swept up the mess and emptied the grains into a bin. Stood up and put the box back on the table.

'More Snaps, then?'

Nathan thought for a few seconds, then said, 'No. I don't think so.'

‘Fine. Want some eggs then? Or just toast?’

‘Just toast please, Daddy.’

‘Okay. Let me just finish the eggs.’

Matt turned back to the pan of eggs.

‘Just toast please, Daddy.’

‘Yes, I heard, sport. Just hold a second.’

‘And jelly.’

Matt raised his eyes. Was just about to say something when he heard footsteps coming down the stairs. He looked up as his wife Ruth wandered into the kitchen.

‘Do you want eggs?’ he asked again.

Ruth started to pour herself a cup of coffee.

‘French toast?’ she asked, taking a sip.

Matt said nothing. Just stared at her.

‘Forget the French toast. Eggs will be fine,’ Ruth said, sitting down at the table. She sniffed. ‘Don’t burn the bacon.’

‘Shoot.’ Matt pulled the tray of bacon from the stove. Just in time.

He served two plates of bacon strips and eggs and sat down at the table with Ruth and Nathan.

‘Daddy, you forgot the toast,’ said Nathan insistently just as Matt picked up a piece of bacon.

‘I’ll get it,’ Ruth mumbled as she got up and put a slice of bread in the toaster.

‘Two slices,’ said Nathan.

‘Two?’ asked Ruth. ‘You sure?’

‘Sure, Mommy. One for me and one for Mr Rex.’ Nathan held up a rubber Tyrannosaurus Rex.

Matt looked up. ‘I thought Mr Rex was a meat eater.’

Nathan grinned.

‘Silly me. One piece of toast. And some bacon for Mr Rex.’

Matt picked up a strip of bacon and tossed it over to his son.

'You taking the car today?' Matt asked as Ruth sat back down again. 'Or walking?'

Ruth looked up at the wall clock. 'Oh, I'll walk in today. Take advantage of the fresh air. Then you can have the car at least.'

'Well, don't go across the common tonight.'

'Do I ever in the dark?' Ruth asked as she got up and buttered Nathan's toast.

'Well, come back via Charles.'

'No. I'll use Tremont and Beacon.'

'Charles is quicker.'

'Yeah, but my route is more interesting.'

Matt shrugged and finished his eggs.

'What's your plan for the day?' Ruth asked, wiping her mouth and straightening her clothing.

'Well, after I've dropped little Mr G off at Bambinos, I'll double back here. I'll need to fix that broken guttering out back and the handrail down to the cellar needs fixing.'

'Should keep you busy.'

'Only got two days vacation. Plan to make the most of it.'

'You back to work Thursday, then?'

Matt finished his coffee. 'U-huh.'

Ruth walked over to him. 'Well, I'll be off now. See you tonight.' She reached up and kissed Matt, then leaned over to kiss Nathan on the top of the head. 'Bye, sweetie.'

'Bye to Mr Rex!' Nathan called out, spraying the table with toast and jelly.

'Bye Mr Rex!' Ruth called out from the front door.

‘Right, Mister,’ Matt said after he heard the door close. ‘Time to get you ready for Bambinos.’

Half an hour later, Matt and Nathan were walking slowly down the street.

‘Are you coming to pick me up tonight?’ asked Nathan. ‘Or is Mommy?’

‘Me tonight, sport. I’m not at work today, but Mommy is. So you drew the short straw.’

Nathan frowned. ‘Short…?’

Matt laughed and ruffled his hair.

‘Forget it. I’ll pick you up tonight.’

Bambinos kindergarten was on Chestnut and Spruce, just three blocks away from Matt and Ruth’s. Matt kissed Nathan goodbye, said he would see him at four that afternoon, then walked back home, picking up that morning’s *Boston Herald* on the way back. Another cup of coffee while he scanned the newspaper and cleared away the breakfast things, then out to the garage for the stepladder to start his list of chores for the day. He had two days’ off from his job at the bank; or rather time off earned for working the last four Saturdays to cover absent colleagues. Either way, he intended to make the most of it.

He had lunch at twelve as he finished the *Herald*, then that cellar stair rail. At one o’clock precisely, his cell phone bleeped. As expected, it was a text from Ruth.

Hi, hows ur day? x

He replied: *v busy. cu tonite x*

He noticed the cellar walls needed a fresh coat of whitewash. A job for tomorrow.

It was beginning to get dark as he walked Nathan back home later. As they turned the corner into West Cedar Street he pulled his coat collar tighter and shivered. He looked over in the direction of Boston Common. Ruth always enjoyed walking home, but on nights like this, he wished she had taken the car, or the bus.

'Come on, sport,' he said, ruffling Nathan's hair.

Being off, it was Matt's turn to prepare dinner. While Nathan sat on the couch watching Scooby-Doo, Matt made a start on the meal: fried chicken, green beans and mashed potato.

Just after five, his cell bleeped again. *Leaving now x.*

Ok x he replied.

The digital clock on the stove read 5:42 as the front door opened and Ruth arrived home.

'Welcome home,' Matt said as they embraced.

'Glad to be home. Mm, that smells nice. Where's Nathan?' Ruth replied.

'In there watching TV.'

Ruth leaned into the other room.

'Hi, honey. Have a good day?'

'Yes, Mommy,' Nathan replied, his gaze not leaving the television screen.

'He's so interested,' Ruth said as she joined Matt in the kitchen.

'Come on honey,' said Matt as he handed her a glass of red wine. 'How can you compete with Scooby, Shaggy, and co?'

The rest of the evening proceeded as normal. Matt told Ruth what he had done that day; Ruth did the same. Neither could find out exactly what Nathan had done at kindergarten, as he was only interested in Mr Rex and Mrs Brontosaurus. Then it was bath time for Nathan. Ruth read his bedtime story: a tale of three dinosaurs searching for a missing egg; the twentieth night in a row that he had wanted that story. When she came downstairs, Matt had just finished loading the dishwasher. He poured them both another glass of wine and they collapsed on the sofa.

'He asleep?' Matt asked.

'Went straight off.'

Matt smiled and leaned back on the sofa.

'What?' she asked.

'What what?'

'You were going to say something.'

Matt thought a second.

'Whatever it was, it's gone. What's the time, anyway?'

'Seven fifty.'

'That late, eh?'

'That late.'

They both took another mouthful of red wine and leaned back on the sofa. Matt slowly closed his eyes. By eight thirty they had both fallen asleep. Woke up around ten thirty and went to bed.

As he brushed his teeth, Matt started to feel amorous. It has been a busy day for both of them, but it was only ten forty-five…

He checked on Nathan, and walked back into his and Ruth's bedroom. Ruth was fast asleep. Matt got in beside her, leaned over, kissed her forehead, then lay down beside her.

He switched off the bedside lamps and was asleep in minutes.

Breakfast. Work. Dinner. Bed.

A normal day.

Their last normal day.

Chapter Two

AT THAT TIME of year sunrise was just after seven and sunset at four thirty. It was still dark when Matt awoke the next morning. Still heavy eyed, he checked his watch. It was six forty. On a normal weekday, he would get up at just after seven. Ruth would follow twenty minutes or so later, as Matt always liked to be first in the shower. If Nathan had not woken by himself by seven thirty, then one of them would wake him. After a normally hurried breakfast Ruth would set off for her job in the Boston offices of Cambridge Pharmaceuticals. She worked just under two miles from home and most days walked to and from the office. If the weather was too bad, and it was only heavy rain that affected her routine, she would take the bus. She could drive, but hated the regular gridlock on Boston's streets. Her morning route would take her across Boston Common between Beacon Street and Tremont Street and would take her twenty-five minutes. On the way home during the winter months when it was dark, mainly due to Matt's insistence, she would in effect walk around the park, up Tremont as far as the Park Street subway station, up Park Street, then along Beacon as far as Spruce, to resume her normal route. This circumnavigation of the Common would add another ten to fifteen minutes to her journey.

Ruth tended to leave around eight fifteen, ten minutes or so earlier if it was her turn to drop Nathan off at Bambinos. Matt would leave ten minutes later, unless it was his turn to drop off Nathan. Matt worked as a Personal Banker for the Bank of New England in the bank's branch in the Custom House District. He would generally drive, braving the traffic. As Personal Banker, he had the luxury of a parking space at the rear of the bank. The bank opened its doors at 9:30, and Matt would arrive a few minutes before nine.

This morning seemed to be starting differently. In the darkness of their bedroom, Matt turned over and felt for Ruth's sleeping body. Maybe they could start the day doing what he was hoping to finish the previous day doing…

Instead of Ruth's waist the first thing Matt could feel was the sheet. He moved his hand around searching for Ruth, but found nothing. Sleepily, he half sat up and looked across to her side. It was empty. He sat up further, blinking. He thought he could just make out the sound of the shower running. He pulled his hand out from under the covers. Ruth's side felt cold to the touch; she must have been up for a while.

He checked the time again, groaned, and lay back down, rubbing his eyes. A few seconds later he reached over and switched on the small bedside light. The room was bathed in a faint yellow light.

At that moment the bedroom door opened and Ruth came in. She was wrapped in a black towel and rubbing her hair with a smaller matching towel.

'How long have you been up for?' Matt asked, still not fully awake.

Ruth looked over at the gold carriage clock on her dresser.

'Half an hour or so, I guess,' she answered, sitting down at the dresser. She picked up a brush and started to brush her wet hair.

'Couldn't you sleep then?' Matt asked, now sitting up on the bed.

'No.'

A little surprised at the brevity of his wife's reply, Matt stood up, fumbled in his shorts, then shuffled over to the bedroom door.

'Might as well get up myself,' he said quietly, scratching the back of his head.

'You don't need to. It's still early.'

'Too late. I'm awake now.'

As he wandered down the hallway to the bathroom, he stuck his head round the half opened door to Nathan's room. In the faint green glow of the night-light, he could see the top of Nathan's head, sharing the pillow with a plastic stegosaurus. Nathan stirred slightly as Matt gently closed the door.

As he stepped into the shower, Matt could hear Ruth switch on the hair dryer. He showered himself, shampooed his hair – twice, as he normally did – then blindly reached out of the shower cubicle for the towel rail. Almost dry, he wrapped the towel around his waist, and returned to the bedroom. As he passed Nathan's room, the door slowly opened, and his son was standing in the doorway, blinking and scratching the top of his head. Clinging onto Mr Stegosaurus, he was wearing blue and yellow pyjamas decorated with various dinosaurs.

'Good morning, sport,' Matt said, ruffling his son's hair. 'Sleep well?'

Nathan nodded, yawning.

'You want to come in and watch some TV while Mommy and I get up?' Matt asked.

Nathan nodded and shuffled after his father.

'Look who I found outside,' said Matt as he returned to the bedroom.

'Morning sweetie,' said Ruth, turning round as she dried her hair. Nathan jumped up onto his parents' bed, reached over for the TV remote, switched it on, and tabbed down to a cartoon channel. Ruth turned round and continued with her hair.

Matt was the first to get dressed. 'I'll go put the coffee on,' he said. 'Come with me, sport; let's get you dressed.'

After getting Nathan dressed, Matt went down to the kitchen and started the coffee. Out of the corner of his eye, he saw Ruth come in the kitchen.

'You want eggs?' he asked, pouring out two cups of coffee.

Ruth said nothing.

'Well?' Matt said, passing her a cup.

'Well what?' she asked.

'Do you want eggs?'

Ruth sipped her coffee and looked at him blankly.

'Eggs?'

'Sorry, miles away. No, no eggs thanks. Think I'll just have this.'

Matt shrugged.

'Suit yourself. Where's Nathan?'

'He- oh, he's still upstairs playing with the dinosaurs.'

'He'd better come down for breakfast,' said Matt walking to the foot of the stairs. 'Or he'll be late for Bambinos. Nathan! Breakfast!' he called out. Shortly they could hear Nathan's footsteps running down the stairs. Now clutching both a stegosaurus and a tyrannosaurus rex, he sat up at the table.

'Cereal and toast?' Matt asked.

'Yes please, Daddy,' answered Nathan, as the T Rex began to chase the stegosaurus around the table.

'I'll take Nathan to Bambinos today, if you like,'

said Ruth from the back of the kitchen.

'No, it's all right, I'm off today -'

'I can walk in via Bambinos. Drop him off on the way.'

'Fine by me. I can make an early start.'

'Early start on what?'

'Whatever I do today. Might start off by tidying up downstairs.'

'Mm. Good idea.' Ruth finished her coffee and stood up. 'I'm just going upstairs to get ready for work. Nathan, ten minutes, okay?'

'Okay, Mommy.'

Nathan finished his toast and ran upstairs to brush his teeth. Then he and Ruth reappeared in the doorway, ready to go. Matt went over to kiss his son goodbye.

'Have a nice day, sport,' he said, bending down. 'Don't be too hard on Mrs Hardy.'

'Harding,' corrected Nathan.

'Harding. Right. I'll pick you up this afternoon.' More of a question, directed at Ruth.

Ruth nodded. Reached up and kissed Matt.

'See you,' she said, and led Nathan to the front door. Her hand stopped at the lock and she turned back and went over to Matt, who was still in the kitchen doorway. She reached up and kissed Matt again, more tenderly than before brushing her fingers down his cheek. She smiled and went back to the door, where Nathan was waiting.

'See you both tonight,' said Matt. 'Pizza okay for you, sport?'

'Yes please, Daddy.'

'Pizza okay?' he mouthed at Ruth.

'Sure,' she nodded, then opened the door and left with Nathan.

*****

Not having anything particular planned, Matt intended to have a leisurely day. A few chores to attend to, but nothing major. Just to potter about in the house and the yard, pick up Nathan, then prepare dinner. As dinner was frozen pizza, the meal wouldn't need much preparation.

Mid-afternoon, he strolled round to Bambinos, picking up a *Herald* on the way.

'We still having pizza tonight?' asked Nathan as they walked home.

'Sure thing, sport.'

'Cool,' said Nathan, as he skipped along next to his father.

Just before five, Matt took some trash out to the garbage can. It had been dark for some time, a cold wind was picking up, and it was beginning to rain. Once back inside, he shivered and picked up his cell phone.

Beginning 2 rain, why not get bus? he texted Ruth, knowing what her response would be. There needed to be at least twelve inches of snow before she gave up her walk home.

Sure enough, a couple of minutes later came the reply: *leaving now*.

Matt laughed, shook his head, and switched the oven on to cook the pizza. The clock on the stove read 5:05. Ruth should be home around 5:45. The pizzas should be ready about then.

At 5:50 he turned off the oven and pulled out the well-cooked pizzas.

'I'm hungry,' said Nathan, who had wandered in from watching TV in the den. 'Where's Mommy?'

‘Just running a bit late, sport,’ said Matt. ‘Should be home by six.’

But Ruth didn’t come home by six.

Or seven.

Or eight.

Chapter Three

POLICE LIEUTENANT DETECTIVE Sam Weber shifted in his chair. After two hours sitting in the same spot, it was becoming really uncomfortable. His partner, Detective Frances Mancini, looked over.

'Getting restless? You want another coffee?' she asked, standing up and stretching.

'Yeah; go on,' Weber grunted. He stood up, stretched, and hitched his pants up. As Mancini walked down the hospital corridor to the vending machines, Weber tucked his shirt more into his pants. Strange, he thought: would have thought the more weight you put on, the tighter your clothes would get. Seemed to be the opposite with him. Maybe he should set about losing some weight. Last time he checked, he was 210 pounds; overweight according to the department medic. That's the price you pay, he told the doc, when all you eat is fast food on stakeouts. And your wife leaves you for a twenty year old. And you give up smoking.

'Why not eat healthier?' the doctor had asked. 'More salads for example?'

'Doc, you gotta be kidding,' Weber had replied. 'If you think I'm sitting all night in the freezing rain and snow eating just a Caesar salad, you're on a different planet.'

He watched Mancini as she walked back with two paper cups. Hell, she kept her figure. But then she was fifteen years younger than him, and probably got more exercise.

'Here you go, Sam,' she said, passing him a cup

of black coffee. 'Number six, is it?'

'You forgot breakfast. Eight or nine,' he grunted, swigging back some coffee.

'Jeez, if I had that many in one day I'd be walking on the ceiling.'

Weber looked at his watch.

'It's just after eight now,' he said. 'Assuming she doesn't wake up between now and nine, then we're out of here.'

Weber and Mancini were in the Massachusetts General Hospital. Around midday they had taken a call about a mugging at the Brigham Circle T station. The attack had left the victim, a woman in her sixties, unconscious. The only two people who witnessed the attack, albeit from a distance, described the assailants as white youths wearing hoods. Both witnesses said the two ran down Huntingdon Avenue. Weber and Mancini drove around the Huntingdon area in case they saw anybody answering that description, but had no luck. It all happened out of range of any CCTV cameras, so Weber and Mancini's best option was to wait for Ms Washington to regain consciousness.

The ambulance went direct to Massachusetts General, or MGH. The nearest hospital to the Brigham Circle was in fact the Beth Israel facility on Brookline, but since just before last Christmas had been partly closed for refurbishment, so the nearest was Mass General, a couple of miles further on. Weber and Mancini arrived just after the ambulance, at just before one o'clock. They had no option but to wait for Ms Washington to regain consciousness, but five hours later she had not done so. At seven they would be relieved by the night duty, unless she woke before then, in which case they would leave after they had taken her statement. They both had mixed feelings: keen to get away after a twelve hour shift, but determined to catch whoever had given this little old lady the head injuries she had sustained.

Whilst waiting, they had speculated on the motive for the attack. Quite early on, they had dismissed race as a motive, as the attack was quick, opportunistic, and her purse had been taken. Assuming she was carrying anything. Violent crime had been a problem in that part of the city for some time; in fact statistically a person had a 1 in 101 chance of being a victim in the past five years.

'Eight forty.' Weber stepped over to the door of the room where Ms Washington was lying. He peered through the small rectangular window. She was still in a coma.

'Is it true,' asked Mancini, 'that the longer they're unconscious for, the lower the chances of her waking up?'

Weber looked over at his partner. He shrugged.

'Possibly. Possibly not.'

Mancini looked through the window.

'She looks so sad, lying alone there.'

'Eh?'

'All alone, I mean. No relatives at her bedside.'

'Well, until she wakes up, or somebody reports her missing, or somebody finds her purse with all her ID, she'll only have us at her bedside.'

'She must have been on her way to work,' said Mancini. 'Hence the name badge. She must be missed there.'

'Or on her way home. Nobody at home to miss her. No wedding band, remember. No ID. Just a little blue badge,' said Weber, looking through the glass again. 'Celeste Washington,' he muttered. 'Who are you?'

‘Sam, it’s time,’ said Mancini. Weber looked round and saw Detectives Anderson and Troy walking down the corridor. The night shift.

‘Hey guys,’ said Troy. ‘No luck yet, I take it?’

‘Nah,’ said Weber. ‘Nothing yet.’

‘O’Riordan wants us to stay here for the duration if need be,’ Anderson said. ‘Says to catch these bastards is a priority.’

‘He wants you to stay here all night?’ asked Weber.

‘He figures the old lady probably won’t make it, so it’ll be a homicide. More pressure to clear that up. Says even if she comes round for a while, she might give us something to go on.’

Weber shrugged. ‘Guess we’ll leave you to it then. Relieve you here in the morning. Unless something happens in the meantime,’ he added.

‘Sure,’ said Troy as he and Anderson took their places on the orange plastic chairs.

‘I bet you twenty bucks,’ said Weber as he and Mancini walked back to their car, ‘that she won’t make it. She's been like that for too long.'

‘Then it’s murder.’

‘You got it in one.’

Just as they reached their car, Weber’s cell phone rang.

‘It’s O’Riordan,’ he said as he pressed the button to answer. Mancini sat in the car while her partner took the call.

‘What is it?’ she asked as he joined her in the car.

‘O’Riordan called to ask a favour.’

‘Which we can’t turn down.’

‘Mm. Anyway, a call’s come in about a reported missing person over in Beacon Hill.’

‘Not her back there?’

‘Unlikely. Did she look to you as if she came from Beacon Hill?’

‘Not really.’

‘No. Some guy’s wife three or four hours overdue from work. Asked if we could go over, take some details to pass over to the MPU.’

‘Why us? Surely he knows we’re on overtime now?’

‘He said we’re the nearest. Should only take half hour or so.’

‘Great,’ said Mancini, fastening her seat belt. ‘Another night when I don’t see my kids.’

Weber started the car and pulled away. Turned into Fruit Street then left into Charles. A couple of minutes later he pulled up outside the Charles/MGH T station.

‘What are you doing?’ Mancini asked.

‘Get the subway home,’ said Weber. ‘I can take care of this.’

‘You sure?’

‘Get out before I change my mind. Go kiss your kids goodnight.’

‘Will you be okay?’

‘It’s Beacon Hill. I should be all right,’ Weber said sarcastically.

‘Lieutenant, I owe you one.’

‘Tell me about it. Now get.’

After Mancini had left, Weber took the car along Cambridge, then down W Cedar. Pulled up outside the address he had been given. He got out of the car and looked around. With its red-brick Federalist townhouses and vintage gaslights, this street was typical of those in Beacon Hill, one of the most exclusive residential neighbourhoods of the city. Some months ago, he was involved in a case in an apartment building a few blocks away from here. The case involved the beneficiary of an elderly woman's will trying to sell her apartment. Only thing is, the woman wasn't dead yet. Weber remembered the place was on the market for close to half a million dollars; slightly underpriced according to the real estate agent. This house here - Weber assumed three bedrooms, maybe two bathrooms, a yard out back, a garage somewhere - must be close to a million, maybe more. He wondered if that was why O'Riordan wanted this guy interviewed tonight. Would have had to have waited till morning if it had been some other parts of the city.

Weber took a deep breath, climbed the four steps to the front door, and rang the doorbell.

Chapter Four

MATT LOOKED ANXIOUSLY at the kitchen clock. It read six twenty. Nathan was busy munching his fourth slice of pizza, oblivious to his father's concern. Matt picked up his phone and sent Ruth a text, asking where she was, was she okay?

After five minutes there was still no answer, so he rang her number. After six rings, it went to voicemail.

'Hi, it's me. Where are you? Have you stopped off somewhere on the way? Call me back soon as you can.'

He pressed the red button to disconnect and, rubbing his chin with the phone, walked to the front door. Looking back to check that Nathan was still occupied, he opened the front door and stood at the foot of the four steps that led down from their door to the street. He looked up and down the street. A couple of cars went past and a man and a woman walked by the other side of the road. Matt looked down the road, in the direction of Mount Vernon Street, searching for Ruth's figure coming up the road. He saw nothing. What the hell was keeping her? It was unlikely, he thought, that something had happened to her walking home, a mugging or such like; the route she took was well-lit and at this time of the evening there were still plenty of people around. Unless she went across the common. When it was still light at this time, she would take a shortcut using one of the many paths across Boston Common, past the Boston Massacre Monument, the Soldiers and Sailors Monument on Flagstaff Hill, and the Founder's

Monument just as she approached Beacon Street. Sometimes she would pause a while by Frog Pond, to do some people watching.

Matt had never been a great fan of the Common: it was never maintained to the standard of the parks he was used to back home, and even he would make a point of avoiding it after dusk. The north west corner of the park was the location of Park Street subway station, and since an incident two or three years ago when he, Ruth and Nathan were approached by one of the many panhandlers congregating around the station environs, he would always try an alternative route. Especially if he was with Nathan. He had turned down the guy's request to stand him for a meal, and, expecting him to move onto someone else, was surprised and unnerved when he followed them right up to Beacon Street, shouting at them.

He would frequently check with Ruth that she was not walking across the Common after dark, and she would always confirm she took the street route. The pathways across the park were used by tourists heading for the Visitor Center on Tremont, although rarely after dark, and by pedestrian commuters on their way to and from the office towers. Like Ruth. In all the time they had lived there, he could not recall an incident on the Common with a commuter, but Matt was naturally cautious. Ruth would always say he was being too cautious, and she was quite safe walking home, even in the dark. Maybe it was the fact that she had grown up on the streets of Boston, whereas Matt had not.

He turned back up the stairs and went back indoors, closing the door. Joined Nathan in the kitchen.

'Enjoying your pizza, sport?' he asked.

‘Mm,’ replied Nathan, his mouth full. ‘When’s Mommy coming home?’

‘Soon,’ Matt said distractedly. ‘Soon. She – she’s been held up at work, and so she’ll be a bit late home.’

‘Can I have some more pizza?’ asked Nathan.

Matt looked over at him. ‘Sure,’ he said. ‘Have a piece of mine.’ He passed over a slice from his plate. Suddenly he was not so hungry.

It was now six forty. He rang Ruth’s cell again, hanging up before it went to voicemail. Maybe she had been delayed after all. He found his contacts list, tabbed to the entry *Ruth – Office* and dialled. The line clicked a few times, then he heard an automated voice telling him his call could not be completed as dialled. Wrong number. Strange: maybe he had programmed his phone incorrectly; he would always use Ruth’s cell phone when he contacted her. He called 411 and gave name and address of where Ruth worked. He dialled this number, which was nothing like the number he had on his cell, and listened. The number rang four or five times, then a recorded message saying that the offices were now closed and would reopen at 9am the next morning.

He hung up and decided to try some friends. Tabbed down to the number for Ruth’s best friend, Gail Smith, and dialled. As he waited for a ring tone, he thought about Gail. She lived the other side of the city, so it was unlikely that Ruth would have gone there; maybe they had arranged to meet up after work, and Ruth had forgotten to tell him. Or had, and he had forgotten.

‘Nathan,’ he called out. ‘Did Mommy say anything about Auntie Gail the other day? About meeting her?’

'No,' said Nathan, as he threw Mr Tyrannosaurus up and down. 'Daddy, can I have some ice cream now?'

'I'm just on the phone. Help yourself. Not too much now. Just two scoops.'

Gail's phone rang five or six times, then went to voicemail. Matt left a message, then hung up. Who else to call? No point calling his parents, and Ruth had none. Or rather they had both died a few years before he and Ruth met.

Rubbing the side of his phone, Matt returned to the kitchen. He took a slice of cold pizza from his plate, and started to chew. It took a long time to chew; he had lost his appetite. Nathan, on the other hand, had covered his face with chocolate ice cream.

'It's getting late, sport,' said Matt. 'Let's get you cleaned up and in the bath.'

'When's Mommy back?' Nathan asked.

'A bit later. If you'll already asleep, she'll go up and tuck you in.'

After twenty minutes in the bath and a bedtime story – involving dinosaurs – Nathan was tucked up in bed. He yawned.

'When Mommy gets home, you will get her to come up and tuck me in again, won't you?'

'Promise,' whispered Matt, kissing Nathan on the forehead and straightening his quilt. He turned the night light on and the room light off.

'Night, sport,' he whispered from the bedroom doorway. There was no answer: Nathan was asleep already.

Matt quietly made his way downstairs and back into the kitchen. Threw away his uneaten pizza and put the dishes into the dishwasher. Dialled Gail's number again. Left the same message again.

He went online, found local new pages for the online pages for the *Herald*, the *Globe*, and the *Beacon Hill Times*. Looked for any traffic reports, any accidents. Any crimes reported for that evening. It was probably too early, he reflected.

He tried ringing Ruth's phone again, and Gail's. Both times the call went to voicemail; both times he left the same message as before.

He stepped outside again, and looked up and down the street. No sign of anybody. A bus roared past the end of the street, along Mount Vernon. He went back indoors.

He wondered about putting Nathan in the back of the car and driving round the streets looking for Ruth, but decided against this as it would be unlikely he would see her in the dark. And he didn't want to alarm Nathan.

He made himself a cup of hot tea and sat down in the kitchen. Almost nine o'clock. Something had to be wrong. He crept upstairs and looked in on Nathan. He was fast asleep. Good. Matt went back downstairs, picked up his phone and sat down in the kitchen. Took a sip of his tea. Looked up at the clock: past nine now. Time to call the police.

He got up the website for the Boston Police Department. His nearest station was in Sudbury Street. It gave a phone number. He started to dial, and then paused. Maybe he should be dialling 911. Thought again: as he had the actual station number: that might be quicker. If it got answered.

It did. A woman officer's voice answered the phone.

'Hello,' Matt said. 'I want to report a missing person.'

'A child, or an adult?' the officer asked.

'An adult. My wife. She's been missing over three hours.'

'Sir, how do you mean missing?'

'She was due home from work at six, but still hasn't arrived. I've tried calling her, on her cell phone and at her office, and to call one of her friends, but I can't get hold of anybody. She's *always* home by six. Always.' His voice started to quiver.

'What's your address sir, and where does your wife work?'

Matt gave the officer the addresses.

'Can you hold the line just one moment, please sir?' said the officer.

Matt was put on hold for half a minute or so, then the officer returned and said, 'Thank you for holding, sir. Somebody will be calling round to take some details in about the next half hour.'

'Thank you very much, officer.'

'You're very welcome, sir.'

Matt hung up and wandered over to the window. Looked out, and up and down the street, as best he could from the window. After a while he thought he could see a car moving slowly up the road, as if looking for a space to park.

Then came a bleep from his phone, advising of the receipt of a text message. His heart pounding, he ran back into the kitchen and grabbed the phone.

'For God's sake,' he hissed as he read the message. It was a text from his manager at work reminding him of a meeting he had to attend at 9 o'clock next Friday morning.

Just as he deleted the message, the doorbell rang. Glancing upstairs to make sure Nathan was still asleep, he went to answer the door. In the light from the hall, he could see that the figure at the door was early middle-aged, around five-six, overweight, and wearing a dark suit and blue shirt. His tie was loose with the top shirt button undone.

'Matthew Gibbons?' the figure asked.

'Yes, that's right,' Matt answered breathlessly. 'The police?'

The officer held out his badge and identity. 'Lieutenant Weber,' he said. 'In response to your call.'

'Yes, of course; please come in,' said Matt as he opened the door. 'Follow me through to the kitchen.' Weber closed the door and followed Matt.

'My son's asleep upstairs,' Matt said quietly. 'I don't want to disturb him. I had just made some hot tea; would you like a cup?'

'No thank you sir; I'm a coffee man myself,' said Weber. He indicated to a chair. 'May I...?'

'Sorry; please do. Please sit down.'

'Thank you, sir,' said Weber, half collapsing onto the chair. He took out a notepad and a pen. 'Now, you said when you called that your wife is missing.'

'Yes, she is,' said Matt. 'And I'm worried.'

He took a mouthful of tea.

'Very worried.'

Chapter Five

WEBER SCRIBBLED ON the front page of his notepad as if to test his pen was working. 'If we could take it from the top,' he said. 'I'll need some names first. Your first name, Mr Gibbons, and your wife's.'

'Matt. Matthew. Matthew Gibbons. And my wife's name is Ruth.'

'Okay. Now, Mr Gibbons: just tell me, in your own words, what has happened.'

'My wife hasn't gotten home from work.'

'I understand that, sir. But I need the sequence of events of tonight; what makes you believe she has gone missing.'

'All right.' Matt sipped some more tea. 'She went to work as normal this morning.'

'Where does she work?' asked Weber. 'What does she do?'

'She works in the offices of Cambridge Pharmaceuticals.'

'Offices in the city?'

'That's right.'

'What does she do there?'

'She's been there a number of years, and has had a number of different jobs there. She did tell me what her latest position there is, but frankly it was so technical, I didn't understand. Still don't understand exactly what she does there.'

'And what about you, Mr Gibbons. Are you at work? I noticed...' Weber indicated to the dinosaur backpack Nathan had left in the corner.

'I work for a bank. Downtown.'

‘Which bank? What do you do there?’

‘I’m a Personal Banker at the Bank of New England. I’ve had a couple of days vacation. Due back tomorrow. Is all this relevant?’

‘Just collecting information, Mr Gibbons.’

‘You don’t think her disappearance has anything to do with my job at the bank? I mean – we get shown security training videos where staff members’ family members get kidnapped for safe combinations, that sort of thing.’

Weber put a hand up.

‘Whoa, Mr Gibbons. Let’s not get ahead of ourselves. I am just collecting background information, that’s all. Standard procedure.’

‘Okay, okay. I’m sorry.’

‘No problem. Now, when your wife left for work this morning, did anything unusual happen? I mean, every household has their getting up and leave for work routine; was there any deviation from yours this morning?’

Matt considered for a moment. ‘No. No, I don’t think so.’

‘You sure?’

‘Yeah, sure.’

‘Okay. When she -’

‘Wait – there was one thing, I guess. I normally get up first, but this morning when I woke up, she was already in the shower.’

Weber nodded, as he continued writing.

‘Why? Do you think that’s important?’

Weber shrugged. ‘Going back to what I was asking: when she goes to work, how does she commute? By car? The T?’

‘No, she walks.’

Weber looked up. ‘Walks?’ he asked.

'Most days. Unless the snow's too bad or it's raining too hard. Always has done. Says she enjoys it.'

'And how long does the journey take her?'

'That depends. Mornings and in the summer – when it's daylight – she cuts across the Common.'

Weber nodded. 'It's quite a busy commuter route.'

'I know. But when it's dark, she takes a detour around the park. Tremont and Beacon. My idea, not hers. She does it to humour me.'

'And she would have taken this detour tonight?'

'Should have done, yes.'

'Sure. Backtracking to during the day. Some couples just say goodbye in the morning and don't speak until that night. Others are calling or texting each other every five minutes. Know what I mean?'

Matt nodded.

'Which category are you in?' asked Weber.

'The former,' said Matt. 'Unless there's anything that can't wait. A couple of guys at work are the other category. Drives me mad: I could be having a conversation with them, then bleep bleep, it's all over.'

'My partner's the same,' Weber smiled. 'Drives me mad too.'

'Your work partner?'

'What? Oh yeah. My work partner. Detective Mancini. Always on her cell. Don't understand what they can have to say all the time.

'Anyhows,' he continued, 'when she left for work, that was the last contact you had with her. Is that right?'

'Until around five. Just before she's about to leave, she sends me a brief text.'

'What does the text say?'

‘I’ll show you.’ Matt retrieved Ruth’s last message and showed it to Weber.

‘“Leaving now”,’ read Weber. ‘Is that pretty standard?’

‘Word for word. I think it’s saved as a template on her phone.’

‘So, when she does that, you have an idea when to expect her home? What about when you are at work?’

‘We both do the same thing. So, for example, I might text her at five thirty; so she knows I’ll be home about six.’

Weber turned again to the backpack. ‘How many kids?’

‘Just the one. Nathan. He goes to kindergarten. He’s upstairs asleep, I hope.’

‘Who takes and collects him?’

‘We take turns. In the morning Ruth drops him off, and I’ll pick him up. Next day I’ll do the drop off, and she’ll pick up.’

‘Generous employers,’ Weber commented.

‘Not entirely. Ruth’s contract is drawn up to reflect that, and she’s only paid the hours she actually works. I have to make the time up, on Saturdays or something.’

‘You said you’re on vacation. What happened then?’

‘Only yesterday and today. If one of us is off, we do both duties.’

‘Got it. So: she sent you this text just after five; so you would reasonably expect her home at...?’

‘Around five forty.’

‘And when she didn’t show?’

‘I left it till six then called her.’

‘Called or sent a text?’

‘Both. Several times.’

'Did you try her office landline?'

'Eventually.'

'Eventually?'

'I tried the number saved on my cell, but it wouldn't connect. Then I called 411 and got a totally different number.'

'Which you dialled?'

'Yes, but I got the office voicemail saying please call back in the morning.'

Weber raised his eyes to the ceiling. 'Great,' he said. 'Don't you just love that?'

He turned the page on his notebook.

'How long have you been married, Mr Gibbons?'

'Three years. But we've been together as a couple six. Almost seven. Nathan will be six this summer.'

'Happily married?'

'Sure.'

'Has there ever been – I'm sorry, I have to ask this – anybody else?'

'No. Never.'

Weber looked up at Matt and gave a brief smile. 'Any rows, or arguments, over the last few days? Anything to make her pissed off; making her stay away just to get back at you?'

'No, nothing. But she'd never leave Nathan.'

Weber looked up again. 'You'd be surprised, Mr Gibbons.' He paused a beat. 'Is there anywhere, anyone, she would visit rather than come home? Friends, girlfriends, her parents, your parents?'

Matt shook his head slowly. 'Can't say so. I tried her best friend's number when I couldn't get through to Ruth. But it went to voicemail.'

'Any call back?'

'Nothing yet.'

'Parents? Brothers and sisters?'

‘We’re both only children. Ruth’s parents died some years ago; before we got together, so I’ve never met them. My parents live on Cape Cod; we go see them every so often, so Nathan can see his grandparents. They and Ruth: well, they get on, I guess, but they’re not what you’d call really close. I think they disapprove, to be honest.’

‘Why?’

‘I’ve no idea.’

Weber paused.

‘Is your wife dependant on drugs?’

‘No. No way.’

‘Sorry. Procedural questions. When you last saw her, this morning, what was her mental, her emotional state?’

‘Normal. Nothing out of the ordinary.’

‘Nothing to give you concern?’

‘No. Nothing.’

‘Has she ever gone missing before?’

‘No. Never.’

‘Okay.’

Weber paused again. Then said, ‘Anything else you can tell me? That might be relevant.’

Matt thought and shook his head. ‘No, I don’t think so.’

‘Do you have a picture of her I can take?’ Weber asked.

‘Surely.’ Matt flicked through a letter rack behind the TV and pulled out a picture. It was a vacation picture of him, Ruth and Nathan. ‘All three of us,’ he said as he passed it to Weber. ‘Down at Busch Gardens, Virginia last summer.’

‘Thanks,’ said Weber as he put the picture inside the notebook and stood up. ‘We’ll get it copied and return it.’

'So what next?' asked Matt.

Weber scratched his nose as he spoke. 'This is what happens now. I take this information back to my Captain. He then passes everything to the MPU. The Missing Persons Unit.'

'And then?'

'And then they follow their procedures. Even though I have a lot of information here,' – he tapped his notebook – 'somebody from the MPU will be in touch with you. Most likely tomorrow. May have other questions to ask you. Then will liaise with you, keep you in the loop. They'll also give you a contact number just in case you think of any other information that might be helpful. Or if your wife reappears.'

'Okay,' said Matt. 'Thanks for your help. And for coming so promptly.'

'No problem,' said Weber, making his way to the front door. 'Hope it all gets sorted for you.'

He paused and glanced up the stairs. 'How's your son?'

'I told him Ruth had to work late. He's expecting to see her in the morning.'

'Don't focus on the worst case scenario. There could be a perfectly good explanation.'

'Sure. Thanks again,' said Matt as he let the Lieutenant out.

Matt slowly shut and locked the door, then quietly made his way upstairs to check on Nathan. His son was sound asleep, sharing his pillow with a pterodactyl. Matt moved the dinosaur onto the dresser and ran his fingers through Nathan's hair. Nathan stirred slightly. Matt leaned over and kissed him gently on the temple. Stepped over to the window, parted the drape and looked out.

Their neighbourhood was on a hill, and from Nathan's bedroom, Matt could see the lights from the vehicles travelling along Charles Street. He could also make out the flickering of light from a vessel on the Charles River Basin in the distance. It was a clear night, and the sky was full of stars, and the white and red lights from a couple of aircraft in the sky.

Yes, as the Lieutenant said, there could be a perfectly reasonable explanation. Maybe she had gotten fed up with him, but to leave Nathan?

His thoughts went to a guy he used to know years ago at High School, and a phrase he would always be using. For one, it was apposite.

I've got a bad feeling about this.

Chapter Six

MATT SLEPT VERY little that night. After the Lieutenant had left, and he had checked on Nathan, he tried Ruth's cell phone one more time. Then Gail's. Again, both phones went direct to voicemail.

In bed, he lay awake for hours, thinking over some of the things Weber had asked, and why he had asked them. He had *assumed* there was nobody else; at any rate, not as far as he was concerned, and Ruth had said or done nothing to indicate anything of that nature. In any case, walking out on him was one thing; leaving Nathan was another. In fact, the only variation on their normal routine was her getting up before him that morning. Hardly an indication that something was wrong.

After three or four hours' fitful and restless sleep, Matt came to just before six. Instinctively, he turned over to Ruth's side of the bed. It was empty, and cold: it hit Matt that she really was not around; it had not all been a dream. He sat on the edge of the bed and rubbed his eyes. What to do first?

He had to return to work for one thing; then try Ruth's phone again. If not her cell phone, then her work landline. Maybe try Gail again if he had no luck there. Presumably he would hear from the Missing Persons Unit Lieutenant Weber spoke about last night. And then there was Nathan. What to tell him?

By the time Nathan woke an hour later Matt had decided what to tell him.

'Where's Mommy?' he asked, scratching his head and yawning.

‘Oh, you missed her, sport,’ said Matt, ruffling his hair.

‘What?’

‘She’s very busy at work right now. She came in late, and had to go in extra early.’

‘Will she be back tonight?’

‘Should be, sport. Should be.’

Matt froze for a second, wondering if Nathan would accept what he had said, or ask more awkward questions.

‘Okay.’ Nathan turned round and shuffled into the bathroom.

Matt breathed a sigh of relief. That worked for now, but he would have to tell him more soon. Unless Ruth turned up.

Matt and Nathan had breakfast as normal, and set off for Bambinos, then Bank of New England. Matt would be taking the car, a 2008 Toyota Camry, and Nathan skipped a few feet ahead of his father as they walked round to their parking garage. As he climbed into his seat and fiddled with his safety strap, Nathan looked up at Matt.

‘Will Mommy be home tonight?’ he asked.

Matt leaned down and kissed his son on the top of the head. ‘She should be. If she’s not too busy at work.’

He quickly closed Nathan’s door and climbed into the driver’s seat. Bambinos was only a two minute ride away, and after Nathan was safely handed over, Matt set off for his office.

His normal route would be to head east along Cambridge Street, turn onto Court Street at the Government Center; then, negotiating Boston’s infamous one-way streets, he would take a right down Congress Street, left down Water Street onto Milk. Then up India Street to the small parking lot at the back of his branch building. The Bank of New England was situated on State and India. The journey would in normal circumstances take around half an hour – he always wondered why he didn't walk – but today the streets were gridlocked. According to the traffic reports on WBUR, there had been a collision at 5:40 that morning on the I-93 Expressway between an SUV and a tractor-trailer. Although the debris had been cleared, the knock-on effect had not. Therefore, Matt was parking his Toyota behind the branch at 9:50.

In spite of the cold, he was hot and flustered, and ran up the steps into the branch. Inside, it seemed quite busy. Unusual for a Wednesday. He hurried over to his desk and sat down.

'Afternoon,' said a familiar voice.

Matt looked up and saw Larry Mason, a fellow Personal Banker and one of Matt's closest colleagues at this branch. He grinned up at Larry.

'Very funny. Traffic's at a standstill out there. A smash on the 93 apparently.'

'I know,' Larry replied. 'Why do you think it's so busy here? Half the staff haven't gotten in yet. My nine thirty client hasn't shown up yet. When's your first one in?'

While they were chatting, Matt had logged onto his personal computer.

'Not until ten thirty, thank God,' he said breathlessly. 'Gives me a chance to get myself sorted out.'

'Well, if you get any grief from Ms Barber,' said Larry, 'ignore it. She only just arrived ten minutes ago herself.'

'Right; thanks for the heads-up.'

'How was the vacation, by the way?' asked Larry. 'Do anything particular?'

'Nah. Just a few things around the house.'

'Ruth off too?'

Matt shook his head. 'No.'

'Well, I'll leave you to it. Catch up lunchtime?'

'Sure. See you later.'

Matt nodded and started to shuffle some paperwork. Once Larry had gone, he put down the paperwork and pulled out his cell phone. He looked around: the part of the branch where his desk was situated was quiet. The longer than normal line of customers was around the teller area. He could see that only two positions were manned: normally there were four. Perhaps the missing two were stuck in traffic. Larry was talking to one of the customers waiting in line, and José Vasquez, the third Personal Banker, was missing. Larry lived in the Forest Hills district of Boston and used the Orange Line subway; Matt had forgotten exactly where José lived, but remembered him saying that he was having to use a replacement bus service as his branch of the T was being refurbished; so he would be stuck in traffic too.

While he was looking at the line of customers, he noticed his manager, Debra Grant Barber, walk past the line. One of the customers attracted her attention and from what Matt could hear was complaining about the length of time he was having to wait in line.

Debra Grant Barber was the bank's New Business Manager, Matt's supervisor. Early forties, she was always immaculately presented, with not a hair out of place. Heavily lacquered, Matt always assumed; and he was in no doubt how she had gotten to the position she was in at such a comparatively young age. The two surnames: not yet forty-five and already two husbands under her belt.

Allowing himself a brief smile, Matt found Ruth's cell number on his phone, and used the office landline to dial. A trick he had learned from Larry: if you use the office landline, as well as not paying for the call, it would not look like a personal call.

Matt could hear the dial tone, and then the click as it went over to voicemail. Rather than just hang up as he did the last couple of times the day before, he left another message.

'Ruth, it's Matt. Again. Look, what's going on? I'm worried. Nathan keeps asking where you are. Give me a call as soon as you pick up this message.'

He pressed the red key, then retrieved her office number. Dialled. A few rings, a click, then a recorded voice saying the call could not be completed as dialled. He had forgotten the number stored in his cell was wrong, but he couldn't remember the correct number.

He called directory assistance and got the number for Cambridge Pharmaceuticals. He was just about to dial when his cell phone rang. His heart missed a beat. The caller was showing as unlisted.

'Matthew Gibbons?'

'Mr Gibbons, my name is Sergeant Paula Edwards. I work for the Missing Persons Unit of the Boston Police Department.'

'Oh, hello.'

'Good morning, sir. How are you this morning?'

'I'm fine, thank you. How are you?'

'I'm good, thank you sir. Mr Gibbons, I have been passed your details by Captain O'Riordan of the Department -'

‘O’Riordan?’

There was a brief pause. Matt could hear some papers being shuffled.

Edwards continued, ‘Yes, although I understand you filed your report with Lieutenant Weber last night.’

‘That’s right. He said to expect a call from you’

‘Sure. I was just -’

‘Have you any news yet?’

‘Not as yet, sir. I was just about to say, this is a preliminary courtesy call to you to let you know the report of your wife’s failure to return home has been passed to us here at the MPU. No news yet, I’m afraid, but the Lieutenant’s report was very thorough.’

‘Do you need any more information from me? He did pass you the photograph of Ruth, didn’t he?’

‘He did, absolutely. I just want to let you know that I will be acting as your point of contact with the Unit, and will keep you up to date with what’s happening.’

‘How often?’

‘Unless there is anything specific to report, I’ll give you a call every couple of days.’

‘Okay.’

‘Mr Gibbons, I’m going to give you a contact number for the Unit, for you to use if Mrs Gibbons returns, or if you hear from her. Or have any more information above that which you gave the Lieutenant which would be of interest to us.’

‘Okay.’ Matt jotted down the number Sergeant Edwards gave him.

‘So I’ll call you in a couple of days, Mr Gibbons.’

‘Okay. Fine.’

‘You have a good day now, sir,’ she said, then

hung up.

Matt replaced the phone. He looked around: the line at the other side of the branch was shorter now; it looked as if four tellers were on duty now. He checked the clock: he should just have time before his client arrived to make this call.

He dialled the number for Cambridge Pharmaceuticals. After a few rings a female voice answered.

'Thank you for calling Cambridge Pharmaceuticals. My name is Roxanne. How can I help you this morning?'

'I'd like to speak to Ruth Gibbons please.'

'Hold the line, please sir.'

There was a click and Matt was put on hold. A moment later, Roxanne returned.

'Sir, can you repeat the name?'

'Ruth Gibbons.'

'I'm sorry sir, I can't trace her. What department does she work in?'

'I'm sorry, I don't -' said Matt. 'Wait a minute – she works in Product Control?' The end of his sentence was more of a question.

'Product Control,' Roxanne repeated. 'I'll try again.'

A minute on hold and then, 'I'm sorry sir; I can't find her under Product Control.'

'She might have moved departments again. Could you check again, please?'

'Hold the line, sir.'

Matt was on hold again, for two minutes this time before Roxanne came back to him.

'I'm sorry to keep you waiting, sir, but I still can't locate her.'

'Can't locate her? What does that mean?'

‘Sir, I’ve trawled through the entire employee database, and haven’t been able to find the name.’

‘I – I don’t understand. What does that mean?’

‘Sir, it means nobody by the name of Ruth Gibbons works here.’

Chapter Seven

MATT RAN ALONG State Street towards the subway station. He had considered getting in the Toyota and driving down to Cambridge Pharmaceuticals, but the traffic problems he had experienced that morning made him decide against it. After his conversation with Roxanne, his mind was going every which way. How on earth could nobody by Ruth's name work there? Surely she wouldn't be using her maiden name? They had been married three years now. She would have used her maiden name of Levene before they were married: maybe she was still using it.

He reached the station, paid his $2.50 for a ticket, and then ran down the escalator to the platform. He checked at the indicator: 5 minutes for the next Orange Line to Forest Hills. Out of breath, he collapsed onto the metal bench. An Oak Grove train arrived at the northbound platform: Matt stared at the faces looking out of the windows.

As the train pulled away for the short journey to Haymarket, Matt thought back again to what Roxanne had told him. After hanging up on her he barely had time to gather his thoughts when his ten thirty client arrived. It was a Mrs Hyman, a widowed lady in her early seventies who, after losing three husbands to cancer, heart failure and a traffic accident, had a considerable amount of wealth. All of her money, as far as she would reveal to Matt anyway, was already with Bank of New England in various accounts and trusts: the purpose of her visit today was to review whether any other accounts Matt could offer her would pay her more interest. They could not. Mrs Hyman was a regular client of Matt's, paying him a visit every three months or so. Nine times out of ten Matt confirmed to her that her savings were in the best place. He suspected that Mrs Hyman knew this all along, and that she was a little lonely, and just came in to see him for the company and a free coffee.

He tried not to prolong his interviews with Mrs Hyman unnecessarily: he felt it was necessary to keep her happy so he could retain her business, but all the time he spent listening to her talk again and again about her three husbands, he could be getting new business. He needed the commission. Normally, unless there was some actual business to transact, their meetings would last no more than an hour; today he was showing her out after half that time.

After he had seen her out he looked around. No sign of Debra, Larry was sitting talking to two of his clients, and José was standing by a brochure stand checking the literature.

'Hey man,' said José as Matt approached him. 'You get stuck in that traffic too?'

Matt nodded.

'Some gridlock,' José went on. 'All down to a wreck on the expressway.'

'So I heard,' said Matt. 'Look, José – when's your next appointment?'

'Not till one. That's why I'm goofing around here.'

'Can I ask a favour?'

'Shoot.'

'I have someone coming in at eleven thirty, then two thirty. But I have to go out for a while. There – there's some kind of emergency at Ruth's place -'

‘Jeez, what’s happened?’

‘Not sure yet. But I need to go down there. Now. Can you cover my eleven thirty?’

‘No sweat man. But will you be back for two thirty?’

‘I hope so. But if I’m not, maybe you and Larry could -’

‘Sure, no problem.’

Matt looked around. ‘Do you know where Debra is?’ he asked.

‘Lying in her coffin somewhere, most like. No, I think she’s on a conference call.’

‘I’ve no time to wait. Can you let her know what’s happened? Say I’ll explain when I get back, and it’s an emergency.’

‘I will, man. Go on. Get off.’

‘Thanks José, I owe you.’

Matt was brought back to the present by the sound of his train arriving at the station. With a screech of brakes and the hiss of air it pulled to a halt and the doors slid open. It was only a third full and Matt easily found a seat, one by the opposite window. With a warning horn, the doors slid shut and the train pulled away. Three stops later, after Downtown Crossing and Chinatown, Matt arrived at his stop: Tufts Medical Center. Matt left the train and made his way up the escalator to street level. Once on the street, he looked around. The Medical Center was on the opposite side of Washington Street. A large metal 800 was on the wall next to the entrance drive. Matt knew – or thought he knew – the address of Cambridge Pharmaceuticals was 1100, so he pulled his collar up as some protection against the biting wind, and began his walk three blocks down.

He proceeded down Washington Street, across the bridge which goes over the I-90 Massachusetts Turnpike, and after five or six minutes' brisk walk he arrived at 1100 block.

Situated on Washington and East Berkeley, the Cambridge Pharmaceuticals Building was an imposing ten floor red brick structure. Matt pushed open the glass doors and walked in. The lobby was decorated in a cream coloured marble. There was a bank of four elevators across the lobby, a waiting area comprising a low table and five chairs on his left and a reception desk on his right. Apart from the young black woman sitting at the desk, the lobby was empty.

'How can I help you, sir?' asked the young woman as Matt approached her.

'Are you Roxanne?' he asked, immediately noticing her name badge showing she was called Ayesha.

'Excuse me?' she asked.

'Sorry, I didn't notice your badge. I was talking to somebody called Roxanne earlier. On the telephone.'

'Oh, she must be upstairs. Do you want me to get her?' Ayesha asked, reaching for the phone.

'No, it's all right. I've come to see someone else. Ruth Gibbons,' said Matt, his palms sweating.

'Ruth Gibbons,' Ayesha repeated, tabbing down a list of names on the screen. 'Sorry, no Ruth Gibbons here.'

'Try Ruth Levene.'

Ayesha glanced up at him and checked again.

'Sorry. No Ruth Levene either.'

'But you must have. In Product Control. Look again. Please.'

Ayesha took a deep breath and looked again.

'Nobody here, sir.'

'This is ridiculous. I know she works there. I'm going up to see them myself.'

'Sir, you can't -' Ayesha started to say, but Matt was already in the elevator. There was a display on the wall showing which department occupied which floor: Product Control was on the eighth floor. Matt stabbed at the button and the doors shut.

When they opened at the eighth floor he was met by a man in his thirties, in shirtsleeves, open shirt, no tie.

'Sir, you must go back down,' he said.

'I'm looking for Ruth Gibbons,' Matt said. 'She may call herself Ruth Levene.'

'No-one of that name here, sir.'

Matt looked around. 'This is Product Control, is it?'

'Yes sir, it is, but -'

'Then Ruth works here.'

The man shook his head. 'I'm sorry, sir. You have the wrong place.'

'Look,' said Matt. He put his hand in his pocket and got out his phone. The man flinched as he did this.

'Look, here's her picture,' said Matt as he retrieved a picture he kept of Ruth.

The man looked at the picture, then shook his head again. 'Sorry, sir. I've not seen her.'

'What about the others who work here? They might know her.'

'Sir, I'm the office manager. I know everyone who works here. And I've never seen her before. Now please, sir; you must leave. Before I call security.'

'Don't bother,' said Matt, stepping back into the

elevator.

He went back down to the lobby, back out to Washington Street and started to slowly walk back to the T station. He paused while he crossed over the expressway and looked down at the traffic below.

Things are getting weird, he thought. Apart from Ruth not coming home. The number he had stored in his cell last night was wrong. Very wrong, nothing like the number he had gotten from directory assistance. And that was the number Ruth gave him. And now he is told that she doesn't work at Cambridge Pharmaceuticals. So where did she go yesterday? For that matter where has she been going every day?

Matt turned round and looked back down Washington. He could see the Cambridge Pharmaceuticals building on the next block. One question kept running through his mind.

What the hell was going on?

Chapter Eight

AFTER GETTING OFF the T, Matt made his way along State Street back to his work. Even though he had to quicken his pace because of the rain, he was walking as if in a trance. His mind was searching for possible explanations: an explanation of where Ruth was and why she had failed to return home or even contact him; an explanation of why there was no record of her, even in her maiden name, at her place of work.

As he walked through the door to his branch, he caught Larry's eye. Larry was standing talking to one of his clients. It looked as if he had just finished a meeting, and he was seeing the client out. Without breaking off his conversation, Larry glanced over at Matt and cocked his head slightly in the direction of Matt's desk. Matt followed Larry's eyes and to his dismay Debra Grant Barber was hovering around his desk.

'Great,' Matt muttered as he walked down to his desk. Debra noticed him arrive and looked up.

'Extended lunch break?' she asked, her voice thick with sarcasm.

'Not exactly,' Matt said, taking off his wet raincoat.

'Not exactly? How so?'

'I – er, had some personal business to take care of. Urgent personal business.'

She raised her eyebrows.

'Oh, really? I wasn't aware of that.' *Meaning you should have asked me first.*

'I said it was urgent,' Matt snapped back. 'You were in your room, with your door shut. Talking on the telephone. I am owed many hours. I arranged for Larry and José to cover my next two appointments.'

The sharpness of Matt's reply took Debra by surprise. Momentarily.

'Maybe we need to talk about it,' she said.

Matt nodded. She was right. It was possible that Ruth's disappearance might impact on his work, so he had an obligation to advise her.

'Let's go to my room,' she said, leading him over to her office.

'Shut the door, Matt. Sit down,' she said from the other side of her desk. Matt did so.

Debra sat down. She took off her glasses and leaned forward, elbows on the desk, hands steepled 'So,' she said. 'From the top. What's going on?'

Matt rubbed his temple.

'It's Ruth,' he said. 'My wife.'

Debra raised her eyebrows inquisitively.

'She didn't come home last night,' Matt continued.

'You mean you guys have split? She's left home?'

Matt shrugged.

'So what's the situation now?' Debra asked.

'The situation now,' answered Matt, 'is that I've no idea where she is. I, or should I say our son and I, haven't heard from her since yesterday morning.'

'Is that where you have been today? Looking for her?'

'In a way. She works down Washington, near the Medical Center. I caught the T down there to see if she was there.'

'And was she?'

'No.' Matt decided not to give her the whole

picture.

She sat back in her chair; rubbed the bridge of her nose.

'Well, I'm sorry to hear all this,' she said. Matt couldn't tell if she was being sincere or sarcastic. 'How much vacation time do you have left?'

'I've no idea. Not without checking it out.'

'Mm.' She paused, thoughtfully. 'And I guess with your wife not in the picture right now, you have to take your – son?' - Matt nodded to confirm - 'to and from school?'

'That's right. For the moment, anyway.'

She leaned forward again, paused a beat, then spoke.

'Look. Today's Wednesday. Wednesday afternoon. Clear up your things and go now. Come back Friday. That gives you a day to do what you have to do. Yes?'

Matt nodded, a little taken back. 'Yes, that would be great.'

'Were you due to work Saturday?'

'I –er, no I don't think I was -'

'Let's be as flexible as we can, then. Take the rest of the day off, and tomorrow. Work Friday and Saturday. Then you'll be up to date, won't you?'

'Yes, I guess I will. I just -'

'Well, that's that sorted. Let's catch up Friday, then,' she said, swinging her chair and loading up her laptop.

Meeting over, Matt thought. 'Thanks,' he said, getting up and leaving Debra to her laptop.

As he walked back to his desk, still clutching his raincoat, he bumped into Larry.

'Hey, guy,' Larry said. 'Everything okay? José said you had to take care of some business. What's going on?'

Matt looked around.

'It's Ruth,' he said quietly. 'She didn't come home last night.'

'Didn't…?'

'Just didn't come home. Saw her in the morning, before she left for work. She sent me a text around five saying she was about to leave, but didn't show.'

'Jeez. But I don't get it. She not answering her cell?'

'No. Kept going to voicemail.'

'Any friends or anything? Someone she could have gone to?'

'She has one best friend. Gail. Gail Smith. You might have even met her. I've tried her a few times, but she's gone to voicemail also.'

'What about her work? What do they say?'

'That's the weirdest thing. Another weirdest thing. I called her office, but nobody knows her there. That's where I went. I got the T down there; spoke to the office manager who said he had never heard of her. Even using her old name.'

'You're kidding.'

'I wish I was.'

'What about Nathan?'

'I've told him she was working late and had to set off early this morning, but I can't keep that up for ever.'

'No.'

'I've ended up calling the police.'

'Jeez. What did they say?'

'Some Lieutenant came round last night. Took some details. Said he'd pass it to the - er, Missing Persons Unit. I got a call from them here this morning.'

'Saying what?'

'Just saying they had her details and were beginning their investigations.'

'Nothing, in other words.'

Matt shrugged. 'Early days, I guess.'

'What are you going to do now?'

Matt nodded over in the direction of Debra's closed door.

'I had to tell her what had happened. Not every detail, but the gist.'

'What did she say?'

'Told me to go home now. Take the rest of today and tomorrow off. "To do what I need to do," she said. I need to get home and start calling around.'

'Friends. Her parents? Yours?'

'I'll keep trying Gail. They're pretty close. Ruth's parents both died before we met, and she and mine aren't exactly close.' Matt paused. 'I need to start calling round the hospitals too, I guess.'

'Jesus, Matt.'

'I know. But it's gotta be done.'

Larry nodded. 'Bet you have to work Saturday,' he said.

'Got it in one. Look, buddy, I'd better get off now. See you Friday. When you see José, can you thank him for covering and get him up to speed.'

Larry put his hand on Matt's arm.

'Sure thing, pal. Good luck. See you Friday.'

Matt checked his watch as he hurried out to the parking lot. With his extended lunch hour and his conversations with Debra and Larry, it was almost the time he would normally leave when it was his turn to pick up Nathan. Hoping the gridlock from that morning had cleared, he started the Toyota and eased it into the traffic in India Street. As he turned left along State, he felt a pain in his stomach. With all the activity, he had forgotten to eat. Now he was starving. No time to stop: early dinner for him and Nathan.

As it turned out, he made it back to Beacon Hill earlier than expected, so had time to drive home, park the car, get a candy bar and walk round to Bambinos. The rain had stopped, but it was getting bitterly cold. As he and Nathan walked home, the question Matt had been dreading came up.

'Daddy, is Mommy coming home tonight?'

Matt paused. For too long maybe.

'I think she has to work late again.'

'Aw, I wanted to see her. So did Mr Bronto.' Nathan skipped along, bouncing a brontosaurus along the sides of the houses they passed.

'Tomorrow, for sure,' said Matt, ruffling his son's hair. 'Tomorrow for sure,' he repeated, quietly.

Matt rustled up an omelette for them both for dinner, and Nathan had chocolate ice cream for dessert. After a bath, he lay in bed while Matt read him a story.

'If I'm still awake when Mommy gets home,' said Nathan, 'can you get her to tuck me in and say good night.'

With a lump in his throat, Matt leaned down to kiss Nathan.

'Sure will, sport.'

'Night night, Daddy.'

'Night night. Don't let the bed bugs bite,' whispered Matt as he dimmed Nathan's light and pulled the door to.

Matt slowly went downstairs, thinking over what

he should tell Nathan and when. Maybe he should call his own parents for advice.

First things first, though. He went into the kitchen, tidied up a bit, then picked up the Yellow Pages and the telephone, and sat down at the kitchen table. He opened the Yellow Pages and found the entries for Hospitals. He found the first entry and started to dial. As the number was ringing, the doorbell rang.

He hung up, leapt off his chair and ran over to the door. His heart was pounding: maybe it was Ruth; maybe she had forgotten or lost her door key?

He flung open the door, hoping to see Ruth. Instead it was Gail.

'Hey, Matt,' she said.

'Gail,' he replied, not knowing exactly what to say.

'You left some messages on my cell,' Gail said. 'I was passing, so I…'

'Come in, come in,' Matt said, opening the door wider.

'Thanks,' she said, stepping inside and going straight into the kitchen. She turned round as Matt closed the front door and followed her. 'I couldn't understand what the messages were about. What's happened?'

It was then that Matt finally broke down.

Chapter Nine

'YOU WANT TO tell me all about it?' asked Gail, after Matt had pulled himself together.

'Sorry.' Matt wiped his eyes and blew his nose on a Kleenex.

'Don't worry about it.' Gail sat down and smoothed down her skirt. As long as Matt had known either of them, Gail had been Ruth's best friend. By coincidence, their birthdays fell on the same day. Gail was born one year before Ruth, thirty-one years ago. Physically, they were similar: both around five feet six tall, both with shoulder length dark hair, although Ruth's was wavy in contrast to Gail's, which was dead straight. Gail was slimmer than Ruth, who always used to joke about her 'child rearing hips'. Gail had no children, a fact which never seemed to bother her; she was more accustomed to exotic holidays. Since Matt first met her, Gail had had two partners, the latest of which, Ryan, held a high position with Nantucket Airlines; hence the frequent travel abroad. They had obviously just returned from one of these trips: as she sat down in Matt's kitchen she crossed her legs and ran a hand down a thin, tanned leg. 'Your messages,' she asked. 'What were they all about?'

'Do you know where Ruth is?' Matt asked.

Gail gave him an inquisitive look and held her palms out. Meaning no.

Matt sat down and rubbed his face with one hand.

'She's gone missing.'

'Missing?'

‘Tuesday, she left for work as normal. Walked to work as normal. I was here all day; I had some vacation days to take. She sent me the usual text we send to each other when we’re on our way home. I expected her sometime between five thirty and six, but she never arrived.

‘I tried calling her and texting her, but she has never texted me back and her phone went to voicemail every time I call.’

‘What about at work?’

‘That’s a really strange one. That night I tried to call her office using the number she had given me, but it wasn’t a right number. So I called 411, got a totally different number. I called that number the next day, only to be told Ruth didn’t work there.’

‘I don’t get it,’ Gail said, frowning. ‘This was Cambridge Pharmaceuticals down on Washington, wasn’t it?’

‘U-huh. I even went down there, and they told me the same thing. I even thought she might be still using her maiden name, but no.’

‘Matt, I don’t know what to say. I don’t understand it.’

‘When was the last time you spoke to her, Gail?’

‘It was – about a week or so. We talked about the four of us getting together some time, When Ryan got back from Europe.’

‘And you’ve not seen or heard from her since then. Not since Tuesday?’

‘No. Honestly, Matt.’

‘Sorry, I didn’t mean to… It’s just…’

‘I know, Matt. I know.’

‘Did she say anything to you about us? Anything to suggest she wasn’t happy?’

Gail shook her head.

'No. Nothing. Nothing at all like that.'

'Gail, you've known her longer than I have. How long is it?'

'Since I've known her? Ten, twelve years, I guess. Around ten as friends.'

'Can you think of what she might be doing? Where she might go?'

'Sorry, I can't imagine. It's not like her.'

They both sat in silence for a moment, and then Gail said, 'What about Nathan? How's he?'

Matt looked up at the ceiling, in the general direction of Nathan's bedroom upstairs.

'He keeps asking where she is. The last couple of nights I've told him it's very busy at her work, so she's having to work late and leave very early in the morning. He seems to have accepted that.'

'For now. You can't tell him that for ever.'

'That's what the police said.'

'The police? You've called the police?' Gail seemed surprised.

'Well, yes. I had to. Did it about nine that night.'

'What did they say?'

'A Lieutenant – er, Weber, called round that night. Took a load of information about Ruth. Oh, and a photo of her. Said he'd pass it to the Missing Persons Unit.'

'I see. Right.'

'I had a call from them this morning, saying they had received the report and they were on the case, as it were.'

'Anything else?'

'Is that you, Mommy?'

Matt and Gail turned round to see Nathan standing in his pyjamas in the kitchen doorway.

'I thought you were asleep, sport,' Matt said,

going over to him.

'I thought I heard Mommy,' Nathan yawned.

'No, it's only Auntie Gail,' Gail smiled. She stood up and knelt down in front of him.

'Is Mommy home?' Nathan asked, looking around the kitchen sleepily.

'No, not yet,' Matt said quietly. 'She's still at work. Time you were in bed.'

'Okay, Daddy,' Nathan yawned. He turned round and started to walk to the stairs.

'I'll take him upstairs,' Gail said, standing up.

'No, it's okay. I'll only be a minute.' Matt walked past Gail and put his arm round Nathan's shoulders. They both slowly went upstairs.

'Do you want to pee first?' Matt asked as they walked past the bathroom. Nathan nodded. After he had peed and returned to bed, Matt tucked him in and kissed him on the top of his head.

'Sleep tight, sport,' Matt whispered. 'Love you.'

'Love you too, Daddy,' Nathan murmured in his sleep.

Swallowing, Matt crept out of his son's room and went downstairs to Gail.

'That's another thing,' he said as he rejoined her in the kitchen. 'Walking out on me is one thing, but she would never walk out on Nathan.'

'Unless she had reason to.'

'What reason could there be? Why would a mother walk out on her child?'

Gail shrugged.

'I'm sorry Matt; I don't know. I just…'

'I think something's happened to her,' said Matt. 'There's no other explanation.'

'Like what?'

'Anything. She would have gone to you if she was

just leaving me. But neither of us have heard anything. So something *must* have happened.'

'So what are you going to do?'

'Well, just before you rang the doorbell, I was about to start calling round the local hospitals. I'm guessing that's something the cops do, but I can't just sit here doing nothing.'

'Are you still going to work?'

'Went in today. Had to tell my boss. She's said to take tomorrow off to do what I have to do, in her words. I go back in Friday.'

'Well, look: if there's anything Ryan and I can do…'

'There is something, yes.'

'Shoot.'

'I have to work Saturday. Till two. I wasn't due to be in, so I don't know what do about Nathan. Are you able to look after him for a few hours?'

'Shit, Matt. Any other time I'd say yes. You know that. But this Saturday I'm due to go down to -'

'Don't worry. I know it's short notice. I'll take him in with me. Sit him in the staff room with a couple of DVDs.'

'No, it's all right. We'll rearrange. We'd love to have Nathan.'

'Great. Thanks. I'll give you a call Friday to arrange. Is that okay?'

'Absolutely. No problem.'

Again a few moments' silence, then Gail spoke.

'I'll be off now, Matt. Speak Friday, yes?' she said as she stood up.

'Sure. Thanks for calling in.'

'No problem. Let me know if you hear anything, won't you?'

'Of course.' Matt walked Gail over to the front

door. She paused just as he was about to open it.

'Do you mind if I use your bathroom first?' she asked. 'Cold night.'

'Sure, no problem,' Matt smiled. 'You know the way.'

He wandered back into the kitchen while Gail went upstairs. Tidied a few things up until he heard the toilet flush and Gail come downstairs.

'I hope everything… Well, you know what I mean,' she said quietly, kissing him on the cheek.

'Thanks.'

Matt stood in the doorway and watched Gail walk down the street to her car. He stayed there until he saw her tail lights turn right at the intersection. Closed the door and returned to the kitchen. He picked up the phone and sat back down.

'Right,' he quietly said to himself. 'Hospitals.'

He began to dial the first number.

Chapter Ten

THURSDAY MORNING AND again Matt woke to find his arm stretched over the empty space that was Ruth's side of the bed. He shot up, sat bolt upright in bed as his brain again processed the fact that Ruth was not there.

He looked over at the clock: just after seven. At least he had slept last night. Time to wake up Nathan and get him off to kindergarten. Then spend the day doing whatever he had to do, to quote Debra Grant Barber. Whatever that meant, he thought. Well, at least the calls to the hospitals produced nothing. Assuming she was not in a hospital outside Massachusetts. If she had gone out of State… He rubbed his stubbly chin as he sat on the edge of the bed. Maybe he should also try places in Connecticut, or Vermont, or Rhode Island. Something to think about.

He decided he would try to hurry Nathan through the getting up, eating breakfast, and setting off routine: maybe if he was in a rush he would not think about where his mother was. Foolish.

'Has Mommy left for work?' Nathan asked as Matt poured him a bowl of cereal.

'Yes, sport, she has. Still very busy at work,' Matt lied as he sat down to eat his own breakfast. He waited for a follow up question. To his relief, none came.

As he dropped Nathan off at Bambinos, Nathan asked one more time, 'Daddy, are you picking me up tonight, or is Mommy?'

Matt ruffled his son's hair. 'Not sure yet, pal. Depends on how much Mommy has on at work. Probably be me.'

'Will she be at home soon?'

'Soon. You'll be able to see her at the weekend. Only two more sleeps.'

'Okay. Bye, Daddy.'

'Bye, sport. Love you.' Matt leaned over to kiss Nathan goodbye. He watched his son get safely inside, then turned and walked back home. Picked up a copy of that morning's *Globe* on the way. As he walked home, he decided if Ruth had not returned by Friday night, he would tell Nathan the truth then. Or maybe he would give it until Saturday evening, after he picked him up from Gail and Ryan.

Back indoors, he scanned the *Globe* for any reports of traffic accidents, or anything at all that mentioned Ruth. He found nothing.

After clearing up the breakfast things, he decided to take a walk down to Boston Common. Maybe retrace Ruth's steps; take the route she would have taken. He felt he needed to think things through: something he could not do indoors. He needed some open space.

He strolled down to Beacon Street, crossed over the road, and entered the Common. He headed over to the Frog Pond. In its original state, it was the home of tadpoles, a mini nature reserve and somewhere he would like to have taken Nathan; a few years back it had been converted into a concrete wading pool. In the winter months it would be transformed into a skating rink. He sat down on a bench nearby and watched two teenagers skate around the rink. One kept falling over, to the great amusement of the other, a girl wearing a pink scarf. Matt wondered why they weren't in school.

As he sat watching the skaters, Matt began to think through the events of the last couple of days. He felt that basically there were two reasons for Ruth's disappearance. One, she had gone involuntarily; something had happened to her. He had reported her disappearance to the police; that was obviously the right thing to do. He had called the local hospitals. None of them had had an emergency admission answering Ruth's description. Then he had a thought: supposing hospitals had some kind of confidentiality rule; supposing they always said no when somebody called to ask that question. To protect the person, who might be admitted with injuries caused by a violent partner. In any case, surely they would have to give the police correct information, and he was sure the Missing Persons Unit would think of contacting hospitals. Or the morgue. He started to hyperventilate as this thought crossed his mind: this was one thing he had not previously considered.

He managed to slow his breathing down to normal as he dismissed the possibility that Ruth was dead. Or even injured; surely to God if she had been admitted to hospital somebody would have been in contact by now. No, he decided, her disappearance must be intentional. But why? They were both happy together; well, so he thought. She had certainly never given any indication otherwise. Gail said the same thing last night. In any case, she would never leave Nathan. So what was going on?

And then there was the situation with Cambridge Pharmaceuticals. He *knew* that was where she worked: sure, he had never been to any Christmas parties there, but he was certain he had been to the offices in the past, and had met some of her colleagues. Though not for some time. She always kept work and home life separate. So what was that jerk talking about yesterday? Maybe she *was* having an affair; and it was with him. That was why he was denying all knowledge of her. But then it all came back to Nathan again: she would *never* desert him.

He got up, and continued his walk through the Common. He decided he would walk down to Ruth's office again. No point trying to gain entry, but by the time he got there it would be lunchtime. If he waited outside, maybe he would catch Ruth taking her lunch break. Or perhaps he would recognise a workmate.

He took the path away from Frog Pond, and walked across the common, past the Soldiers and Sailors Monument, veering slightly to the right as he passed the sports field. Even on this cold morning, four hardy souls were playing tennis on the courts adjacent to the Central Burying Ground. He paused momentarily as he passed a plaque stating that portrait painter Gilbert Stuart was buried nearby.

He reached Tremont Street and crossed over outside the Boylston Green Line stop. Two more blocks and he was on Washington. Turned right and headed down to Cambridge Pharmaceuticals. He paused as he passed an HSBC branch and headed for the ATM. Inserted his card, keyed his PIN and requested fifty dollars. With all the events of the last two days, he had forgotten to get any cash. Something he and Ruth always joked about: he worked in a bank, but always forgot to make use of his branch's ATM.

Suddenly a thought hit him. If Ruth had left voluntarily, she would have needed money. They had a joint account, so he could see if and where she had made any withdrawals from their account. That might at least give him an idea of where she was. That was why that policewoman had asked about their accounts. He could leave it for the police to handle, but he felt he had to do something. Slight hitch here though: their account was with the Bank of New England and this was an HSBC machine. He wouldn't be able to get a list of transactions here. He took his cash, then pressed a couple of other buttons to get the balance. He frowned as he read the account balance on the screen: it was inconclusive, as he wasn't sure how much should be in the account. He needed a Bank of New England branch, and he knew there wasn't one in this part of the city. Or he would have to wait until he got home, and then go online. He looked around as he pondered: he needed to know about the account urgently, yet didn't have time to go home.

He stepped into a doorway where he found shelter from passers-by and from the wind, and speed dialled Larry Mason. It went to voicemail. He left Larry a message asking him to call him back ASAP, and continued his walk down to Ruth's offices.

He had just covered one block when Larry returned his call.

'Hey, Matt; how you doing?' Larry asked.

'I'm good. Well, as good as yesterday,' Matt replied, stepping into another doorway. 'I just need a favour.'

'Sure thing. Shoot.'

'If I give you my checking account number, could you check the recent transactions on it?'

'Sure, pal. Whatever you need.'

Matt read out the account number and held on while Larry retrieved the list of transactions.

'There's been a fifty dollar ATM withdrawal on the... Today. It was today.'

‘Yes. That was me. Go back the last couple of weeks.’

‘A hundred out on the tenth. At one of our machines here.’

‘Yes, that was me again.

‘I have two hundred on the eleventh. That was at the Safeway on Tremont.’

‘Okay. That would have been Ruth. She goes there after work sometimes.’

‘And a three hundred on the thirteenth. Again, Safeway on Tremont. Man, that’s a lot of shopping.’

‘Yeah. Okay, Larry. Thanks. See you tomorrow.’

‘Sure thing, buddy. You take care, now.’

Matt put the phone back in his pocket and looked up at the sky. It was clear and blue, but there were some heavy clouds building up to the west. He looked up and down the street, as he tried to figure out these withdrawals. Five hundred dollars in the space of two or three days. Ever since they had moved in together, he and Ruth had divided up the household expenditure into two areas of responsibility. Matt dealt with household bills: the mortgage, insurances, electricity, that sort of thing. Ruth took care of the groceries. Sometimes on a Saturday or Sunday they would all make a trip to an out-of-town mall, but normally she would call in somewhere on the way home. She would quite frequently use that particular Safeway store during her lunch break. Or so Matt thought. Because that was what Ruth told him. He knew she would normally pay in cash: she owned a credit card, but she preferred to withdraw cash at an ATM before she went shopping. Said she found it easier to keep track of the account that way. Hence the transactions at that ATM. But the amounts: two hundred did seem a large amount for groceries, considering she would have had to walk home with them. Perhaps that was to take care of several days' visits. Her knew she liked to shop little and often, preferring fresh produce. But why three hundred two days later? Sure, it was a holiday weekend then, but even so…

He stepped out from the doorway and over to a bench by a bus stop. An elderly lady with two large plastic bags was sitting in the centre of the bench, and moved to the other end when Matt sat down.

He slumped onto the bench and rubbed his face. What the hell was happening? Where the hell was Ruth?

And why the hell would she need five hundred dollars just days before she disappeared?

Chapter Eleven

STILL TRYING TO figure out why Ruth would need five hundred dollars other than to finance leaving him, Matt hurried down Washington Street. It was nearly midday, and presumably the workers at Cambridge Pharmaceuticals would be starting their lunch breaks very soon. There was another bus stop with a bench right outside the building – the next bus stop from the one he had previously stopped at, in fact – and he stood by the stop, leaning on a *Boston Globe* vending machine, as the bench was full of people waiting for a bus. He made himself as comfortable as he could, half sitting on the machine and began to watch the glass doors of the building.

Just before twelve a man – Matt estimated mid-twenties – dressed in a suit and having an animated conversation on his cell phone entered the building. Matt jumped slightly as there was a loud hiss behind him. A bus had arrived at the stop. Matt turned his head ninety degrees and looked up at the dot matrix indicator display: the bus was Route 275 heading Downtown. All but one of the occupants of the bench got on the bus; the remaining occupant shuffled up to the opposite end and buried himself back in that day's *USA Today*.

Matt winced as he caught the full force of the roar of the bus's engines as it accelerated away from the stop and headed Downtown. As he rubbed the inside of his ear with one finger he noticed some figures leave the Cambridge Pharmaceuticals building: two men and three women. He recognized none of them;

certainly Ruth was not one of the group. As he watched them walk down Washington, talking and laughing, he considered catching them up and asking if they knew Ruth. He decided against it – for now.

A few minutes later, a middle-aged woman left the building, followed shortly by two younger men.

Over the next ten minutes, around a dozen people left the building: all headed in the same direction, down Washington. Two of the three women he saw leave earlier returned, each carrying a small brown paper bag, presumably with a sandwich or something.

'Excuse me dear, it this where I catch the airport bus?'

Matt looked up into the face of a white haired elderly woman.

'Excuse me?' he asked.

'I am looking for where I can catch the bus for Logan,' she repeated.

Matt looked around, trying to make sure he wasn't missing anybody leaving the building.

'I-I don't know, sorry. I…' he stuttered.

The man at the other end of the bench looked up from his newspaper.

'You're best walking up to the Medical Center and catching the Orange Line for Oak Grove,' he said. 'Transfer to the Blue Line at State, and then you can get a free shuttle bus from Airport.'

'Right, thank you very much,' she said, then turned and began to wheel her little case up towards the station.

'You're welcome,' the man said, and returned to his newspaper.

Involuntarily, Matt looked in the direction of the man as he gave the directions, and out of the corner of his eye he saw two figures – a man and a woman –

walk past. As the man looked at the woman, Matt recognized his face. It was the jerk he spoke to at Ruth's office yesterday. And the woman he was with…

She was unmistakable, even from behind. The five feet six slim figure, the way her hips swayed as she walked, the dark hair, slightly wavy, down to halfway down her back. He didn't recognize the clothes, but she was always shopping anyway. As they walked, their arms got closer and closer. The body language was not that of two colleagues picking up a sandwich. Then he put his arm around her waist and pulled her closer.

'I knew it,' Matt muttered as he got up and followed them down Washington. Suddenly his concern and worry turned to anger: so she was having an affair with this asshole. Why not just tell him? Why put him – and Nathan – through all the worry of not knowing? And was she really walking out on their son?

He quickened his pace as they ran across the first street before the *Don't Walk* sign lit up. He braved the traffic as he crossed the street after them; only one driver sounded his horn at him.

As he got back onto the sidewalk, he could no longer see them. He had lost them. Muttering an oath, he looked around. He was now outside the Safeway store. Standing on tiptoe, he looked through the glass doors to try to pick them up.

He ran his hands through his hair. How could he lose them? No problem, he thought; they would have to go back to the office within the hour. He would return to the bus stop and wait there. Then confront them.

He returned to the street. Just before turning to go

back to the bus stop, he glanced to his left. And saw them again. Now they both had an arm round the other's waist. They had stopped and were going in somewhere. Matt walked briskly down the street, checking the premises to see which was the most likely one. After half a block he found a bar. The fascia was cream with green borders. He looked up at the sign: McGann's Irish Pub. One of many hundred in Boston. He paused a moment, then went in.

The bar was quite full, as one would expect this time of day. He looked around, as his eyes started to get accustomed to the dim lighting. He looked round at the tables: all were occupied, but not by Ruth and her co-worker. There were around a dozen people sitting at the bar. Squinting, Matt looked down the backs of the customers there. At the end of the bar, he saw them. They had just been served: he had a glass of dark beer; Matt couldn't make out what Ruth was drinking. She normally had white wine when they went out.

Matt walked up to them. As he got to six feet away, the man got up.

'Sorry; bathroom, honey,' he laughed, rubbing her shoulder. She put a hand up to her shoulder to touch his.

As he turned to go to the restroom he caught sight of Matt. A couple of seconds passed as he figured out why he recognised Matt. He opened his mouth to say something.

'Very cosy,' said Matt, sarcastically.

The man straightened up, keeping his hand on her shoulder.

Ruth turned round.

Chapter Twelve

ONLY IT WASN'T Ruth.

Remarkably similar to be sure, but definitely not Matt's wife.

The figure was the same, the walk was the same, as were the hair colour and style; as she turned round to face Matt, he could see she was of Asian descent – Japanese, Matt assumed.

Matt froze, lost for words.

'I – I…' was all he could manage.

'It's you,' said the guy. 'The guy from the elevator yesterday.'

Matt said nothing.

'Who is he, Danny?' asked the woman, in a worried voice. She reached up and put her hand on his arm. 'Who is this man?'

'Nobody, baby,' Danny replied, resting his hand on hers. 'Just nobody.'

'I – I'm sorry,' said Matt. 'I saw the two of you, and I assumed…'

'You assumed she was Ruth Gibbons,' Danny said. 'That was her name, wasn't it?'

Matt nodded.

'I said I'm sorry,' he said. Then turned to the woman. 'I thought you were someone else.'

'Well, you were wrong,' Danny said. 'This is Aki, my girlfriend. She's just met me for lunch.'

Matt nodded and began to back away.

'Like I said, I'm sorry,' he said quietly, turned and made his way out of the bar. Back on Washington, he rubbed his chin and looked up and down the street.

He stood outside the bar a moment while he considered what to do next. He decided he would take up his place by the bus stop and continue his vigil. If this abortive trip to the bar meant he had missed Ruth going out, he could still catch her returning. He walked back up to the bus stop and sat down again on the concrete bench. The man reading the *USA Today* was still there.

After five minutes he saw a figure he knew. She was a young African American returning to the Cambridge Pharmaceuticals building carrying a brown *Subway* bag. Matt recognized her as the receptionist he spoke to yesterday.

'Ayesha,' he called out, getting up from the bench. She paused momentarily, and began to hurry on once she realised who he was.

'Ayesha, please,' Matt said, catching her up.

'Please go away, mister. I don't want no trouble,' Ayesha said nervously.

'I just want to show you a picture,' Matt said. 'That's all. Then I'll leave you.'

She nodded hurriedly. Matt retrieved a picture of Ruth on his phone and showed it to her.

'This is Ruth Gibbons,' he said. 'My wife. She might be calling herself Ruth Levene.'

'I told you yesterday, mister. I don't know her.'

'But have you ever seen her going in and out of the building? Please?'

She took a closer look at the photograph, then shook her head.

'I'm sorry, mister. I never seen her. Never.'

'Okay. Thanks anyway. Sorry to have troubled you.'

Ayesha nodded, and hurried off, and through the glass doors. Matt returned to the bench.

Over the next hour, he witnessed a dozen or so more groups and individuals leave the building, and return, normally with some type of bag containing their lunch. Just before one thirty, two young women walked past, both talking and laughing, each carrying a *Subway* bag. Matt recognized them as having left the building a little earlier. One was very tall, well over six feet, and towered over her companion, who was at least eighteen inches shorter.

'Excuse me,' he said, standing up and walking over to them. They stopped and looked over to him.

'I'm so sorry to trouble you,' he asked, 'but do you work for Cambridge Pharmaceuticals?'

They looked at each other, and then nodded. Both had a puzzled expression.

'I was just wondering if either of you knew a Ruth Gibbons. Ruth Levene, maybe.'

Before they had the chance to reply, he took out his phone and showed them Ruth's picture. The taller one looked down at the other, then back to the picture.

'No. I'm sorry, I don't,' she said.

Matt nodded and turned to the shorter one.

'And you? Do you know -?'

'No. I've never seen her before.'

The two women turned and walked away, back to work, the taller one a couple of paces behind.

Putting the phone back in his pocket, Matt returned to the bench. He checked his watch: it was almost one thirty. He considered if there was any value staying there any longer. If he was going to catch Ruth leaving the building for lunch – and that was if she *was* working there – he would have seen her by now. He needed to get back to Beacon Hill to pick up Nathan, and the last thing he wanted was to bump into – what were their names? Danny and Aki – as they returned.

He gave it another ten minutes, then stood up, stretched and began to walk up the street. He called in at a Starbucks on the next block and bought himself a coffee and a roast beef sandwich.

Pausing at a trash can to throw away the empty cup and sandwich wrapper, Matt wiped his mouth with a napkin, tossed that away also, and started to walk briskly up Washington Street. He passed the Medical Center, decided against taking the T, and continued up the street. The heavy clouds he saw earlier had come to nothing: now the sky was a clear blue, crisp and cold. He crossed over Kneeland, and made a left at Boylston Square. Soon he was back at the Common, and the Central Burying Ground. Rather than cross the Common, he carried on Boylston and took a right up Charles Street, which is the division between Boston Common and the Public Gardens. He checked his watch again: even though he now had plenty of time before Nathan finished, he wanted to get home first, get online, and check their bank accounts.

He got home just before two thirty, logged onto the Bank of New England website, and retrieved his and Ruth's accounts. As well as the joint checking account, they had a savings account, also in joint names, and an account for Nathan. First of all, he went to the checking account. The screen confirmed what Larry had told him earlier: the two withdrawals totalling five hundred dollars from the ATM at the Safeway store. Matt went back three months, but there were no unusual transactions. Then he clicked onto their savings account. It occurred to him that if Ruth had drawn the five hundred to finance her disappearance, she may have done the same with their savings account. Withdrawals from there might not come to light for months.

Matt checked the account: all was in order.

He logged off and sat back in his chair. Now he felt guilty. Sure, there was still the question of those two withdrawals, but what was he doing suspecting his wife of absconding with their savings? When he first saw that office manager – Danny – and his girlfriend, he was sure that it was Ruth he was with, that they were having an affair, and that was the explanation. But of course it wasn't. Once again, it all came back to Nathan – she would never ever leave him.

Nathan. He checked his watch: almost time to go to Bambinos. Time for one more phone call. One call he was not looking forward to making. To his parents.

Matt's parents – Matthew and Estelle – were both retired, now in their early seventies. When Matthew Snr retired from his job with the City of Charleston, they bought a small white clap-board house a short walk from the coast in Sandwich, the first town you find when arriving on the island of Cape Cod. Matt was relatively close – he felt – to his parents, but for some reason they and Ruth never quite hit it off. It had always been as if they had reservations about her suitability as a wife for Matt, and for her part, Ruth was always reserved towards them. All parties denied this, saying it was Matt's imagination. Ruth's own parents had died long before Matt met her. One thing which was in no doubt, however, was how much they loved their grandson. Matt would visit them at least once a month, always with Nathan; sometimes Ruth was unable to accompany them, due to work commitments. Neither Matthew Snr nor Estelle would seem particularly bothered that Ruth had to work.

How would they react now? Matt picked up the phone and dialled. His mother answered the phone.

'Hello, Mom. It's Matt.'

'Oh hello, dear. What's the time? Are you calling from work?'

'No, I'm not at work today. Listen: I have something to tell you.'

'Oh, what's that, dear?'

'It's Ruth. She – she didn't come home Tuesday night. I don't know where she is.'

As Matt expected, Estelle said, 'Matt, here's your father. Speak to him.'

As Estelle passed the phone across, Matt could hear her whisper, 'It's Matt. He says Ruth's left him.'

'Matt? It's your father here,' came a gruff voice.

'I didn't say she's left me, Dad; I just said she didn't come home the other night.'

Then Matt spent the next ten minutes relating to his father the events of the last two days. His father said nothing, just grunting and muttering 'u-huh' every so often.

'So what are you going to do now?' his father asked.

'I guess I'll just have to carry on at present. There's nothing else I can do. Make sure Nathan's okay, and wait until the police contact me.'

'Here. Your mother wants to speak to you.' With that, Estelle came back on the line.

'Matt, why don't you and Nathan come down at the weekend? We can all talk then. Be nice to see you both.'

Not Ruth.

'That'd be nice. Wait though: I have to work Saturday till around three. We'll make an early start

Sunday morning.'

'You're working Saturday? What about Nathan?'

'Ruth's friend Gail and her partner Ryan have agreed to look after him. Nathan likes them; he'll be okay.'

'Right,' said his mother, not entirely approvingly.

'Listen, Mom, I have to go now. Have to pick Nathan up from kindergarten. See you Sunday.'

'Right you are, dear.'

'Call you if I get any news.'

'Yes, please. Do that.'

With that Matt hung up and left the house to pick up Nathan. On the way to Bambinos he decided to tell Nathan that his mother had gone away on a training course and would be back at the weekend. Nathan seemed to accept what Matt had told him, and to his surprise and relief asked no further questions. Matt was dreading being asked if they could telephone Ruth, but his son was more interested in the southern fried chicken and the DVD of *Land Before Time VIII.*

By eight, Nathan was bathed, had brushed his teeth, had been read a story and was snoring soundly.

For the first time since Tuesday night, Matt poured himself a whisky and soda and slumped into an armchair. *What a wasted day*, he thought. He was so convinced he would see Ruth that lunchtime. And still more questions, like where did that five hundred bucks go? Maybe she had had her purse stolen? He shook his head: no, that just raised more questions. In any case, she was very punctilious about PIN security.

Back to work tomorrow.

He looked up at the ceiling, in the direction of Nathan's room. He thought about his story of Ruth being on a training course. He said that on impulse.

As he said it, he knew it was a bad idea, but he swore he would tell his son the truth on Saturday night.

Whatever the truth was on Saturday night.

Chapter Thirteen

'I'LL BE PERFECTLY honest with you,' the man said, as he rubbed his chin. 'We are shopping around, you see.'

Matt nodded. Not as if this was the first time an interview he had conducted began with that line.

'I understand,' he said.

Matt's customer leaned back in his chair and brushed some imaginary dust off his sleeve. 'We've been to Bank of America, Mellon Bank, and – where was it yesterday, dear?' He turned and looked at his wife, a smartly dressed lady also in her early sixties.

'Sovereign Bank, John,' Mrs Thomas replied.

'That's right, Sovereign,' Mr Thomas continued. 'So basically, today I want you to tell me what you and New England Bank can offer me. Offer us, I mean. Then I and my wife will decide.'

'Bank of New England,' Matt corrected, instantly wishing he had kept his mouth shut.

'Whatever,' Mr Thomas said, icily.

Shut your mouth Gibbons, you can't afford to screw up was the thought passing through Matt's head as he turned slightly to his right and fired up his computer.

'Well,' he said. 'Can I start first by taking down some information about yourselves, your personal circumstances, so I can begin to match your requirements to our products and services?'

Mrs Thomas started to say, 'I don't see -'

'That will be satisfactory,' Mr Thomas interrupted her. 'Proceed.' He leaned back further in his chair, folding his arms. Mrs Thomas remained poised upright on her chair, clutching her blue sequined bag.

So for the next ten minutes Matt proceeded to ask Mr and Mrs Thomas questions about their personal financial circumstances, their income and outgoings, what type of insurance they had, what their aspirations were. He learned that Mr Thomas had been retired for seven years, having previously been an executive with the Exxon Mobil Corporation. Mrs Thomas left work in the early sixties, since when she has raised their four children and made cakes and sat on committees. Before he retired, they lived in Irving, Texas, close by Exxon's headquarters. Mr Thomas was raised in New Jersey, and on his retirement wanted to move back to the North East. Their main home was just outside the town of Concord, a select community around twenty miles west of Boston; they also had another residence, 'our winter home', as Mrs Thomas called it, in Fort Lauderdale. They had spent Christmas and New Year there, and had come back to Massachusetts to take care of some business, as Mr Thomas called it. After they had decided what to do after visiting all the banks in Boston, they would return to Florida.

So, thought Matt, you're *just wasting my time really. No intention of doing any business with me.*

Trying to keep positive, and going for that one in ten chance that Mr and Mrs Thomas might pass him their accounts, Matt began to talk about the best type of accounts for the couple.

'If we can look first of all at checking accounts…'

'Go ahead. What can you offer us?'

'Well, how much do you intend to be keeping in the account?'

Mr Thomas sniffed and checked his fingernails.

‘Only a few thousand, just for expenses. Most of our money is in property or in our savings accounts.’

‘I ask the question because our Premium account has a tiered interest rate structure.’

‘Oh yes?’ Mr Thomas seemed interested.

‘If the balance is less than ten thousand dollars, the interest rate is 0.05%; between ten thousand and -’

‘Forget it. That rate’s too low. What about the rates on your savings accounts?’

Matt’s attention was momentarily diverted away from the couple to his top right hand desk drawer. The drawer was open six inches or so, and Matt’s cell phone was lying, with a calculator, on top of a note pad in the drawer. The phone screen remained blank: no messages or missed calls.

‘Are you still with us?’ snapped Mr Thomas.

‘Mm?’ asked Matt, his attention returning to his customer.

‘I asked what are the interest rates on your savings accounts.’

‘If I could just go through the checking accounts first, then -’

Mr Thomas gave Matt a smug, self-satisfied smile. ‘The savings accounts.’

Matt took a deep breath.

‘Well, that would depend on the type of account you want, how much you have in the accounts -’

Mr Thomas held his hand up.

‘Mr Gibbons,’ he said, still with that smug look on his face. ‘I just want the savings rates.’

Matt had had enough. Giving his phone another glance, he took a decision. If these people were just wasting his time, then he had nothing to lose. Maybe he was in with a chance to get their business, but it was a slim one. In any case, there was no way this guy was going to speak to him like he was Nathan's age.

He leaned forward, resting both arms on the desk.

'Mr Thomas. Mr and Mrs Thomas,' he said quietly. Politely but firmly. 'If you just want to know what our interest rates are, then fine; take a brochure. But it was my understanding that you came to see me for *advice*. If that is the case, then you must allow me to go through my procedures, gather all the information I need so I can match your needs to what we can offer. Then you can make your decision. With all the facts.'

Mr Thomas straightened in his chair. His face lost the smug expression.

'How did you get on?'

Matt looked up from his desk.

'Get on with what?' he asked Larry Mason.

'The old couple. They looked like they weren't short of a few bucks. How did you get on with them?'

'Oh, them. They're taking away all the information I gave them. To think it all over.

'Right. Well, fingers crossed.'

'Thanks.' Matt took his cell phone from his drawer and checked it. Nothing.

'You okay, Matt?' Larry asked.

'Yeah, fine.'

Larry opened his mouth the say something else, but stopped when the phone on Matt's desk rang.

'Matt Gibbons,' Matt said into the phone. 'Right. I'll be right along.'

He put the phone and shook his head.

'Problem?' asked Larry.

'Debra wants to see me,' Matt said as he stood up.

'Uh-uh. Better take your crucifix and garlic. Chin up, buddy,' chuckled Larry as he slapped Matt on the shoulder.

'Come in,' Debra called out as Matt knocked on her door.

As he pushed the door open and went in she was engrossed in something on her laptop.

'Sit down, Matt. Won't keep you a moment.'

Mind games, he thought as he silently sat down.

After a couple of minutes she shut the laptop.

'Matt,' she said, giving him a brief smile, pushing the laptop to one side. She took her glasses off and laid them on the desk. Matt caught a whiff of an expensive perfume.

'How did you get on with your customers?' she asked. 'Mr and Mrs'- she glanced down at some notes on her desk - 'Thomas?'

'They were interested in what we had to offer. They were shopping around.'

'Shopping around?'

'They said they had been to four or five other banks. Taking details of what we can offer. Then make their decision.'

'But our products are the best on the market. I just don't understand why you couldn't close the deal.'

Matt shrugged. 'As I said, they are shopping around.'

'How optimistic are you about them returning?'

'Reasonably.'

She put her glasses back on and opened the laptop. Stared at Matt for a second.

'I hope so, Matt. I hope so. Keep me up to speed on them.'

She returned to her laptop, so Matt stood up and began to leave.

'How are you, in any case?' she asked, looking up.

'Fine. Thanks for asking.'

'Any news?'

Matt knew what she meant. 'No. No news.'

'And how is your son? Ethan, isn't it?'

'Nathan, you mean?'

'Yes, that's right. Nathan. How is he bearing up?'

'As well as can be expected, thanks.'

'If you need any more time off…'

'No thanks. Need to keep occupied.'

'And keep a pay check coming in.'

Matt started to answer when she cut him off with, 'Thanks for dropping by Matt. Fingers crossed for your next customer. Let's hope for some success with *them*.'

As Matt shut the door on his way out, he thought a moment. Success with *them*: was she implying failure with Mr and Mrs Thomas? And *keep a pay check coming in*? Was that a veiled threat?

Standing outside Debra's door he checked his phone again. Then walked back to his desk. He had one word for his conversation with Debra.

Bitch.

Chapter Fourteen

LARRY MASON LEANED back in the armchair he was occupying in the staff room. He looked up as Matt came in and headed straight for the coffee machine.

'You still with us then, buddy?' he asked.

'What?' asked Matt, as he added his normal two spoons of sugar.

'After your interview with the devil woman,' Larry replied.

'Oh nothing really,' said Matt as he sat in the chair opposite Larry. 'Just the usual stuff: you know, how she couldn't understand why I couldn't sign them up there and then. Then how she understood how much I needed my pay check.'

'Subtle as ever,' said Larry.

'I wouldn't worry,' said José. José and Matt had both worked at this branch for around the same length of time. 'I had the same conversation with her the other day. We all have. And there's no way she's gonna get rid of us all.'

'Well,' replied Matt, swirling his coffee and studying the movement of the liquid. 'That was the conversation we had.'

'The thing is though,' said Larry, 'she says the sort of things she says; like with you, Matt, but it's always the same thing. How she can't understand why we couldn't do something.'

'Yeah,' said Matt. 'Your point being?'

'My point is this. When I worked up at Bangor a few years back -'

'I never knew you worked there,' José cut in. 'How long ago?'

'Five or six years. Anyway – what I was going to say: when I was there, the Branch Manager, a guy called – what was his name? Terrance, no Torrance – he really had a grip on the sales part of the job. He used to have a meeting before we opened the doors with all the Personal Bankers.'

'Cruella doesn't,' said José.

'No. Quite. Well, in this meeting, we all discussed all the people who were coming in that day. You know, their personal and money stuff, then we all talked about what potential each client had. And the thing is – and this is where he differs from her so much – he always had lots of ideas and suggestions.'

'What sort of ideas?' Matt asked.

'Things like the best way to get a client interested in an account, or he'd suggest a way to overcome an objection a client might make.'

'I see,' said Matt. 'Interesting.'

'The thing is,' continued Larry, 'he had done the job himself for years so he knew everything inside out. Unlike -'

'Unlike that bitch out there,' José said, also sitting down with Matt and Larry. 'She's just got to that job on her back.'

'I would suggest then,' said Larry, 'that the next time she says that she is surprised a client didn't sign up we all ask her what she would have done in the circumstances. Put her on the spot for a change.' As he spoke he looked up at the corner of the room and closed his eyes as if in meditation.

'Sounds cool,' said José. 'About time she showed an interest. Other than in her frigging laptop.' He walked over to the sink, threw the dregs of his coffee away and walked over to the door. 'Time for my next one. See you later guys.'

'Later,' Larry said, then turned to Matt.

'You sure that's it, Matt? You seem awful quiet.'

Matt swirled his coffee. 'No, I'm fine, thanks. Just a lot going on, I guess.'

'Your wife, you mean?'

Matt nodded.

'No more news, then?'

Matt shook his head.

'What have the police said? I assume you've been to the police?'

'Straight away. They were very sympathetic, took all the details. Then started to – to follow their processes, I guess.'

Larry's cell phone buzzed. He pulled it out.

'Sorry, Matt. My next client's arrived.'

He stood up and ruffled Matt's hair as he walked past.

'Stay focussed, buddy. No news is good news.'

Left alone in the staff room, Matt sat back in his chair. Drained his cup. Checked his watch. It would soon be time to leave to pick Nathan up from the kindergarten. That was one concession he had managed to get out of Debra: her permission for him to leave early to meet Nathan. He had to make up the time of course: out of vacation time or working extra Saturdays. Always a price to pay.

Ten minutes before he had to leave. Just time to call Lieutenant Weber.

He speed dialled Weber's number and waited for the Lieutenant to answer.

'Weber,' came the voice.

'Hello, Lieutenant, it's Matthew Gibbons.'

There was a brief silence.

‘Ah, Mr Gibbons. I thought I recognized the number.’

‘I was just wondering if there was any news.’

‘I’m not aware of any. Look, Mr Gibbons, do you remember when I called round to see you? I said I had to pass the information you gave me about your wife to my Captain. He then passes it to the Missing Persons Unit. They’ve been in touch with you, haven’t they?’

‘They have, yes. I just thought you might have heard something.’

‘Look, Mr Gibbons. I’ll tell you what I’ll do. I’ll get hold of my counterpart in the MPU; get them to call you to give you an update. Okay?’

‘Okay. That would be much appreciated. Thanks.’

‘You’re welcome, Mr Gibbons. You take care now.’

Matt slowly disconnected the phone, put it into his pocket, and wandered back to his desk. He tidied up what paperwork he had left on the desk, and made his way to the parking lot. Larry, José, and the others were all seeing clients, so he avoided any awkward goodbyes. Everybody knew why he was leaving early.

‘Was that him again?’ Detective Mancini asked, as she dragged her index finger down the patrol car window, wiping a clear line through the condensation.

‘U-huh,’ replied Weber, as he slipped the phone back into his shirt pocket.

‘What does the guy want?’

‘What the hell do you think he wants? His wife back, that’s what he wants.’

'His wife back? Like that's going to happen.'

Weber shrugged. 'Let's just say he wants to know where she is.'

'And he keeps calling you?'

He shrugged again. 'Desperate, I guess. I might've been the same. Anyhow, I've done all I can do. I can't do no more. It's up to the MPU guys now. They should keep in touch with him.'

'And are they?'

'Of course they are. Well, they were three days ago when I checked. That was the last time he called me.'

'Jes-us.'

'Give the guy a break, Mancini. He just wants to know, that's all. Wouldn't you be the same if Joe never came home from work?'

'No.'

'Mancini…'

'Yeah. I know. I'd be the same.'

There was a moment's silence, then Mancini spoke again.

'There again, he could already know where she is.'

Weber looked over at his partner. 'Haven't we had this conversation before? You know he had nothing to do with it. He was eliminated from the investigation after the first day.'

'Yeah. I remember.'

'Oh, what the hell.' Weber picked up his phone and dialled.

'Who you calling now?'

'Edwards from the MPU. Get him to call Gibbons one more time.'

*****

The parking lot Matt used was at the rear of the building. As he walked out of the branch doors he took a left, then another left down the side street which led to the lot. Checked his watch again. Yes, traffic permitting, he would get to Bambinos in time. Then a detour via the 711 store to pick up something for their dinner. Tell Nathan another bullshit story about where his mother was. Still away on that work course, probably. Then when Nathan was asleep, make another load of calls. Still thinking things through, he walked across the lot to the space where he had left the Toyota that morning.

As he got to the space, he stopped.

The car had gone.

Chapter Fifteen

LIEUTENANT WEBER WAS just about to dial the MPU to check up on the Gibbons case when it rang. The caller number was not shown. He answered, listened for a moment, said, 'We'll be right over,' and then hung up.

'What is it?' Mancini asked.

'MGH,' Weber answered, starting the car. 'Celeste Washington came round ten minutes ago.'

Mancini fastened the blue light on the car roof as Weber accelerated out of South Shore Plaza where they had been investigating a case of suspected arson.

'You taking the 93?' she asked, as they swung round a bend and he took the ramp leading up to the Interstate. He was already doing seventy as they joined the highway and swiftly moved into the number 4 lane.

'Quickest way I know,' Weber muttered. 'Should be there in half an hour,' he added, giving a black sports car a blast on the horn to get the driver to move over.

'What's the hurry?' Mancini asked, glancing down to the speedo dial, which was now showing ninety.

'I want to get the sons of bitches that did what they did to her,' Weber said. 'And we need to talk to the lady herself. While she's -'

'Still alive?'

'I was going to say while she's conscious. She could slip into a coma again. But, yeah; while she's still alive maybe. And don't forget: the sooner we get to them, the less chance there is of them doing the same thing to another little old lady.'

'Let's just get there in one piece, Sam,' Mancini said as she tightened her grip on the door handle. Weber was doing ninety-five.

'Relax Mancini,' Weber grinned. 'I've done the advanced driving course, remember?'

'Oh yeah. I'd forgotten,' she said sardonically. She watched as they sped past the traffic in the other lanes.

Weber swung off the 93 just after they left the tunnel section and was soon pulling up outside the Massachusetts General Hospital. They both ran into the hospital and to the room where Ms Washington was being kept.

Matt contemplated returning to his office to report his car stolen, but he would rather do it from home. In any case, he had to pick Nathan up. He hurried up to State, and along to the subway station; not to get a train, but one of the many taxi cabs that were always parked outside the station.

The cab dropped him off outside Nathan's kindergarten. Matt had ten minutes or so to spare, so he walked around the block a couple of times, trying to get his head round what was going on. First Ruth, her disappearance, the mystery of where she worked; now his car being stolen.

He picked up Nathan and they walked home, calling in at the 711 two blocks from Matt's house. Picked up two microwave lasagnes and set off home.

'You wanna watch some TV?' he asked Nathan as they got in. 'Daddy needs to make a couple of phone calls.'

'Sure thing, Daddy,' the little boy replied, heading straight for his favourite seat opposite the television. 'Can I see *Jurassic Park*? Please, please.'

'No, I don't think so,' Matt said slowly as he looked through their collection of DVDs. 'How about *Ice Age 3*?'

'Cool. Yeah, yeah,' Nathan replied excitedly.

'Coming right up.' Matt started playing the disc of *Ice Age 3: Dawn of the Dinosaurs* and left his son glued to the television while he went into the kitchen to call the police. Again. 911 not being appropriate he felt, he looked up what number to dial, and did so.

The call took about ten minutes. He felt slightly disappointed afterwards: never having had to report a stolen car before, he was not sure what to expect, but got the impression he was just going through the motions. The officer he spoke to gave Matt a crime reference number, which he would need for the insurance. He had read somewhere that the percentage of stolen vehicles recovered was in single figures: at least there was nothing valuable in the car, he reflected.

'You looking forward to seeing Gail tomorrow?' he asked Nathan, as they both attacked their lasagnes.

'Mm,' mumbled Nathan, nodding. 'Will Mommy be coming home tomorrow?' he asked.

'Should be. Maybe after you get back from Gail's.'

'Cool.' Nathan returned to his food.

After Nathan had gone to bed, Matt poured himself a glass of red wine and sat down. The chair was still warm from when Nathan was watching television earlier. He had a thought. He drank the last of his wine, and went upstairs. He peeked into Nathan's room to check on him, made a bathroom stop, then back downstairs. Booted up their computer, and logged on again to the Bank of New England site. He keyed in the necessary passwords, and got access again to their accounts. He scanned the transactions again, this time back to the twenty-fifth of the month before. The twenty-fifth was payday for them both. For the last month, and the twelve months before, every twenty-fifth, or twenty-fourth, or twenty-third, depending on the day of the week, there were two credits to their account, representing their respective pay. Sure enough, in the details column for Ruth's pay, was the comment *Cam Pharm*. Matt made a clicking noise with his tongue, something he did sometimes while in thought: so she *does* work there. So that asshole – what was his name? Danny – was bullshitting him. But why? What was it all about?

He leaned back in his chair, slowly shaking his head.

'What in the hell's going on?' he said aloud. 'Danny whatever your name is, you're full of shit,' he added. 'And you're gonna be straight with me tomorrow.'

He logged off, determined to make another trip to Ruth's office the next morning.

Until he realised it was Friday night. Ruth never worked weekends, so the offices were bound to be closed till Monday. Shit; would have to wait till then. But the police would need to know. Matt realised he had not told them about the question about where Ruth worked. Not Lieutenant Weber, nor the officer from the Missing Persons Unit.

He checked the time: it was getting late, and he had an early start the next morning. Gail and her partner Ryan were looking after Nathan while he was at work, and he had to leave early to drive Nathan to their house.

Drive.

No car.

Damn.

Groaning, Matt retrieved his phone from the kitchen and dialled Gail's number, praying it would not go to voicemail. It didn't.

'Hello?'

Matt was at first surprised she failed to recognize the number, but realised it was Ruth who always called her.

'Gail, it's Matt. Sorry to call you so late.'

'No problem. What's up? Do you still need us to look after Nathan tomorrow?'

'I do, yes; but there's a problem. My car was stolen today. I've reported it already, but have no transportation right now. It's not really practical to take him to yours using public transportation; any chance you and Ryan could come and get him?'

'Oh, shit. Sorry, Matt. Ryan has to take the car in the morning, so I can't. Maybe -'

'Don't worry. I'll get a cab. I'll get it from here, drop Nathan off, then the driver can take me up to the office. When is Ryan due back?'

'Around lunchtime.'

'So you could bring Nathan home in the afternoon?'

'Sure. Maybe the three of us can play some ball or something in the park, then get over to yours around four.'

'Sounds good. Do you want to stay for dinner? My way of saying thank you for helping with Nathan.'

‘Gee, any other time, I’d say yes, but we already have plans for tomorrow night.’

‘Some other time then.’

‘Sure. Absolutely.’

‘Well, I’ll get Nathan over to yours for around eight thirty tomorrow.’

‘Sure Matt. See you then.’

‘See you.’

‘Oh Matt,’ Gail added. ‘Is there any news? About Ruth, I mean.’

‘No. Nothing yet.’

‘Well, call me if there is. Any time. Sorry about the car, too.’

‘Thanks. See you in the morning.’

Matt ended the call and tossed the phone down onto the table. ‘Don’t concern yourself too much,’ he muttered, as if continuing his conversation with Gail. ‘If it was my best friend listed as a missing person, I’d be more interested than you seem to be. Then you always were a narcissistic bitch.’

Matt looked over at the clock. It was now just gone ten. He stretched and rubbed his eyes. Time for bed: it was an early start tomorrow, and he had a lot to do – again. Maybe he would get some quiet times at work tomorrow so he can do something about the car. He was sure the insurance policy gave him so many days’ use of a courtesy car. There was that trip to the Cape on Sunday: postponing would not normally be a problem, but this time, he needed to go.

He switched off the television and the downstairs lights and started to climb the stairs. As he was half way up, the doorbell rang. He quickly listened out in case the sound had woken Nathan, and then went back down.

Through the spy hole he could make out two

figures. One was slight – female he guessed – and the other taller and rounder. He recognized Lieutenant Weber. He started breathing quickly as he fumbled with the lock and swung the door open.

'Lieutenant,' he said breathlessly. 'Have you any news? Has Ruth turned up yet?'

Weber swung round to look at the female officer. She remained expressionless.

'Mr Gibbons,' the Lieutenant said. 'This is my partner, Detective Mancini.'

Matt and Mancini gave each other a slight nod.

'Well?' Matt asked again.

'No,' Weber continued, 'your wife has not turned up yet, but the investigation – the search – is still ongoing.'

'You've come about my car, then?' Matt asked.

Weber looked puzzled. 'Your car?'

'It was stolen today. I reported it earlier this evening. I thought -'

'We haven't come about your car, Mr Gibbons. We have come in regard to the investigation into your wife's disappearance.'

Matt had a sudden uneasy feeling.

'We need to ask you some more questions,' Weber went on.

Then he paused. Matt wondered if it was for effect.

'Downtown.'

Chapter Sixteen

'WHAT?' ASKED MATT, uncertain if he heard the Lieutenant correctly. 'You want me to answer more questions?'

Mancini answered. 'Downtown.'

'Look,' Matt said, trying to speak louder but still keeping his voice down. He did not want to wake Nathan, nor did he want the woman who was walking by the opposite side of the street and watching them, to hear them. 'I have a five year old boy upstairs asleep. It's late. Why do you need me to come to the station with you? Now? What's so important it can't wait, or can't be done here?'

Weber glanced over at Mancini, who remained expressionless. 'All right,' he said, looking back at Mancini. 'Let us in now, and we'll see how we get on.'

Matt's eyes flickered over to Mancini, whose eyes had just opened wide. Saying nothing, he held the door fully open and let the two police officers in.

'Go into the kitchen,' he said. 'Lieutenant, you know where that is.'

Weber nodded, and stepped in, followed by Mancini, who was not looking happy. As Matt watched Weber lead his partner into the kitchen, he thought what an unlikely partnership this was. Weber, the middle-aged, overweight, African American cop, dressed in a scruffy suit and open raincoat and looking like something out of the fifties; Mancini, much younger, a slighter figure dressed in a black leather jacket, blue denims and black shoes. Her red hair was cut in a boyish style. Strange, Matt thought, she doesn't look Italian.

'May we?' asked Weber, indicating to one of the chairs.

'Be my guest,' Matt said as he joined them. Weber pulled out a chair – the same one he used the last time. Mancini looked as if she was determined to stand until Weber flashed her a stare. Reluctantly, she pulled out the next chair and sat down. As she put her hands on the table, Matt noticed a wedding band. That explains the surname, thought Matt.

'Coffee?' Matt offered. He felt Weber was about to say yes, but after a quick look at Mancini, who declined, the Lieutenant waved his hand.

Matt leaned on the sink.

'Well?' he said. 'You said you had more questions.'

'Yes, we do,' said Weber. 'First of all, I want to clarify some points from our conversation the other day.'

'Clarify?' queried Matt.

'Yeah. Mainly for Detective Mancini's benefit. So she's up to speed.'

Mancini looked over at Weber, then back at Matt.

'It was Tuesday night when you reported your wife missing,' she said. Matt was surprised: not so much at the question, but that out of the blue, she was asking the questions. Maybe this is what they meant by good cop bad cop, he reflected.

'It was. Tuesday night.'

'And when did she disappear?'

'Tuesday night. And she didn't disappear as you put it. She didn't come home.'

The look on Mancini's face said *whatever*.

'Tell me again: what time was she due home?'

asked Weber.

'Between five thirty and quarter of six. She finished work at five.'

'Was that when she normally finished?' asked Weber.

'U-huh. Generally.'

'But you don't know that she did finish at five that night,' said Mancini.

'I do.'

'How so?'

'She sent me a text to say she was leaving work. She did every night when she left. I would do the same. It was just our way of letting the other know we were on our way, and what time we could be expected home.'

Mancini said, 'So you got this text, when?'

'At five,' said Matt, slightly impatiently.

'Is it still on your cell?' Weber asked. 'Could I..?'

'Surely.' Matt retrieved the message on his phone and passed it to Weber. The Lieutenant checked it, nodded and showed it to Mancini. She looked and nodded to Weber.

'You can check the day before,' said Matt. 'And the day before. Or Friday last week, rather.'

Weber silently tabbed down to the previous day's messages, then passed the phone back to Matt.

'But you agree,' Weber said, 'that this is just a text: you don't know for sure where she was when she sent it.'

Matt took a deep breath. 'No, that's true, but -'

'Or that it was your wife who sent it,' added Mancini.

'What do you mean?' asked Matt.

'I mean anybody could have sent it. Even you.'

'Even me? What the hell are you talking about?'

'What we're trying to say,' said Weber, 'is that nobody can be one hundred percent sure that it *was* your wife who sent the text, or that she *was* at work when she sent it.'

'Mm. I see.' Matt was beginning to get the picture.

'Which brings us to the next question,' said Weber. 'Where does your wife work?'

'I told you the other day: Cambridge Pharmaceuticals on Washington,' Matt replied. He paused a moment, then added, 'But you're gonna tell me they've never heard of her.'

Weber and Mancini glanced at each other, then Weber said, 'No. I was going to tell you she hasn't been to work since last Friday.'

'What?' Matt couldn't believe this.

'She hasn't shown up all this week. Nobody has seen her since last Friday.'

'But – but,' Matt stammered, shaking his head, 'that's not what they told me.'

'You called them to see where she was?' Weber asked.

'Well, eventually.'

'Eventually?' Mancini queried.

'Could I just check on my son?' Matt asked. 'Make sure he's asleep.'

Mancini opened her mouth as if to protest, but Weber cut in.

'Sure. Be quick, though.'

'One minute.'

As Matt crept up the stairs, he could hear whispering from the kitchen. He was unable to make out what was being said, but it sounded like *sotto voce* arguing. He peered in Nathan's room: his son was still fast asleep, clutching a dinosaur Matt couldn't identify. He was lying on his front, his left leg hanging down the side of the bed. Matt leaned down and gently lifted the leg back onto the bed, covered it with the *Jurassic Park* quilt, which he smoothed down. Nathan stirred slightly as Matt tenderly ran his hands through his son's hair.

He returned to the kitchen. Weber looked up at him and said, 'You were going to tell us about calling your wife.'

Matt pulled out a chair from the opposite side of the table and sat down.

'When Ruth was overdue by fifteen, twenty minutes, I started to call her cell phone. Did it several times. Got voicemail each time. I figured maybe she's in a meeting, maybe she put it on silent earlier, forgot to change it, so I rang her office landline.'

'And?'

'The number I had stored in here,' - he held up his cell phone – 'seemed to be wrong.'

'Wrong? As in…'

'As in this call cannot be completed as dialled. I was surprised; after all it was the number Ruth gave me herself. I figured I must have programmed the phone wrong.'

'Had you not called her on that number before?'

'Don't recall doing it. Always used her cell.'

'So you called Information?' asked Weber.

'That's right. And the number they gave me was totally different from the one I had.'

'It's possible,' Mancini said. 'Sometimes phone companies change numbers. Upgrading an exchange. Converting to digital, maybe.'

Matt shrugged.

'Anyway,' he continued, 'I called that number and it was the right number, but I got a recording saying the offices were closed and to call back the next morning.'

'Which you did, presumably,' said Mancini.

'I tried Ruth's cell a couple more times. Then her friend Gail.'

'Gail?' Weber asked.

'Gail Smith. She's Ruth's best friend. I wondered if Ruth had gone over to hers, or maybe she knew where Ruth had gone.'

'Where does this Gail live?' asked Weber.

'Her precise address – that's -'

'In Boston?' said Weber.

'Yeah, it's here.' Matt reached over for the address book they kept by the house phone and looked up Gail's address. Mancini made a note while Matt read it out.

'Did she know where your wife was?' asked Mancini, looking up from her notepad.

'I got voicemail. Same as Ruth.'

'Okay,' said Weber. 'You were saying you called the offices the next morning.'

'That's the whole point. I did – and they told me nobody with Ruth's name worked there. I even tried her maiden name – Levene – and still they said the same thing. I even went down to the office in my lunch hour and they told me the same thing.'

'Well,' said Weber, leaning back in his seat, 'they told us she does work there; only she hasn't been in since Friday. They've tried calling her, but keep getting voicemail.'

'See? Same as me,' said Matt, banging his hand on the table. Who did you speak to?'

'Sorry.' Weber shook his head. 'Can't say at this time.'

'Was it that office manager? Danny – Danny

something?'

Weber and Mancini said nothing.

After a few moments of silence Weber spoke up.

'You said something earlier about a stolen car.'

'Yes, I took it to work this morning. Parked it as I always do in the lot at the rear of the bank. When I left this afternoon to pick up Nathan, it was gone.'

'Stolen?' said Mancini.

'Absolutely stolen. I wouldn't have mislaid it.'

'And you've reported it?' Weber asked.

Matt nodded. 'This afternoon. I did think at first that was why you called round.'

Weber shook his head. 'No, Mr Gibbons. Not our department.'

'No, of course not,' said Matt. 'So I got a cab back here, got Nathan, and called you guys about it.'

'Mm,' said Weber, slowly nodding his head. 'What make and model is your car?'

'A Toyota. A Camry. 2008. Why? Has it been found?'

'No.' Weber shook his head. 'Just routine. Who normally drives it? You? Do you have a car each?'

'No. Just one between us.'

'And who normally drives it?

'I do. I work in a bank on State Street. The journey by public transit would take two hours almost.'

Weber whistled softly. 'So your wife – she would use the bus, the T?'

'She'd normally walk.'

'Walk?' asked a surprised Mancini.

'U-huh. She's always walked. Unless the weather was really bad, then she'd go by bus. Says it saved her fifty bucks a week gym membership.'

'Can she drive?' asked Weber.

'She can, but as she walks, I normally take the car in.'

'I see,' said Weber. 'Where are the car keys now?'

'Over here.' Matt stood up and stepped over to a row of small hooks on the wall. There was an assortment of keys hanging: house keys, garage keys, and the Toyota keys. He held up the car keys for Weber to see. Weber held out his hand for the keys. Matt passed them over. Weber checked for the Toyota logo engraved on the key, and passed them back.

'Are there any spare keys?' Weber asked.

'Sure. We keep them upstairs.'

'Could you..?'

'I checked them already. The other night I couldn't sleep. I had all sorts of weird ideas about how and why Ruth had disappeared. So I checked where we keep the spare keys. Just to make sure they were there.'

'And?'

'They were there, of course. Why? Do you want me to check again?'

Weber nodded. 'Yes please. If you don't mind. The keys are there?'

'I told you: I checked already. The other night.'

Matt stood up. 'I'll go get them,' he said.

'Mr Gibbons,' asked Mancini as Matt left the kitchen, 'why do you keep the spare keys upstairs. Why not over there?' She indicated to the row of key hooks.

'Force of habit. Before we moved here we had an apartment. One floor. One day we needed the spare keys, but couldn't find them Turned out Nathan had put them in the toilet. So from then on we've kept them in a drawer upstairs.'

Mancini smiled slightly as Matt left her and Weber.

'What?' asked Weber.

'Nothing,' said Mancini. 'My youngest did that once.' She shook her head. 'O'Riordan's gonna be pissed you didn't take him Downtown for questioning.'

'Screw O'Riordan. If we did, what are we gonna do about the kid? Call Social Services? At this time of night? Get real. Anyhow: let's see what he has to say here, then take a view in the morning. He's not going anywhere. And I can handle O'Riordan. If he thinks...'

Weber stopped when he saw Matt standing in the kitchen doorway.

'The other night, like I told you, I checked the drawer where we keep all the spare keys. They were all there,' Matt said.

'And?'

'The spare car keys have gone.'

Chapter Seventeen

SINCE THE EARLY 1950s, Connie's Bar on Hawkins and Bowker Streets has been the first port of call for the officers of District A-1 of the Boston Police Department. Connie, the original proprietor, died in the late seventies at the ripe old age of ninety-three, and now her grandson George, himself in his late sixties, ran the establishment. Whenever his shift finished late, Lieutenant Weber always made a point of dropping in for a drink or two on his way home. Whenever his shift finished on time, he made a point of dropping in on his way home. Whenever his shift finished early, he made a point of dropping in on his way home. But he was always fit to drive afterwards, and had never been worse for wear the next morning.

He had finished his customary two drinks: normally now he would make his way home, but as it was Friday night, one more would be in order. He nodded his thanks across the bar to George, and took a mouthful.

'What part of bring him in for questioning didn't you understand?' said a familiar voice behind him, making him splash his beer. He looked up and saw Captain O'Riordan standing over him.

'Oh, it's you,' he said, shuffling his stool slightly to the left so O'Riordan could fit in next to him. George ambled over and the Captain ordered a Guinness.

'I was asking what part of bring him in for questioning?' O'Riordan said.

'Didn't think it was necessary,' said Weber. 'How

did you know anyway?'

'How do you think?'

'Ah, yes: the good Detective Mancini.'

'Yes, and the fact that you weren't occupying the interview rooms.'

'Ambitious girl, Mrs Mancini.'

O'Riordan laughed. 'You should worry. I think she's after *my* job.'

'Not the Commissioners?'

'Probably. Now, to get back to my original question: why didn't you bring him in?'

Weber half drained his glass.

'Didn't think it was necessary.'

'Oh?'

'Look Ciarán: do you think he's going to go on the run?'

'You tell me.'

'For a start, he had a five year old boy asleep upstairs. You can't seriously be suspecting him of anything?'

O'Riordan shrugged his shoulders.

'How long have we known each other?' Weber asked.

'Best part of twenty years, I guess. Three as rookies, fifteen as partners -'

'And friends.'

'And friends. And two as captain.'

'So you trust my judgement?'

'Of course I do, Sam. I just suggested -'

'Suggested?'

'Kind of suggested. That Gibbons be questioned Downtown, that is. It's just that the enquiries at the MPU don't seem to be going anywhere, and I figured that if he was trying to hide something, being questioned here might kind of -'

'Intimidate him?'

'No; just move things on a bit.'

'The MPU had no luck yet?' Weber asked.

'Not really. They told me they called her workplace -'

'And she's not been seen since last Friday.'

'Oh,' said O'Riordan. 'You know that, then.'

'Yes, and that's an interesting point,' said Weber.

'How so?' enquired the Captain.

'They told me they spoke to a guy called Clark. Er – Danny Clark. The office manager apparently.'

'And?'

'Well, Gibbons has spoken to him also. Went down there the other day. Says he spoke to Clark himself, but Clark told him he had never heard of her; that nobody of his wife's name – and maiden name – worked there.'

O'Riordan drank his Guinness down to half full. 'Interesting,' he said, licking the cream off his lips. 'Didn't know about that. What do you propose to do?'

'The offices'll be closed through Monday,' said Weber. 'Thought I might have a word with the MPU, then talk to Clark myself Monday?'

'What about the Washington case? And the others?' O'Riordan asked.

'Ciarán, it's only gonna take an hour or so to speak with Clark. Bear with me, hey?'

'Do you think it's about the money?' O'Riordan asked. 'I mean: he only works in a bank, and she's a PA or something. That house of theirs must be worth a packet. The mortgage payments must be astronomical.'

Weber shook his head. 'Nah. I did some research on that the other day. It's quite a large house, for sure;

I checked with a couple of Real Estate offices and we're looking at four fifty, four seventy-five.'

O'Riordan whistled.

'But – Gibbons and his wife bought it a couple of years back for three eighty. But the mortgage was only for seventy-five.'

'Where'd the other $305,000 come from then?'

'Gibbons's family are moneyed. His old man's retired on Cape Cod now, but he had a good job, but the grandfather owned a small chain of hardware stores. Sold them off years ago for a tidy sum, and so a lot of that went into the Gibbons family home. So your theory – and Mancini's, no doubt – of him doing her in for the insurance is all bull.' He paused. 'I think.'

The Captain finished his drink, and motioned over to George for another.

'What's your theory then?' he asked.

'I think she's left him. Not sure if he's being a hundred percent straight with us when he says everything was fine between them, and he has no idea what's happening, but I think she's moved out.'

'With a third party?'

'Not sure. That's why I want to talk to this Clark guy face to face. You know, to check out what Gibbons said about being told his old lady never worked there.'

'You mean he could be the third party?'

'Possible. Then there's some other factors. I was able to check activity on their checking account. There were some unusual cash withdrawals on the account before she disappeared.'

'How much?'

'Over five hundred, all taken out at an ATM near where she works. Then there's the car.'

'The car?'

'He reported it stolen.'

'Jesus.'

'Quite. Said it was taken from his office parking lot while he was at work. But when Mancini and I called round tonight, he said he wondered at first if she had left, so checked for keys and the like, and everything was there. But while we were there, he checked again, and the spare keys,' – he tapped on the bar – 'were gone.'

O'Riordan said nothing; just scratched his stubbly chin.

'So I think,' continued Weber, 'that she has left him. On her own or with another person, Clark maybe. I figure she's taken the car keys. So she has some transportation. Even if Gibbons did check that her stuff was there earlier, she could easily have gone to the house while he was at work and taken them.'

'But what about the kid? She wouldn't have walked out on him.'

'Mothers have done worse things. In any case, how do we know the kid's hers? She could be a wicked stepmother.'

O'Riordan yawned and rubbed his chin again. 'How's the Washington case progressing?'

'We spoke to her once she came round. But she can't identify the assailants for sure. Just guys wearing hoods. Local CCTV shows the same.'

'Damn. 'I was hoping we might get a break. This is the third.'

'I know,' agreed Weber. 'One of these days a victim's gonna die.'

'Sam, we need to get the sons of bitches before then.'

'Think I don't know that?'

O'Riordan patted Weber's arm.

'I know, I know,' he said, standing up. 'Just keep on with the enquiries. Maybe revisit the other two cases. Talk to the witnesses again – maybe something's come back to them.'

'And the Gibbons case?'

'Okay. But *minimal* involvement. Talk to this Clark guy Monday; see what you think. But don't spend time on it to the detriment of your other cases. Especially Washington. And for Christ's sake keep liaising with the MPU.'

'Sure, I will. Thanks, Ciarán.'

Weber finished his drink and the two of them wished George good night, and walked to the door. O'Riordan patted the back of an officer who was sitting at a table as they went past.

'See you Monday, Sam,' O'Riordan said, and turned to the right.

Weber nodded and walked the other way, back to the station lot.

Got to the car and sat down in the driver's seat.

He sat in silence a few moments, thinking.

Then started the engine, left the lot and drove home.

Chapter Eighteen

'ARE WE GOING on a mystery trip, Daddy?' asked Nathan eagerly as he and Matt climbed into the taxi at seven o'clock the next morning.

'Kind of. We're going down to Auntie Gail's place.'

'Will she have candy?'

'I would imagine so. I have to go to work until just after lunch time. You and Auntie Gail are going to have a few hours' fun together, and then I'll come back and take you home for dinner. Maybe pizza tonight.'

'Cool,' exclaimed Nathan and settled back down in his seat with his plastic Tyrannosaurus Rex at the rear of the taxi and started to study the buildings as they rushed past.

'Tell me if you see any dinosaurs.'

'Okay, Daddy.'

That was the last Matt heard from his son for most of the journey; much to his relief the subject of Ruth did not come up.

Gail and her partner Ryan lived in a small but select apartment block in the West Medford area of Boston, halfway between the 93 Highway and the Mystic Lakes, which were around ten minutes' drive from their street. Whenever they used to visit, Gail would suggest driving out to the lakes: Matt suspected it was not so much giving Nathan an opportunity to see some unspoiled countryside, more a desire to minimise the amount of time he spent in their third floor place, which was clearly not furnished with young children in mind. He and Ruth would wince every time Nathan climbed onto a comfortable but expensive leather sofa and pick up what looked like an antique ornament. When Nathan was younger, Ruth would always carry a small bottle of wood scratch remover, and if and when Nathan happened to cause a scratch or chip on a piece of furniture, she would dab the scratch with the remover, rub it furiously with a Kleenex, and hope that Gail wouldn't notice.

The journey took only twenty-five minutes, much less than Matt had anticipated. He hoped that they were not too early for Gail, as it was his intention that the driver should wait while he took Nathan up to the apartment, then take him Downtown to work.

'I'll just need to take my son up to my friend's apartment,' Matt said as they arrived. 'Will only be five minutes. Can you wait?'

The driver looked up at Gail's building. The four floor block had a secure entrance and was surrounded by willow trees and bushes. Matt and Nathan would be out of view.

'Tell you what,' he said. 'You pay me for the journey so far, and I'll wait here ten minutes.'

Matt handed over the fare.

'You will wait, won't you?' he asked. I have to go back Downtown straight away.'

'I'll stay here ten minutes,' the driver replied. 'That should be enough time, shouldn't it?'

Matt nodded.

'If it puts your mind at rest, save the tip till we get Downtown.'

Matt agreed this and hurried Nathan into the

building, carrying a large plastic T Rex. He pressed Gail's bell. Momentarily she answered.

'Hello Gail, it's us. Sorry we're a bit early. Can we come up?'

'Sure.' There was a click and Matt was able to push the door open. They took the little elevator up to Gail's floor, where she was waiting in the apartment doorway, already fully dressed.

'Sorry we're early,' Matt said. 'The journey was quicker than I expected. The traffic on the 93 was light this morning.'

'No problem. I've been up since six. Ryan had to leave at seven. Hi, Nathan, come on in.'

'My cab's waiting downstairs,' Matt said. I'll be back just after three.'

'That'll be fine,' Gail said, leading Nathan indoors.

'Bye, Nathan,' Matt called out. 'See you this afternoon. Be good for Auntie Gail.'

'Bye Daddy,' Nathan called back.

'Don't worry. He's always good,' smiled Gail. 'Has he had breakfast?'

'About an hour ago.'

'Well, I'll see if he wants anything else now. Thought maybe we'd go down to the Lakes.'

What a surprise, Matt thought.

'That would be nice,' Matt said. 'He always likes it there. See you later. I'll call if I'm running late.'

'Okay.' Gail gave him a slight wave and closed the apartment door.

The elevator had gone, so Matt headed for the stairs and rushed down the two flights. To his relief, the taxi was still waiting. He climbed in, gave the driver his office address, and sat back breathlessly.

'You only took seven minutes, sir. Plenty of time

to spare,' said the driver cheerfully as he headed back to the 93.

Much to Matt's relief, there was very little booked in his diary that day, so he should have plenty of opportunity to make the necessary calls he had to make. He had spent the time in the taxi trying to figure out what had happened to the spare car keys. He was positive he had seen them when he checked the other night. Positive. Maybe he hadn't seen them. Maybe he hadn't even checked; maybe he had dreamed it. He tried to remember the last time they had need of the spare keys. The only time he could recall was when Ruth had to make a business trip to DC. Matt had gotten a ride off José into work; later that morning Ruth had driven Downtown, parked the Toyota in a parking garage and caught the T up to Logan. Matt then picked up the car after work using the spare keys, and drove home. But that was months ago, and the keys had been in the drawer since then. One of a growing list of questions.

Another thing about which Matt was relieved: Debra was not working today. Not that he was surprised at that. For somebody who regularly lectured the staff at the branch about how they were working in a six day business, she seldom put in an appearance on a Saturday.

Once he had logged on his workstation and gotten his first cup of coffee, he decided to arrange a temporary car rental. He was about to dial when Larry turned the corner.

'Hey buddy,' Larry said. 'Wasn't sure if you were in today. Didn't notice your car out back.'

'Had to,' replied Matt, cradling the phone in his

hand. 'To make up time I took off because my wife disappeared.'

'Orders?' Larry asked, inclining his head towards the closed door of Debra Grant Barber's empty office.

'U-huh.'

Larry shook his head sadly. 'Any news?' he asked.

'Nothing yet. And the car was stolen.'

'Je-sus. Where from?'

'From out back. On Thursday morning.'

'Damn, Matt. You're not having much – well, you know what I mean.'

Matt nodded. Larry noticed he was about to make a phone call. 'Catch you later, buddy.'

Holding the telephone handset between his chin and shoulder, Matt rummaged in one of his desk drawers and pulled out a copy of the Yellow Pages. He found that Avis had offices only ten minutes away in Center Plaza. He called.

'Good morning, Avis Rental Government Center. Judy speaking, how can I help you?'

'Oh, good morning, I need to rent a car for a couple of days.'

'Until Monday morning then, sir?'

'No, better make it until Tuesday.'

'Three days rental, sir. What type of vehicle are you looking for: Standard Size, Full Size, Premium, Specialty -?'

'I'm looking for the cheapest.'

'The cheapest? Hold the line please sir; I'll just check our system for availability. I'm pleased to say we can offer you a vehicle from our Subcompact range.'

'That sounds ideal.'

'The vehicle is a Hyundai Accent. Four doors,

automatic transmission.'

'How much for three days rental? From today?'

'For rental today through Tuesday morning 9AM is $221.97.'

'Yes, I'll take it.'

'Sir, if you have internet access you can log onto our site and pay only $210.87.'

'No, I'm at work, so I can't log on.'

'In that case $221.97 is your charge, sir.'

Matt carried on the conversation and arranged to pick up the car from the lot behind the Center Plaza office after he had finished work that afternoon. He now had to return the car lunchtime Tuesday. Hopefully by then the Toyota had turned up, or he could arrange rental of a temporary replacement through his insurance company. Then at least he could collect Nathan himself later, and they could still make the trip to the Cape tomorrow.

His first appointment was booked for ten thirty. By now it was ten forty and there was no sign of them. He stood up, stretched and wandered over to the teller area. There were only three customers waiting in line; a very quiet morning. He grabbed another cup of coffee and headed for the restroom. As he stood at the urinal, he heard a flushing sound and Larry emerged from the stall.

'Hey buddy,' Larry said as he began washing his hands. 'How's it going, then?'

'First one is booked for ten thirty. Still waiting on them.'

'Lucky Queen Bitch isn't in today,' Larry said, pumping more liquid soap on his hands. 'It was quiet yesterday too; you wanna know what she had us do? She had us call all our existing clients to get them in next week to discuss the bank's latest products.'

'I guess I have that pleasure to come next week,' said Matt, zipping up.

'Probably. But that wasn't what I was asking. I meant how's things going with you. Any news on Ruth?'

Matt joined Larry at the wash basin. 'Nothing yet. The police have been asking a lot of questions: her friends, her routine, were we happy, our money situation…'

'Surely they can't think you've -'

'I guess it's just routine.'

'Those withdrawals you asked me about the other day: do they have anything to do with it?'

'Possibly. Possibly not.'

'And Nathan?'

'He keeps asking where his mommy is. I've been saying she's away on business.'

'But you can't keep telling him that.'

'No. I've decided to tell him the truth – or what truth a five year old can understand – tonight.'

'And your car – that's a real clusterfuck as well.'

'Yeah; just what I needed. Reported that to the police, but they more or less just said call your insurance company. Did that just now. I made a claim, but luckily my policy gives me four days courtesy car rental while my claim's being sorted. I already arranged something with Avis through Tuesday, so can get the courtesy car after then. So I'll have seven days' wheels at least.'

Larry patted Matt on the shoulder. 'Shit, man; you're really going through it. Don't forget, if there's anything you need…'

'I know, Larry. Thanks.'

Larry stopped in the doorway. He looked over at the stall he had occupied, grinned and said, 'And sorry about that…'

Matt scrunched up his nose. 'I'm coming as well,' he said, and hurried out behind Larry.

Chapter Nineteen

AFTER AN UNPRODUCTIVE morning in which only one of his three scheduled appointments had shown up, Matt hurried down State Street to Avis Car Rental which was based opposite the Government Center. It was bitterly cold, and beginning to snow.

The block in which the offices were situated was undergoing some kind of renovation and was covered with canvas sheets, wooden hoardings and scaffolding. The scaffolding meant that the sidewalks on that block were quite narrow, and Matt had to fight his way through the crowds who were also attempting to take shelter from the weather.

After he had paid his deposit, shown his drivers licence, and completed all the requisite paperwork, the clerk behind the desk led Matt out back to the parking lot. Around twenty shiny new vehicles were parked here. The clerk checked the tag on the key fob and located the maroon Hyundai Accent which Matt had rented.

'There's a full tank of gas,' the clerk said as Matt climbed in. 'Please remember to fill up before you drop off at the end of the rental period.'

'I will, yes,' said Matt as he turned the key and pulled away. As he left the lot and turned into Cambridge Street he noticed the clerk standing by the door, watching him as he drove away. He also noticed the bus pull away sharply without indicating, and he managed to hit the brakes just in time. What he didn't notice was the silver Audi A3 pulling away from its spot just a few yards up Cambridge.

It did not take Matt long to get used to driving the Hyundai, and he made his way around the one-way streets to the John F Fitzgerald Surface Road, then to the I-93 proper. Just as he passed the last set of signals before the 93, they turned amber, then red. He heard a couple of car horns sound behind, and glanced into the mirror. In the distance he could see a silver vehicle – he couldn't pick out the make – shoot across the junction in spite of the red light. Obviously couldn't hold his wad, he thought.

The Saturday afternoon traffic was heavy and slow, not helped by the snow which was falling heavily. At a quarter after four he was driving down the exit ramp for the streets to Gail's place. He had a clear run off the Interstate and along Mystic Valley Parkway as far as the junction with Winthrop Street, where he hit a red.

After a minute or so the signal went to green and Matt moved away, followed by a blue SUV, a *New England Tours* bus, a silver Audi A3 and a red and white Coca Cola truck.

Gail and Ryan's apartment block had a small parking lot at the rear of the building. Matt was quite familiar with it as he and Ruth would park there when they visited. Matt steered the Accent into the Right Turn lane, then into the parking lot. While he was waiting for a gap in traffic, the silver Audi and red truck passed him by.

After parking the car, he walked over to the building. Rather than wait for the elevator, he took the stairs up to their floor. Gail answered the door just as he knocked.

'Saw you coming out the window,' she said, standing in the doorway with Nathan who already had his coat on.

‘Everything okay?’ he asked Gail, whilst ruffling Nathan’s hair.

‘Absolutely fine,’ she replied. ‘We took a ride down to the Lakes for an hour or so; then it looked as if the weather was going to turn bad, so we came back and had pizza for lunch.’

Pizza for lunch. Great. No pizza for dinner then.

‘Yes, it’s just starting to snow,’ said Matt. ‘Snowing quite heavily in the city. Better get back before it gets any worse.’

‘Okay now. You take care,’ Gail said, beginning to close the door.

‘Say thank you to Auntie Gail,’ Matt told Nathan.

‘Thank you Auntie Gail.’

‘You’re very welcome,’ Gail smiled at Nathan, and slowly closed her door.

‘Let’s take the stairs,’ Matt said, as Nathan tried to reach up for the elevator call button.

They were halfway down the first flight of stairs when Nathan grabbed his head.

‘Mr Rex!’ he cried. ‘We left Mr Rex behind!’

Then with Matt trailing behind, he rushed back up to Gail’s floor and banged on her door. As Matt reached the door, Gail opened it. With an irritated look on her face, she had a cell phone in one hand, holding it to her left ear, and in her right hand she was holding out Nathan’s dinosaur.

‘Sorry,’ Matt mouthed as Nathan grabbed the dinosaur. Gail nodded and, continuing with her call, slowly pushed the door to.

‘Have a good time with Auntie Gail?’ Matt asked as he started the car and turned the heating level up slightly.

‘Cool,’ Nathan said. ‘She took me and Mr Rex to play by the side of the lake. Till it got cold.’

'Did you see Uncle Ryan?' Matt asked as he stopped at the entrance to the main road.

'Nah. He was working,' said Nathan, as he bounced the dinosaur up and down in his lap.

'How about Denny's tonight?' Matt asked. 'As you've already had pizza.'

'Cool.'

'I'll take that as a yes,' muttered Matt as he pulled into the traffic.

The nearest Denny's was just off the main route to Logan International Airport, so Matt made a detour when they had been on the I-93 twenty minutes. Just after five they pulled up in the Denny's lot, across the street from the East Boston Skatepark. The restaurant already had at least three other fathers with young sons sitting at tables. For an appetizer they shared a *Basket of Puppies*: ten miniature pancakes rolled in cinnamon and sugar, with a syrup dip. Matt then had a Club Sandwich and fries, and Nathan spaghetti and meatballs. All rounded off with apple pie and ice cream.

After the meal, Nathan yawned heavily as they got back into the car. As Matt waited for a break in the traffic in Meridian Street he had to blink as a car in the lot switched on its lights, illuminating Matt's rear view mirror. Blinking again, he pulled into the traffic. To his relief, it had stopped snowing: there was a little snow settled on the sidewalks, but the roads were cleared.

Nathan was asleep by the time they reached home. Matt carefully reversed the Accent into the space in their parking garage, and gently lifted him out of the car and carried him round the corner to home. Nathan stirred slightly as Matt fumbled with the door keys, but remained asleep as Matt slowly took him upstairs and laid him on his bed. He would have to go without a bath tonight, and could get undressed if and when he awoke that night. Matt looked around: he had left the T Rex in the car. Forget it: that can wait till morning. He looked down at Nathan: poor little guy, he thought, it's been a long day for him. Will be another long day tomorrow, with the drive to the Cape.

Matt quietly closed Nathan's door, made a quick bathroom stop, then went back downstairs. Into the kitchen to make himself a cup of coffee, then into the living room and switched on the TV. It was *American Idol*. He turned the volume down, put his coffee cup on the table and went over to the window to pull the drapes. As he pulled them to, he looked up and down the road. There was no sign of the snow, thank God. A couple of cars passed by on the other side of the road. He could see three more parked on the street: two this side and one the other. He closed the drapes and sat down.

There were more than three cars parked on the street. Not for the first time that day, Matt had missed the fourth vehicle parked across the street, two buildings down.

The figure in the Audi A3 lit a cigarette and sat back in the seat.

Chapter Twenty

THE NEXT MORNING, Matt and Nathan began the fifty-seven mile journey down to Matt's parents just after eight thirty. Matt would normally take the Pilgrim's Highway, cross over to the island on the Sagamore Bridge, then take the Sandwich Road south easterly direction. Once he had passed through the town, he would come across his parents' house. This time on a Sunday morning the drive would take around over ninety minutes; however, as a special treat for Nathan, half an hour into the journey Matt pulled off the main highway and headed for a McDonalds outlet for breakfast.

After breakfast, they rejoined the highway. By now, Matt had gotten used to the Hyundai, and was comfortably cruising at sixty. He looked over at his son, clutching a purple dinosaur model and staring out of the window. Matt smiled down at the boy, relieved at how he had taken the news of his mother's disappearance.

Nathan had woken at just after seven that morning, excited at the prospect of the trip down to the Cape. Matt was still in bed when Nathan wandered in.

'Hey, sport,' Matt said across the bed. 'You're about early. Couldn't sleep?'

Blinking, Nathan said, 'Are we seeing Grandma and Grandpa today?'

'Sure thing. Come over here. I need to tell you something.'

Nathan padded over to the side of the bed. Matt

lifted up the quilt. ‘Come in with me,’ he said. Nathan jumped in.

‘It’s about Mommy,’ Matt said, his heart pounding.

Nathan looked up at his father. ‘When’s she coming home?’ he asked.

‘Not for a while,’ Matt said, cuddling Nathan. ‘She has to go away for a little while, as she’s not well right now.’

He waited for a reaction.

‘Oh dear,’ Nathan said quietly. ‘I hope she gets better soon.’

‘So do I,’ said Matt, not sure how to react. He squeezed Nathan tightly. ‘So do I. But remember, no matter how long she’s away for, she loves you very much. So do I.’

‘This much?’ Nathan asked, stretching his arms out.

‘No, this much,’ Matt said, stretching his arms out now. ‘Times ten.’

Nathan looked into Matt’s eyes. ‘I love you too, Daddy,’ he said. Tears in his eyes, Matt put both arms around his son.

‘Daddy?’ Nathan asked after a moment.

‘Yes, what?’

‘Can I take a dinosaur to see Grandma and Grandpa?’

Matt released his grip and Nathan climbed off the bed.

‘Where you off to now?’

‘I need to peepee, then get ready for Grandma and Grandpa.’

‘Okay then. You go to the bathroom first. You want to have breakfast here, or stop off at Donald’s?’

‘Donald’s, please, please!’ replied Nathan

excitedly.

'Donald's it is then.' Matt lay back on the bed. He looked up as Nathan trotted out of the room, and into the bathroom. A tear ran down his cheek as he watched him leave. Relief that Nathan had taken the news the way he did, or something else?

As each day went by, he found it more and more difficult to understand why Ruth had gone. What kind of mother would abandon her little boy?

Matt was beginning to feel a new emotion.

Anger.

Chapter Twenty-One

'SO WHAT KIND of dinosaur is that?'

Nathan looked up. 'It's a Vossi Raptor.'

'A what?' Matt laughed, switching his glance between the dinosaur and the road ahead.

'A Vossi Raptor.'

'Oh, you mean a Velociraptor.'

'Yes; a Vossi Raptor.'

'I think you can call them Raptors for short.'

'Raptors,' said Nathan slowly, as if trying out a new word. 'Raptors.'

There were a few moments' silence while Nathan pondered this new word, then he spoke again.

'It means *speedy fief.*'

'Speedy what?'

'Speedy fief.'

'You mean speedy thief?

'Speedy fief.'

'Right. What does it mean, anyhow?'

'Daddy, you're not paying attention. Vossi Raptor means speedy fief. It eats little dinosaurs.'

'Okay. Glad I'm not a little dinosaur,' Matt chuckled.

'Raptor. Raptor,' Nathan muttered to himself, staring out of the window. Matt smiled again. He looked up as they passed a green sign declaring Cape Cod was six miles away.

They crossed the bridge just after ten o'clock. There was a slight delay as they turned onto the Mid-Cape Connector: a truck had overturned on the bend, and its cargo of paint drums had spilled onto the road.

Fortunately, all of the drums remained intact, so the traffic was able to negotiate the accident.

Matt sounded the horn as he pulled up outside the picturesque white clap-board house the other side of Sandwich. Simultaneously, his mother emerged from behind the screen door at the front of the house and his father walked round from the rear.

'Grandma! Grandpa!' Nathan shouted as he leapt out of the car and ran up the steps to his grandmother. The old lady bent down to hug him.

'Good to see you, son.' Matthew Senior shook Matt's hand and led him up the steps. Matt turned round to lock the car. His father nodded as the car bleeped and the lights flashed.

'New car?' he asked. 'Don't think I've seen that before. What is it? Hyundai?' he added, peering at the hood.

'U-huh. Hyundai Accent.'

'Right. So you got rid of the Toyota?'

'This is a rental. The Toyota was stolen.'

'Jesus H, when?'

'The other day. Tell you later, Dad,' said Matt as they walked up to the house. By the time they reached the screen door, Nathan had already run inside. Matt's mother held her arms out. They hugged.

'I'm so sorry, Matt,' she said. 'Is there any more news?'

Matt shook his head. 'Nothing.'

'Leave all that till later, Estelle,' Matthew Senior said as he reached the top of the steps. 'Let's have coffee first.'

'Sure,' Estelle smiled and went into the kitchen.

'Let's go out back,' said Matthew. 'Come on. Hey there, Nathan. How's my favourite grandson?' They bumped into Nathan outside the kitchen. He was riding on a large plastic tractor. The Raptor was in the trailer.

'Cool, Grandpa. Look at me!' Nathan giggled as he shot off into the kitchen with Estelle.

Matt and his father sat down on the small porch at the rear of the house. Estelle brought two mugs of coffee out.

'Thanks. Mom,' said Matt. 'Where's Nathan?'

'Oh, he's inside with me. Colouring in some dinosaur pictures. I found a book in town the other day.'

'Don't let him take over,' Matt said.

'Don't worry. He's fine.'

'So tell us about Ruth, then. What's happened?' Matthew asked.

'I thought we were going to wait till later?' asked Estelle.

Matthew shrugged. 'It's later now,' he said. 'And the boy's inside.'

Estelle nodded and sat down.

'Nathan?' she called out. 'Shout if you want me. I'm out here with Daddy and Grandpa. Don't touch anything.'

A voice came from inside. 'Okay.'

'Well?' Matthew asked, slightly impatiently.

Matt drank some coffee, sat back, and started to retell the story of the events since the previous Tuesday. Matthew sat back in his chair, slowly nodding his head.

'How much does Nathan know?' Estelle asked.

'I told him that she's gone away for a while. That she's not well.'

'And how did he react?'

'That's the thing. He didn't really. Just said something like I hope she gets better soon, and then asked if we were still coming here.'

Estelle looked over at Matthew.

'It can't have sunk in yet,' she said.

Matt nodded. 'No, I don't think it has really. He was asking each day in the week, and each time I said she was away through work. Each time he just seemed to accept it. I'm just waiting for him to…'

He paused, took a breath, and a mouthful of coffee.

'What do you plan to do?' Matthew asked.

'About what?' Matt asked. 'About Nathan, or about Ruth? Or something else?'

'Well, I meant about Nathan first.'

'I'm not thinking any further than a day or two ahead. I'm hoping she'll walk back in, and I can tell him she's back, and well again.'

'And about Ruth?'

When recounting the events of the last few days, Matt had omitted the part about her place of work not having heard of her, and about the cash withdrawals. He decided not to fill in the gaps now.

'Nothing else I can do. I've reported her disappearance to the police, they're investigating. Said they would contact me at least every week to update me. Unless there was news earlier.'

'Do you think your car being stolen has anything to do with things?' Matthew asked.

Matt shrugged. 'Can't see how it can. Just one god-awful coincidence.'

'I can't see how she can just leave the boy,' Matthew said as he inclined his head indoors. 'With all due respect, son, I can see her walking out on you; but not on him. What kind of woman would..?' He stopped mid-sentence with a glare from Estelle.

'You don't know what's happened,' Estelle said.

'She might not have gone of her own choice. She might have had a road accident, or been taken ill, or been abducted…'

'Don't be ridiculous,' said Matthew. 'People don't get abducted. At least not people like us. Not that…' Another glare from Estelle.

'Has anybody called the hospitals?' Estelle asked, trying to sound cheerful.

Matt shook his head. 'I called every hospital in Boston. The police told me their procedure included contacting all hospitals in the State. And apparently there's a system of checking out of state hospitals.'

'Well, I think that's what's happened,' Matthew said, nodding his head and folding his arms. 'If we assume that Ruth would never leave Nathan – *if* – then surely a hospital is the obvious place. Jesus Christ, she might be lying in bed with amnesia or something. Or she might be lying…'

'In a ditch somewhere. Yes, I know that.' Matt stood up and walked over to the porch rail and looked out to sea.

His parents said nothing: just looked at each other. Estelle had a pained expression on her face.

'I'll need to start preparing lunch,' she said, standing up. 'I'll enlist Nathan to help.' Matt turned round and nodded, smiling slightly.

There was a moment's silence after she left; then Matthew spoke first.

'Look son, what I said earlier, about… Well, I didn't mean… You know…'

'It's okay Dad, I know.'

'I take it you've already called any friends, workplace; that sort of thing.'

'Work – work said she'd not been in since the previous Friday. The only friend – that I'm aware of anyway – had heard nothing from her either.'

'What about Ruth's own cell phone?'

'Tried it that night again and again. And the next. And the next. Always to voicemail.'

'Try it again now.'

'What?'

'Try her cell again now.'

Matt shrugged and pulled his phone out.

'Wait a minute,' said Matthew as Matt was just about to dial. 'Use this one.' He pulled his own phone from a pouch on his belt.

'What?'

'Use my phone. If she is screening her calls and wants to avoid speaking to you, she might not recognize my number.'

Matt took his father's phone and dialled.

'Well?' Matthew asked after Matt hung up.

'Voicemail again,' said Matt, giving the phone back.

'Just a thought.'

Matt turned as Estelle appeared on the porch.

'Lunch is ready,' she announced.

'Is Nathan okay?' Matt asked.

'He surely is. He's been helping me with lunch, haven't you, darling?'

Nathan nodded, proud of himself.

After lunch, which comprised a massive plate of Boston Baked Beans – a salty stewed mix of pork, onions and beans – followed by apple pie and ice cream, Matthew took Nathan around the back yard to show him how he had reorganised his workshop, while Matt sat on the porch with Estelle.

'Don't mind him too much,' Estelle said. 'The things he says about Ruth, I mean.'

'I don't. It's just right now…'

‘He’s all bull and bluster. He knows you’re hurting, and it hurts him too. That’s just his way of dealing with it. Of not showing it.’

‘I know.’

‘What about that nice young lady who called round when we came to stay Christmas before last?’

‘Gail, you mean?’

‘Gail – that’s right. Does she know anything?’

‘No. Same as me. Heard nothing. As puzzled as I am.’

‘It’s a shame her parents both passed on.’

Matt looked at her, puzzled. ‘Yeah. And…?’

‘What I mean is, if you and Ruth were having problems, for argument’s sake, then at least she would have somewhere to go, to get away for a while.’

‘Oh, I see what you mean. Yes.’

‘You never met either of them, did you?’

‘No, they both died before she and I met. Her father some years back; her mother I think a few months before we got together.’

‘And no brothers or sisters?’

‘No. She was an only child.’

‘What about school friends? I read you can keep in touch on a computer.’

‘No. No; she didn’t do anything like that.’

‘Mm,’ said Estelle, sitting back in her chair.

‘Mom, what are you getting at?’ asked Matt.

‘I’m not getting at anything. I was just thinking aloud about Ruth - where she might go; what reasons she would have for going. If she has gone anywhere. If she’s not -’

‘Lying in a ditch somewhere? Or in a coma in some hospital?’

Estelle laid her hand on Matt’s. ‘Take no notice of

me dear; just my foolishness.' She paused. 'Has your father told you about the boat?'

'The boat?'

'Yes,' she nodded. 'He's talking about getting a boat.'

'What the hell for?'

'Don't ask me. Old Harry Jobs down at Monument Beach has just gotten one, and your father spends more time on the damn thing than he did at the office before he retired.'

'I shouldn't worry. You know these interests soon pass. Something else will come, and he'll have forgotten about the boat.'

'I hope so. He doesn't need to be messing about in some boat at his age. It takes him all his time to maintain the yard here.'

An hour or so later, just as it was getting dark, Matt and Nathan set off for home.

'Good luck, son,' Matthew said as they shook hands. 'Are you okay, you know, for money?' He spoke out of the corner of his mouth.

'Fine, thanks, Dad. Fine.'

'Okay. Well, hope everything - well, you know…'

'I know, Dad. Thanks.'

Estelle reached up and embraced Matt. 'Safe drive back, and come see us again soon. Let us know if there's any news. Or is there anything we can do.'

'I will,' Matt said as he started the engine and turned on the headlights. Estelle and Matthew waved at Nathan who was settling down in the back seat, clutching his velociraptor. He waved back and yawned. Matt waved again as he eased the Hyundai onto the road.

‘You still awake, sport?’ Matt asked about five miles past the Sagamore Bridge. There was no answer. He glanced into the rear view mirror and could see that Nathan had fallen asleep. It was dark by now. Matt decided that unless Nathan woke up during the journey, he would carry straight on till they got home, rather than stop for food on the way. Traffic was relatively light that night, and he could quite comfortably cruise at sixty-five.

Matt pulled in to a gas station to top up at around the halfway point, and also bought a couple of candy bars. Nathan was still asleep, so Matt ate his, then set off again.

As the city lights started to show in the distance, Matt reflected on the day’s trip. He was glad they had gone down there; his parents were the first people with whom he had been able to have an open conversation. His father’s comments about Ruth – well, not for the first time, it was just his bluster. Just like his mother said. But it was what his mother had said which gave him cause to think. Ruth had no family: she was an only child, and he had never met her parents. Or school friends. What school did she go to anyway? Where was she raised? She must have told him; he had just forgotten.

As he joined the Southeast Expressway, he realised just how little he knew about his wife.

Chapter Twenty-Two

MONDAY MORNING AND Lieutenant Weber and Detective Mancini were due to start their shift at ten.

'The timing's just about right,' Weber had said on the phone to Mancini earlier that morning. 'I'll head down to see this Danny Clark guy, then meet up with you at the station for ten.'

'I think you're wasting your time, Sam,' Mancini replied. 'For one thing, it's got nothing to do with you really; let the MPU deal with the case. And don't we have enough work of our own to handle?'

'Frannie, I'm doing this in my own time, aren't I? And I've cleared it with O'Riordan and the MPU. I'll make sure I'm back for ten.'

'Up to you. Just make sure you're on time. And fatso – I've told you before: don't call me Frannie.'

Weber chuckled and hung up. He was in slow moving traffic heading down Washington Street, just three blocks away from the Cambridge Pharmaceuticals building. He managed to park in a side street, and arrived at the offices just after nine.

'Can I help you sir?' asked a young man at the reception desk.

'I'd like to see Mr Clark,' Weber said. 'Mr Danny Clark.'

'I'll just see if he's available,' the receptionist said, picking up the phone. 'Who shall I say wants to see him?'

'My name's Weber,' the Lieutenant said. 'Lieutenant Weber, BPD,' he added holding out his badge.

The young man flushed slightly as he spoke. 'Is Danny Clark there? It's Connor at the desk.' He paused slightly, making an effort to avoid eye contact with Weber. 'Mr Clark? I have a Lieutenant Weber down here to see you. No, he didn't say. Okay, I'll tell him.'

'Mr Clark will be down in a few minutes,' he said, replacing the phone. 'You want to take a seat over there?'

'Okay. Thanks.' Weber stepped over to one of the chairs and sat down. After a few moments the elevator doors opened and a man stepped out. Weber estimated he was aged around thirty, dark pants and open necked blue shirt. His dark hair was slicked back. Weber took an instant dislike to him.

'Lieutenant Weber?' the man asked, walking over to Weber, holding his hand out.

'Sir,' Weber replied, standing up and shaking his hand.

'Danny Clark, office manager here. I must say, this is a coincidence.'

'Coincidence, sir?'

'I had one of your colleagues here the other day, asking me questions.'

'Hm,' Weber grunted. 'I won't take up too much of your time, sir. I just need to ask you a few more questions.'

'More questions. Is this about Ruth Gibbons?'

'Yes, it is.'

'But I told the other officer all about her.'

'I'm aware of that, sir. There are just a few things we need to clarify.'

'Okay. Fire away.'

'Firstly: did Ruth Gibbons work here?'

'Yes, she did – does, I should say. She still does.'

'How long has she worked here?'

Clark shook his head. 'Not sure exactly. I've only been here since the beginning of last year, and she was here when I joined.'

'What did she do here?'

'She was a Quality Auditor.'

'What does that mean – Quality Auditor?'

'It means – in layman's terms, she was responsible for ensuring the purity, the integrity of our products. Entailed checking samples.'

'Quite a responsible job, I imagine?'

'Absolutely. If there were any imperfections in any products, that could have devastating consequences for the company.'

'On a good salary, I imagine?'

'Oh, yes. Not sure exactly how much.'

'Ball park figure?'

'Oh, around $60,000 off the top of my head.'

Weber nodded. 'And did she always work here?'

'I told you, I've only been here a year or so myself.'

'No, I mean, did she work out of the office here all week. Or was she out *sampling*?'

'Oh, I see what you mean. No, she would be here maybe three days a week. Rest of the week she would be visiting our factory.'

'Which is?'

'South Boston. Old Colony Avenue.'

'Okay. Thanks very much.'

Clark appeared relieved. He looked ready to go back upstairs.

'Just a couple more questions, sir. You said she would go down to the factory two days a week?' He looked at Clark for confirmation. Clark nodded.

'Well, I understand she always walked to work.'

‘Mm?’ Clark gave him a puzzled look.

‘I’m just trying to figure out,’ Weber explained, ‘how she would get down to South Boston without a car.’

Clark said nothing.

Weber pressed the point. ‘Do you know?’

‘I’m not sure. I think she mentioned that she walked in. Most days, at any rate. Maybe she used public transportation. No idea. Sorry.’

‘I see. One more question, then I’ll let you get back to work. You told the other detective that the last day she was in work was two Fridays ago. Is that right?’

‘U-huh.’

‘And you’ve heard or seen nothing of her since then?’

‘No.’

‘Has any attempt been made to contact her?’

‘Naturally, we tried to contact her.’

‘How? By phone?’

‘By phone – her cell and home numbers. And Human Resources would have written to her home address.’

‘And still no reply.’

‘Like I said, we’ve heard nothing from her.’

Weber nodded, appeared deep in thought.

‘Why did you tell her husband you never heard of her?’ he asked quickly.

Clark appeared flustered. ‘Her husband?’

‘Yes, a Mr Gibbons. He told us he came down here last week, saw *you*, and you told him you had never heard of his wife.’

‘Er, no – I don’t recollect that.’

‘What don’t you recollect, Mr Clark? Speaking to Mr Gibbons, or telling him you’d never heard of his wife?'

'No, no, no – I recollect speaking with him, of course. But I told him what I told you and the other detective. She's not been in the office since the other Friday.'

'I see. I guess Mr Gibbons misunderstood you.'

'I guess so. He seemed pretty upset.'

Weber nodded. 'Well, thanks for your time, Mr Clark. You can get back to work now.' He held out his hand to shake Clark's.

'No problem,' said Clark, shaking Weber's hand. 'Any time.'

With that, he walked over to the elevator and disappeared from view. Weber stood and watched him leave. Then nodded to Connor on the reception desk and walked back to his car.

He sat in the car and put the key in the ignition. Paused and rested his arm on the window ledge. So Clark confirmed what he had told the guys from the MPU. But there was a discrepancy between his story and Gibbons'. Some misunderstanding; and Gibbons seemed a guy who was keeping it together.

So why was there a discrepancy?

And why was Clark's palm so sweaty?

Chapter Twenty-Three

'IF YOU'D COME with me this morning,' Weber said to Mancini later that morning, 'you'd know what I mean.'

'I didn't need to,' Mancini replied as she emptied the paper cup of latte. 'It's not our case. You shouldn't have gone. Did he know you're not on the case?'

'Does it matter?' Weber replied. 'I told you: O'Riordan sanctioned it, and the MPU okayed me going.'

'What have you gained by going to see him?'

'Just putting my mind at rest, that's all, I guess. It was niggling me – the fact that he told them that Mrs Gibbons did work there – does work there – but he told her husband that he'd never heard of her.'

'What did he say to that?'

'Said he never told Gibbons that. Said he told him the same he told the MPU guys – that he saw her last the Friday before she disappeared. Said Gibbons seemed upset when he called. Said he must have misunderstood.'

'Perhaps he did tell Gibbons that. You know, a polite way of telling him to fuck off. Would you want my husband ranting and raving at you at the station?'

Weber laughed. 'If you disappeared, your husband would be paying the one way fare.'

'Very funny. Hey, we'd better get going. Look at the time.'

Weber checked his watch and got up. 'Hey, can I get another refill?' he asked the barista at the coffee shop they were in, holding out his paper cup. He got his refill and joined Mancini in the car.

'Seriously, though,' she said as they got in, 'who do you believe?'

Weber looked over to her. 'My head tells me to believe Clark. It seems more logical; the MPU told me Clark even checked on their computer records and checked the days she logged onto their system, and that confirmed the last Friday but one, whatever the date was. But…'

Mancini gave him a wry look. 'But…?'

'But I got the right vibes from Gibbons. Sure, he *could* have been so upset when he called on Clark; after all, apparently they had to threaten to call security. But Gibbons seems to have kept it together. He's an intelligent guy – he works in a bank after all – and that's one hell of a misunderstanding.'

'You just didn't like Clark, did you?'

'Well, no.'

'Hardly a reason for arresting him.'

'I know, but listen to this: I asked him about Mrs Gibbons, and I said "did she work there" – you know, past tense.'

'And?'

'And he didn't correct me. Well, not at first. But it seemed to unnerve him.' Weber shook his head. 'Oh, I don't know.'

'O'Riordan thinks Gibbons may have done something to her.'

'O'Riordan's full of crap. Always was. Always will be. When we were on the streets together he didn't have a freakin' idea about most things. Got that promotion on account of his – *connections*. And you can tell him that the next time you have one of those one to one chats with him.'

'Sam, I'm not -'

'Forget it. Remember, I've known Ciarán O'Riordan for more years than I care to remember. He always more interested in the politics and his clear up percentages than what's really going on. No, I don't think Gibbons has done anything to her. If any evidence comes to light, that's a different matter. There's no motive, for a start. Sure, she was earning about 60K, but the mortgage on that house of theirs is tiny compared with how much they paid for it. Tiny compared with mine, for that matter. The rest came from Gibbons' family. I checked out his bank statements -'

'How'd you get to do that?'

'Unofficially. His earnings more than cover all the household bills. Hers, plus some of his, just go into a savings account. So he doesn't need any insurance money.'

'Maybe they had a fight. Maybe she was having an affair.'

'That's possible. But there's no evidence of that. There's little evidence of anything, apparently. No, I'm sorry: the idea of him as a wife killer just doesn't *feel* right.'

'Just don't get too deep, Sam. That's all I'm saying.'

'Sure. Come on; let's go see Ms Washington. See if she remembers anything else.'

'Good news that's she's at home now.'

'Mm. Hey – I've just realised: she's Ms Washington; Mrs Gibbons works on Washington Avenue. Coincidence or what?'

'Let's just go see Ms Washington.'

'I think it's good karma, that's all,' said Weber as he turned the ignition.

'You got her address?' Weber asked.

'Sure, it's in Newton. Whittier Road. I'll take the 90.'

They were five minutes into their journey when there Weber's phone rang. He passed it to Mancini. 'Here, you take it.'

Mancini took the call; listened for half a minute, then said, 'Right; we'll be there in around ten minutes.' Then hung up.

'Ms Washington will have to wait,' she said. 'You need to head up to Winchester.'

'Not another mugging, I hope.'

'No. This one's dead.'

It had started to rain by the time they reached the scene: a small block of apartments just off the Mystic Valley Parkway. Not the heavy, driving rain they had experienced over the last couple of days, but heavy drizzle: half rain, half sleet. It had gotten bitterly cold since dawn.

They walked through the police cordon, past the two blue and whites and into the building. Climbed up to the second floor. Four uniformed police officers were in the corridor, two of them talking with an elderly couple in an apartment doorway. Further down the corridor, an apartment door was wide open with the other two officers in this doorway. As they walked in, nodding to the officers, Weber noticed the corridor carpet was soaking wet, as was the carpet inside the apartment.

The bathroom was to the right immediately as one entered the apartment, and they could see that the water emanated from there. Weber looked inside the white tiled bathroom: the bath was opposite the open door. He looked in further and saw, at the top end of the bath, a body. It was a woman's body, naked, and slumped over the bath. The black hair, long down to just below her neck, was wet and straggly, hanging over both shoulders.

One of the uniformed officers joined Weber and Mancini in the bathroom.

'The super made the call,' the officer said. 'He noticed the water stain on the carpet outside, tried to raise her, then used his master key, and found her. Like this.'

'Who is she?' Weber asked.

'She's a Ms Watanabe,' the officer replied. 'Ms Aki Watanabe.'

'Asian? Sound it from the name.'

'Japanese, apparently. Took this place about a year ago.'

'What do you think happened?' Mancini asked Weber as she looked around. She was hunched over the side of the bath, in the corner. The bath was filled with water, her face partially submerged. There was an integral bath/shower, with the shower hose leading from the faucets to the shower head. The hose and head were lying in the water, coiled like a snake. Weber said nothing, just looked around as well.

'Look,' Mancini said, pointing up to the shower arm, fixed to the wall above the bath. It was hanging in an odd position: at a forty-five degree angle. I reckon I see what's happened. She'd run herself a bath, maybe leaned over to switch off the faucets, the shower head came off the arm up there, hit her on the back of the head there,' – she pointed to a two inch gash on the back of her head, dark matting showing on her black hair – 'rendering her unconscious. Her face falls into the bath, and she drowns.'

‘Was the water running when the super came in?’ Weber asked the uniformed officer. ‘Or did he turn it off?’

‘He said he didn’t touch anything.’

‘Bullshit,’ muttered Weber. ‘Look at all that water. There’s been some displacement due to her body in the water, but not that much. He turned the water off, no doubt about it.’

‘I’ll check with him.’

‘Has he made a formal statement yet?’

‘Leave it until then. If he denies it – well, we’ll take it from there.’

Weber looked back at the bath and the body. He peered down to the submerged shower head. There were small particles of something floating in the water around the head, and red wisps in the water.

‘Well?’ asked Mancini. ‘Do you agree?’

‘Hm?’ Weber asked, still studying the body.

‘She’s crouching here, the shower head falls off, hits her, and she falls unconscious into the water and drowns. Subject to COD being confirmed of course. Has the ME been called?’ The last question was directed at the uniformed officer.

‘Yes. He should be here anytime. Oh, here she is now.’

The officer, Weber and Mancini stepped aside as a woman in her forties, dressed in a blue coat, her red hair tied in a bun, bustled into the bathroom. She grunted a greeting to them, and knelt down to the body. The three officers stepped out of the bathroom while she did her work.

‘You agree?’ Mancini said quietly to Weber. ‘You saw the gash on the back of the head. The shower head must have hit her.’

‘Quite possibly,’ Weber said. ‘It may have fallen

off the arm and hit her on the head.'

He paused a beat.

'But did it also give her those bruises on the back of her neck?'

Chapter Twenty-Four

MONDAY MORNING BLUES.

A feeling with which Matt was more than familiar. Even more so today as he drove to work.

The previous evening, Nathan was still asleep when they arrived home. Matt woke him and they walked back to the house. Lunch in Cape Code was filling, so all they both ate a corned beef sandwich before Nathan went upstairs for a bath and bed. After Matt tucked him in and said good night, he went downstairs, made himself a coffee, and logged on. He checked his emails, none of which was of any consequence, then took a bath himself.

As he lay in the warm soapy water he felt relieved that still there had been no reaction from Nathan about Ruth; or maybe he had just been expecting something different. His mind went back to the enigmatic conversation he had had with his mother earlier, and the early stages of his relationship with Ruth.

Before they met up he had had two what you might call serious relationships, neither of which lasted more than a couple of years. But in each of these relationships, in the early days, he found out things – normal stuff – and took them at face value, as they did about him. Then, as time went on, the things he was told would be evidenced: meeting the parents, the school friends, going through old photographs.

But with Ruth, it was slightly different. Sure, after a few weeks he knew things about her: her background, where she grew up, the fact that she was an only child, and that both her parents were dead. She told him she had a few friends, but only one she kept in touch with – Gail. But nothing had been substantiated. *But,* he thought, *she told me her parents are dead: why wouldn't I believe her?* He wouldn't ask to see a certificate of death.

After his bath, he dressed in the tee shirt and shorts he would wear to bed, checked on Nathan, and sat on their own bed. Sat there pondering a few moments, then stepped over to the six-drawer chest he and Ruth used, top four drawers for Ruth, bottom two for him. He carefully went through the Ruth's drawers, sifting through the underwear, the tee shirts, the jewellery and cosmetics she kept there. He found nothing, although he was not sure what he was looking for.

He then went over to Ruth's closet. He went through the clothes she had hanging inside, then the shelf above. Checked under the shoes she kept on the base of the closet. Again nothing. He did the same for the little cabinet by Ruth's side of the bed.

He sat on the floor, looking around the room, thinking. Then he heard a noise coming from Nathan's room – he was calling out. Matt got up and went to check: a false alarm – Nathan must have been calling out in his sleep.

Back in his bedroom, Matt checked the time and yawned. He was tired after today's journey. He wanted to check some more places for – for God knows what, but it would have to wait until tomorrow.

*****

On arrival in the work parking lot, he hesitated a moment before parking in the space the Toyota had previously occupied. He double locked the doors, checked each one of them manually, and walked across the lot to the steps leading up to the bank. At the foot of the steps, he stopped, went back to the car, and checked the doors again.

In the bank, he was met by Larry Mason, who had a wide grin on his face.

'Morning, Matt,' Larry beamed.

'Hey there, Larry,' Matt replied, pulling his coat off. 'You had a good weekend I guess?'

'Average.'

'So you're just naturally happy this morning?'

Larry laughed. 'It's Queen Bitch. She has the flu.'

'What?'

'She called in five minutes ago. Has the flu.'

'Nothing terminal I trust?'

'Sorry, guy. Just the flu. Couldn't happen to a nicer person.'

'So there is a God.'

'More or less. We still have to call her cell phone close of business. Tell her how much we've sold. Or haven't.'

'Swell,' muttered Matt.

Larry changed the subject. 'How was your weekend anyway? Any news?'

Matt shook his head. 'Nah, no news. Just waiting for the police liaison guys to contact me, give me an update. I took Nathan down to the Cape to see my folks.'

'They both okay?'

'Fine, thanks.'

His Monday morning blues slightly lessened, Matt got to work preparing for that day's appointments.

*****

That evening, after he had put Nathan to bed, he made himself a coffee, and set about resuming a search. If Ruth had something she was hiding from him – and that was a mighty big if – it would not be somewhere he would come across, such as the kitchen.

He stood at the bottom of the stairs and looked around. Then had an idea. The house had in effect four floors. There was a basement, which tended to act as Matt's den, his workshop. Ruth hardly ever ventured down there, and he knew every inch of the place.

Then there was the attic. They used this for storage: small items of furniture they hadn't gotten round to throwing away; clothes and toys Nathan had grown out of. Ruth tended to look after storing the items and keeping the place tidy. Matt only ventured up there twice a year: to bring down the Christmas tree and decorations, and early January to put them back.

He checked Nathan was asleep, and then pulled down the hatch. The little door was just outside Matt and Ruth's bedroom door; as it opened, a stainless steel ladder slowly lowered. Matt climbed up the ladder, slowly so as not to wake Nathan, and went up into the attic, flicking the switch as he got up there to turn on the light.

Once in the attic he looked around. He shivered: it was cold and damp up here. He nodded: Ruth did keep it tidy and in good order. The redundant furniture – six dining chairs and two small tables – was stored on one side; there were five large plastic boxes which Matt knew contained Nathan's old toys and clothes at the far end; the Christmas tree was boxed up as were two cardboard boxes marked *Christmas*. Two other boxes were also there, one marked *4 July*, the other *Halloween*. Matt shivered again and made a start, opening the Christmas boxes first.

He was halfway through the second box, when he looked up: in the rush to leave work to pick up Nathan, he had forgotten to phone Debra Grant Barber with that day's sales figures. Screw her, he thought; she'll have to wait till tomorrow. And doesn't her phone make outgoing calls? Trying to put work out of his mind, he returned to the boxes.

Matt checked his watch after he closed up the last box, one containing Nathan's baby clothes. Allowing for the five minutes or so when he went back down to check on Nathan and visit the bathroom, he had been up here almost two hours. He rubbed his forehead: even though it was cold up here, he was sweating. He sat on the floor and looked around. He was sitting next to one of the roof support beams; there was a horizontal beam running from here to a corresponding beam the other side. He blew the dust off the beam next to him, then coughed as he was engulfed in a cloud.

He looked around again: the floor was covered in dust as he expected; where he had sat and manoeuvred the boxes around, the dust had been disturbed, but there was one patch of the floor, the other side of the horizontal beam where nothing was stored, but the dust had been disturbed here. He frowned slightly: Ruth was always up here, sorting and tidying; maybe she did keep some boxes there. Or maybe they had rats. He shivered again, stood up and climbed over the beam. He looked around this part, but there was nothing stored there. He turned to climb back, but as he lifted his foot up, the board underneath moved slightly, just an eighth of an inch, no more. He knelt down and played with it: it was definitely loose. He played some more, and managed to pull up the board: it was around six inches by three feet. Underneath was the insulation foam which they had installed a couple of years back. He replaced the board, made a mental note to come up here one day and secure the board, and stood up.

As he stood up, he noticed a tiny wooden door, a foot square, in the wall. The piles of furniture were hiding the door, so it could easily be missed when entering the attic. He went over to the door and pulled the handle. It didn't move. He tugged harder, and the door opened with another cloud of dust, smaller than before. He went down on all fours and peered in. It was a tiny cupboard, only five or six inches deep. It seemed empty. He put one hand in and felt around. The space inside appeared to run past the door frame; as he put his fingers around the frame, he felt something hard; whatever it was, it was light, as it moved. He had no idea this cupboard was even here. He got closer and moved his fingers slowly and gently. Whatever it was, he didn't want to push it out of reach.

With his fingers on the object, he moved his hand up and felt a corner and a top. He caught a hold on it and pulled it closer. Once he could, he pulled it into the main cupboard space, then out all together.

He sat down and looked at the object. It was a tin, the sort of thing one could buy cookies in at Christmas. In fact, the faded picture on the lid showed a family sitting round a well laden table, laughing. He opened the tin. Inside was a plastic bag, one of those

Ziploc bags used in food storage. Inside was a brown letter-sized envelope. He zipped open the plastic bag, pulled out the envelope. Inside the envelope were some sheets of paper and some photographs. He pulled out the contents and looked through them.

He sat back, rested his head on the wall and read them again, this time slowly shaking his head.

That feeling of anger that he had felt the other night had returned.

Reading the contents of the envelope, he learned that everything his wife had ever told him had been a lie.

Chapter Twenty-Five

MATT'S EYES MISTED over as he lay on his bed and read through the contents of the envelope for the third time. He had replaced the little door, then slowly climbed down from the attic. Quietly looked in on Nathan, who was sound asleep. He crept over to the little boy's bed, leaned over and kissed him gently on the temple. Nathan stirred slightly.

The first document was a woman's birth certificate. At first, Matt thought this was Ruth's, and then he saw that the name was Ruth Dubois. He frowned: why would she keep another woman's birth certificate? Then he looked further at the certificate, and the date of birth was exactly the same as Ruth's.

He shook his head slowly, trying to take in what this certificate meant. The birth took place at the Highland Maternity Hospital, Rochester NY, to Ira and Elisabeth Dubois. On the same day that Ruth told him she was born. But surely this couldn't be…?

He turned to the other sheets of paper. One was a programme for a school nativity play at the Nazareth Elementary School, dated six years after the birth certificate. Inside, there was a cast list, and playing the part of an angel was Ruth Dubois. Her name had been circled in pencil. The third sheet of paper had on it a drawing, clearly done in crayon by a child, of two stick figures, a man and a woman, holding hands with a smaller female figure. They were standing on a green hill waving. A large round yellow sun was in the middle of the page.

Then Matt turned to the three photographs. One was of a school class, a couple of dozen little boys and girls sitting posing with their teacher. The children looked around five or six, around Nathan's age. The second was of a dark haired girl, maybe early teens, sitting on a wall with an older woman who was wearing a pink floral dress. In the background were a beach and the ocean. The final picture was in the same location: this time the girl was sitting with a man, who was dressed in an open necked white shirt and light grey pants. Matt looked hard at the girl in the picture: maybe it was his imagination, but she bore an uncanny resemblance to Ruth. He turned the photographs over, looking for maybe a description or a date, but they were all blank.

Matt rubbed his eyes. He was tired, but in a state of disbelief. Ruth had told him very little about her childhood. He had no idea where he was raised; whenever he brought the subject up, she would give monosyllabic answers or immediately change the subject. After a while, Matt gave up on asking, figuring she would tell him when she was good and ready. As far as her parents were concerned, right from the start, she had told him they were dead and she was an only child. End of subject. When Nathan was born, the subject of grandparents came up, and Matt tried to ask about her own family, she always changed the subject. When Matt first introduced her to his own parents, as far as he was concerned they made every effort to be welcoming, but the barriers always seemed to come down. Even after Nathan, there was always that aloofness as far as Matt's parents; as if she didn't *want* to get close to them.

He looked up, trying to remember where she said she was born and raised. He couldn't remember where she had said, but he was sure it wasn't Rochester. It must be Ruth's birth certificate: the only difference was the surname. But when they met she had told him her name was Levene. That was the name she used when they got married. So where did the Dubois come in? And why were all these items hidden away somewhere he was unlikely to find them?

The woman he thought he knew better than anybody was becoming a stranger; in the space of an hour or so he was finding he didn't know her after all. She hadn't even told him her parents' names: just that they were deceased. Now that he knew their names, maybe they were still alive; maybe they might shed some light on his wife and where she had gone.

He went downstairs and booted up his computer. A few months back he had tried to trace an old school friend and had successfully used the online directory provided by AT&T. He got onto their website and completed the Surname, First Name, City and State fields.

'What?' he muttered, as the screen returned a *Location Not Found* message. Then he noticed he had entered the wrong State. This field had to be filled using a drop-down menu, and in his haste he had selected NV for Nevada instead of NY for New York. He corrected it and sat back. A few moments later, the screen was populated with three Ira Dubois in New York State. One in Albany, one in Buffalo, and one in Syracuse. None in Rochester.

Matt stared at the screen for a few moments, scratching his chin. Maybe they had moved. If they were still alive. Then he returned to the Search screen and repeated the enquiry, this time for Elisabeth Dubois. He double checked the spelling of Elisabeth to the birth certificate then clicked on the *Find It* button.

'Yes,' he breathed as the screen showed four Elisabeth Dubois in New York State, one of which was in Buffalo. The others were in Poughkeepsie, New York City, and Rochester. The Poughkeepsie and New York City ones he felt he could eliminate, but the other two were possibles.

He clicked on the blue hyperlink for the Buffalo entry. Immediately he was taken to a different screen asking for a payment of a $6.95 registration fee for more information.

'Why am I not surprised?' he muttered, then reached into his back pocket and got out his wallet. He keyed in his credit card details, waited a few seconds for the transaction to be validated, then was returned to the original screen. He clicked again on the link, and got the full Buffalo address for Elisabeth Dubois. He was about to cross check it to the Buffalo Ira Dubois when he noticed her age. She was 96.

'It can't be you, can it?' he said as he searched for Ira Dubois, Buffalo. He was eighty-five, but at a different address.

He sat back and tried to figure out her parents' likely ages. His father had just turned seventy, his mother was three years younger. He was four years older than Ruth, from the age she had told him and from the Ruth Dubois birth certificate. Therefore one would expect her parents to be in their sixties. However, whilst a ninety-six year old woman could never have been her mother, an eighty-five year old man could have been. Unlikely, but possible. He picked out the photograph of the man and girl on the sea wall, and looked closely at the man. He looked in his forties; assuming this was a picture of her father, this man would not be eighty-five now.

He returned to the original screen and clicked on the Rochester Elisabeth Dubois. He had an address for her, and she was 65: just the right age. But there was no corresponding entry for Ira. Maybe he had died; or they had just gotten divorced. Either way, this was a start.

He checked the time: it was almost midnight. Too late to call her, even if he could get a phone number. In any case, he would prefer to visit. Talk to the woman face to face. It would mean a drive to Rochester. He got up Google Maps: it was just under 400 miles if he took the I-90 west; should take around seven hours. It would be possible to make a round trip in one day, but it would be very tiring. And there was Nathan to consider. He couldn't expect Gail and Ryan to babysit him again, and overnight this time. He would have to take him back down to his parents. But what about work? He would have to wait until the weekend before he made the trip.

'To hell with that,' he said aloud. He would call the office first thing tomorrow and arrange to take some personal time: after all, his wife had gone missing after all. Then drive to the Cape. Then hit the 90.

He felt a sense of achievement as he shut down the computer, as if he was finally making progress in finding out where Ruth had gone.

And who she was.

Chapter Twenty-Six

BY NINE THE next morning Matt was speeding down to Cape Cod, taking the same route he had taken two days ago. A rather bemused Nathan was sitting in the back seat, clutching the Velociraptor and an overnight bag. Matt had woken him that morning, told him he would not be going to Bambinos for the next couple of days; instead he would be having a short vacation with Grandma and Grandpa. Nathan made no objection to this.

The call to work was easier than anticipated, probably because Debra Grant Barber was still off with the flu. Matt decided to call Larry Mason's cell phone direct.

'Hey Matt; what's up?' came Larry's cheerful voice.

'Larry, there've been some developments about Ruth.'

'What's happened? Have the police found her or something?'

'Not exactly. Look, I'm going to need to take a few days' personal time. There's something I have to do. I take it Queen Bitch is still off sick?'

'Yep, she sure is. Great, isn't it?'

'Wish I was there to enjoy it. I should be back in say, Thursday.'

'Okay, I'll let everybody know. What are you up to?'

'Can't say right now. Too many questions, not enough answers. Fill you in when I get back. I think I had only two appointments today -'

‘Quit worrying. José and I can take care of them. And tomorrow’s.’

‘Thanks Larry. You’re a real pal.’

‘I know,’ Larry joked. ‘Just remember me on payday.’

‘I will. See you, then.’

‘Sure thing, buddy. Take care now.’

As he pulled in to a gas station for fuel and food he quickly called his parents’ number. His mother answered.

‘Hey Mom, it’s me. Are you and Dad around the next couple of days?’

‘Why, yes of course; where would we be going?’

‘Would you mind looking after Nathan for a couple of days?’

‘Why, of course not. What’s happening?’

‘Long story, Mom. I’ll fill you in when I arrive. We’re just outside Plymouth right now, so we shan’t be too long.’

‘Right you are dear. Your father’s out with that damned boat again, so it’ll be a nice surprise for him.’

‘Are you sure you’re not clutching at straws, dear?’ his mother asked him an hour later. ‘You know, that’s a hell of a long way to drive on a hunch.’

‘It’s more than a hunch, Mom; look at this.’ Matt double checked that Nathan was playing upstairs, and then showed her the birth certificate.

Estelle put her hand to her mouth as she read the certificate. ‘My gosh,’ she exclaimed, ‘it could almost be Ruth’s. Apart from the name.’

‘Even the date of birth’s the same,’ Matt said. ‘And look at these.’ He showed her the photographs. She took a glance, then sat down at the kitchen table and studied them again. Took her glasses off and wiped her eyes.

'It *is* her,' she said. 'I can tell; it's Ruth.'

'And I'm assuming,' Matt said sitting down opposite his mother, 'that they are her parents. Ira and Elisabeth.'

'But you told me her parents are dead. Right from when you and Ruth first got together.'

'That's right. Of course, they both could be. These photos are at least twenty years old. But I did an online directory search -'

Estelle looked puzzled. 'What's that?'

'It's something I can do on the internet. I used AT&T but other companies provide the service. It's the same as going to the library and browsing through telephone directories. Same thing, only much much quicker.'

'I see. So what did you find on this search?'

'Well, I figured like this: you and Dad are in your sixties – well, just about. Ruth is more or less the same age as me, so it's logical to assume her parents are – or would have been – the same age as you two. In those pictures they both look in their forties, wouldn't you say?'

She looked again and nodded.

'Now,' Matt continued. 'The Elisabeth Dubois who lives in Rochester is sixty-five.'

'Which is a reasonable age for Ruth's mother to be. I see. What about her father?'

Matt shook his head. 'No record of him. There was an Ira Dubois in Rochester, but it was a different address, and he was in his eighties.'

'Could be him. They could have split up. She could have had an older father.'

'But look at the photo. He looks about the same

age as the woman.'

Estelle looked at the picture again, shaking her head slowly. 'I can't believe it. She looks so much like Ruth. It has to be.'

'Well, I'm hoping to find out today, or tomorrow.'

'Why would Ruth keep these hidden away?' she asked.

'No idea, Mom. No idea. Maybe I'll find out when I get there.'

'Why not just telephone her?' asked his mother.

'I thought about that. But there's a reason Ruth kept everything hidden away. This woman might be part of it. She might know something anyway. So I want to see her face to face.'

Estelle nodded thoughtfully. 'Do you think Ruth might be there?'

Matt shrugged and shook his head, as if to say *I don't know*.

'Does Nathan know?' she asked looking up at Matt as he got up from the table.

'No. I've just told him I have to go away for work for a couple of days. I wasn't sure how he'd react, seeing as I told him something similar about Ruth, but he was okay about it. He liked the idea of staying with you two.'

'And we like having him. Look - you'd better get off now. You've got a long drive ahead of you.'

'Yeah. I'll just say goodbye to Nathan. Tell Dad I'm sorry I missed him.'

'I will. I'll also tell him the same thing you told Nathan. For now, at any rate.'

Matt paused, then nodded.

He met Nathan at the foot of the stairs.

'Well, I'm off now, sport,' he said, picking him up for a bear hug. 'Be a good boy for Grandma and

Grandpa.'

'He always is,' smiled Estelle from behind.

'I will, Daddy.'

'I'll call you all tonight. Love you all.'

'Love you too, Daddy.'

Estelle nodded and smiled as Matt closed the screen door behind. She and Nathan waved through the screen and watched as Matt took the Hyundai onto the main road and back to the mainland.

Matt took his normal route away from his parents' place, turning west onto the I-90 Massachusetts Turnpike as he reached the city. He did consider turning off and paying another visit to Cambridge Pharmaceuticals, but decided against it. Time was not on his side today – it was almost one-thirty – and he could not see how it could serve any useful purpose.

As he went through the third toll booth of the journey, he realised it would be pushing nine o'clock; too late to drop in on a sixty-five year-old woman. He would find a Holiday Inn or something similar when he arrived at Rochester and see her in the morning. Deciding this, he set the cruise control for sixty and turned on the radio. It was now almost three: it had been a crisp but dry day today, with not a cloud in the sky. So hopefully another couple of hours of daylight. He surfed the radio stations until he found a programme playing hits from the 1980s – just my station, he thought as he settled down in his seat.

After three numbers, the music gave way to a half hourly news, weather and travel bulletin. The news section led with a speech made by the President about a healthcare initiative, then reports about two murders in Boston that day: one outside a night club in the early hours which the police felt was racially motivated, the other was a young woman found drowned in suspicious circumstances in her bath in her apartment in Winchester. Matt glanced down at the radio at this item: the name seemed slightly familiar to him, though he couldn't place it. Overseas news consisted of a report of a car bombing in the Middle East and a report from the East Anglia part of England where three people, a woman and two men had been found in the grounds of a country house dead from shotgun wounds. The report had a graphic description of how the woman had had half her head blown away. Matt shuddered and reached over to change channels, paused for the travel update which said traffic was slow on the I-90 west at Albany and east approaching Boston. The night was due to be cold and clear.

He passed Worcester, then Springfield, approaching Albany around six. The middle of rush hour. Sure enough, the 90 got down to a crawl for around ten miles as they passed the city, then traffic began to speed up again.

Delayed because of the Albany traffic, it was almost ten when Matt approached the town of Victor. Known as the gateway to the Finger Lakes region, the town of Victor is located in upstate New York, just outside of Rochester. It was just a few minutes off the I-90, so convenient for Matt; he just hoped they had some vacancies.

Which there were. $165 got Matt a large room with one king sized bed. The restaurant was closed, so he ordered a hamburger and fries from room service. While he waited for the food to arrive he lay on the bed and called his parents' house.

'Daddy!' came the greeting.

'Hey, what are you doing still up?' he asked.

'Grandma said I could stay up till you rang,' Nathan said.

'Well, I've rung now, so you can go to bed. Call you in the morning. Put Grandma on, will you?'

'Night, Daddy.' Then there was the patter of feet and in the distance: 'Grandma! Daddy wants to talk to you.'

'He insisted on waiting for you,' Estelle said as she came to the phone. 'Dozed off a couple of times on the couch.'

'He must be bushed. Anyway, I've stopped at a Holiday Inn just outside Rochester. I'll go see her tomorrow.'

'All right. Well, good luck, anyway.'

'I said I'd call Nathan breakfast time.'

'All right. Talk to you in the morning.'

Matt hung up and put his cell phone on the room desk. There was a knock on the door: his food. He took the tray and gave the porter a $5 tip. Slouched on the bed and attacked his burger and fries: he had not eaten since he left Cape Cod. His plan was to take a shower after he had eaten, then go to bed for an early start. Although he wanted answers here, ideally he would like to get back home tomorrow night. Thursday at the latest.

As he leaned back eating he flicked the TV remote and switched on. It came on to NBC and the eleven o'clock news. The item about the Damascus car bombing was just finishing and next was the suspicious death in Winchester, MA. The reported gave the name as Ms Akira Watanabe; Matt looked up from his fries as again the name seemed familiar. Then her picture showed on the screen, one the authorities had released from her drivers licence. Matt leaned forward and peered at the screen. Her face seemed familiar as well as the name. But where had he seen her before?

Then it hit him. It was in that Irish pub on Washington last week. When he challenged that jerk Danny Clark. He introduced her as his girlfriend Aki. Akira. From a distance Matt had mistaken her for Ruth.

Now she turns up drowned in her bath.

Coincidence or what?

Chapter Twenty-Seven

MATT WOKE JUST after seven. He showered, dressed and, knowing that Nathan and therefore his parents would have been awake some time, decided to make the promised phone call before he had breakfast.

'Morning, son,' said his father as he answered. 'I'll just get your mother.'

Matt laughed and shook his head while he waited for her to come to the phone. In the background he could hear Nathan crying 'It's Daddy! Daddy!' and little footsteps getting louder.

'Hello Daddy, I was a good boy last night.'

'Well done. What did you do?'

'After my supper Grandma let me watch Sesame Street, then I had a bath, then Grandpa read me a story.'

'Oh, what was the story?'

'Can't remember.'

'Never mind. You just be a good boy for them today, and I'll be back tomorrow. Okay?'

'Okay, Daddy.'

'Now is Grandma there?'

'Yes.'

'Well, give her the phone, can you?'

'Okay, Daddy.'

Nathan passed the phone to Estelle.

'How are you this morning, Matt? Did you sleep well?'

'Kept waking up. Look, I'm going over to see her after breakfast. Depending on what I find, I may or may not be back tonight. If I need to, I'll stop here another night and drive back tomorrow.'

'All right. What about work?'

'Work's sorted, but I'll need to drive back tomorrow at the latest.'

'Well, good luck. Call after you've seen her. Let us know what she said, and when you're coming home.'

'I will. Let me say good-bye to Nathan.'

'He's gone. He's in the kitchen with your father. They're making pancakes.'

'All right. Call you later. Bye.'

Matt hung up and sat back on the bed yawning. He had slept fitfully the night before, trying to figure out where Elisabeth Dubois fitted in with everything. At the end of the day, this could be one big wild goose chase. Trying to figure out what was with the birth certificate, the nativity thing; why it was all hidden away. When they met, he knew her as Ruth Levene: why did she change from Ruth Dubois? Was Elisabeth Dubois her mother? If she was, why tell him she was dead?

Then there was that news item last night about the murder back in Winchester. Was she the same person as the girl he saw with Danny Clark? He couldn't be sure, but maybe he would speak to Lieutenant Weber when he got back to Boston. He may have news for him about this visit also. Other fish to fry today.

He had finally gotten off to sleep around 12:30; he began to stir a couple of hours later, aware of noises. He lifted his head off the pillow and cocked his ears. Through the wall he could hear the regular rhythm of a bed squeaking.

'Jesus, no.' He pulled the duvet over his head to shut out the noise. No use. The squeaking got faster and faster and he heard a faint cry through the walls. Then everything went silent.

'Thank God for that,' he muttered, and curled up tighter. Then, half asleep, he recalled the last time he and Ruth had made love. It must have been two or three weeks ago, but it had not even crossed his mind since she disappeared. Momentarily, the anger he had been feeling turned to concern; he found he was missing her again.

'Thanks guys,' he mumbled, addressing the couple in the next room. Hardly surprising: he saw quite a few people staying on business as he checked in; it was probably somebody banging his secretary.

He checked the clock: 2:50AM. By 2:52 he was asleep again.

As he took the elevator down to the hotel restaurant, he thought about his conversation with his mother, and had a craving for pancakes for breakfast. This he duly ordered, and had a meal of pancakes, bacon, maple syrup and three cups of strong black coffee. As he ate, he looked around the restaurant, trying to identify the couple from the next room. He could not; they were probably still in bed, he reflected.

As he checked out, he asked the receptionist if they were fully booked that night, just in case his business kept him in Rochester an extra day. She assured him that so far they were only sixty percent full, so there was a good chance that he could book a room later. No guarantee, she added, that it would be the same room. Matt replied that would not be a problem.

*****

Matt's rental car had GPS, so all he needed to do when he set off was key in Elisabeth Dubois' zip code and follow instructions. It did occur to him that he would have to phone the car rental office that day, to extend the rental period, as there was still the matter of the insurance claim for the Toyota to attend to.

It was rush hour as he made his way into Rochester. He reflected that it wouldn't have hurt to wait a while longer at the hotel to avoid the traffic. He did regret not checking when he returned to his room after breakfast if his neighbours had put a Do Not Disturb sign on their door. Over breakfast, he had made a mental note to check and if they had, turn the sign round to Please Make Up Room. But he forgot.

The GPS took him off the 390 North at Jefferson. After a dozen or so blocks he turned into the street where Elisabeth Dubois lived. Her house number was 916; he had turned into the street at the 1600 block, so continued down the street until he reached the 900 block, and pulled up across the road from 916.

He remained in the Hyundai, looking across the street at her house. It was a modest looking single storey family home - three bedrooms, Matt estimated. A small but neatly maintained yard out front: grass mown, colourful flower beds, surrounded by a small white picket fence. There was a driveway leading to a garage, but no sign of a car. All of the windows were shut.

Matt stepped out of the car, and crossed the road. He walked up the neat path and knocked on the wooden screen door. Knocked again after a while. Still no answer. Guessing nobody was in, he returned to his car. It was 9:25, and he had not expected her to be out. He had assumed that a lady in her sixties would not be going out until later, so would be in this early in the morning. He slapped the dashboard in frustration. He would have to wait; hopefully she wasn't away on vacation.

He decided to take a walk. Checking the car was okay where he had parked, he wandered up the road. In the distance he could see a busier cross street: maybe he could get a coffee somewhere there. Two blocks later, he found a busy road, the other side of which was a small shopping center. He crossed over and found a diner. It appeared to be privately owned, not a franchise. He bought a *USA Today* and a coffee and sat down in a window booth. He spent the next half hour watching the traffic go by and reading the newspaper while he slowly drank his coffee. Paid his bill and wandered back across the street and down to where he had left the car. He sat back in the car and resumed his vigil.

It was just after ten when he saw a figure walk up the path and let herself into the house. He sat up: it had to be her. She was slight, had grey hair and wore a grey overcoat. She was carrying a bag of shopping in each hand. He waited five minutes, and then crossed over. Knocked again on the screen door. Waited a few moments, then knocked again.

He was about to knock a third time when he heard coughing from inside the house. Through the screen and the glass of the internal door, he could see a figure, that of the old lady, approaching. The inner door opened, and she stepped out.

'Yes, can I help you?' She had taken off her overcoat and was wearing a woollen jumper and a pleated skirt. She still wore outside shoes. Her hair was grey, and her face was lined. He reflected that she looked ten years older than someone in their sixties.

'I am very sorry to bother you, ma'am,' he said. 'I am looking for an Elisabeth Dubois.'

She appeared surprised at first. 'I am she,' she replied. 'How can I help you?'

'Well, I – I am calling about – about your daughter.'

She tensed. 'I'm sorry, I don't have a daughter.'

'I'm so sorry to have troubled you then,' said Matt. 'I must have the wrong person and address. I am looking for an Elisabeth Dubois who has a daughter Ruth.'

She gasped slightly and put her hand to her mouth.

Matt continued, 'I am her husband, you see.'

'I am very sorry. You must have the wrong house.'

'I must have. Sorry to have troubled you.'

Matt smiled and stepped away, back down the path.

'Please, wait,' she called out as he reached the sidewalk. He spun round, then slowly walked back up to the door.

'Why were you calling here about your wife?' she asked. Matt noticed her knuckles were white as she clung onto the door.

'She's disappeared,' Matt answered. 'Just never came home from work the other day. It's a long story, but her birth certificate shows her being born in Rochester to an Ira and Elisabeth Dubois. Is Ira your husband?'

'I'm a widow,' she said. 'But my late husband was named Ira.'

Matt nodded. ‘I see.’

‘Do you have any ID?’ she asked.

‘Surely,’ Matt said. He was rather taken aback, but showed her his drivers licence.

‘Thank you,’ she said. ‘Would you like to come in?’

Matt nodded, as she unlocked the outer door and let him in. She led him through to her lounge. The inside of the house was just as neat and tidy as outside. There were floral pictures on the wall as he followed her, and two vases of flowers, one on a lace mat on the dining table, the other also on a lace mat, but on a bureau. She turned round to him.

‘Do – do you have a picture of your wife?’ she asked, somewhat hesitantly. Matt nodded and took out his wallet. He showed her a small picture he kept in there.

She swallowed. Looked around the room, then said, ‘Wait here, please.’

Matt nodded again while she left the room. She returned a few moments later with a picture. It had a flap on the back, so must have been standing on something. She showed it to Matt. It was a black and white photograph of a dark haired woman sitting at a round glass table, the sort one found outside a bar or a restaurant. She was holding a glass of wine. Matt felt his face flush and a nervous feeling in his stomach as he stared at the woman in the photograph: it was a younger version of Ruth. He turned to Elisabeth Dubois.

‘But… I don’t understand… Who…?’

‘That’s my daughter, Mr Gibbons. That photograph was taken three years ago. Her name was Ruth too.’

‘Three…? I still don’t understand. This is – this

is…'

'My daughter and your wife can't be the same person. Two weeks after that photograph was taken, my daughter was killed in a car crash.'

Chapter Twenty-Eight

MATT STARED AT Mrs Dubois, not understanding what she had just told him. Not sure if he even heard her correctly. He didn't know what to say next.

'Sit down, Mr Gibbons, please,' she said softly. As he looked into her grey eyes, he could see they were moist. He slowly lowered himself into an armchair; she sat on the chair opposite.

'It was almost three years ago,' she told him. 'Three years on the 28th, to be precise.'

Matt paused a moment before speaking.

'What happened?' he asked softly.

She fiddled with the silver necklace she was wearing. 'She was visiting us. Late one morning she had arranged to meet a friend – I don't know who they were – for brunch. The weather was bad that day, very heavy rain…' She paused a moment to compose herself.

'Take your time,' Matt said.

'She was making her way back here. It was dark and raining hard. There was some construction going on on part of her route back here…' She paused again. 'Somehow, in the wet, she lost control of the car, and crashed into the side of an overpass. The car burst into flames.'

Matt put his hand to his mouth. 'Oh my God.'

'The policewoman who called round said she must have been killed or at least rendered unconscious immediately, so she wouldn't have felt…'

Matt nodded rapidly, hoping she would change

the subject, not prolong the pain she was putting herself through. He knew that this could not have been his Ruth, but even so; the poor woman must have been grief-stricken. The pain must still be so raw.

She sat up erect, composing herself. 'So you see, Mr Gibbons: my daughter cannot possibly be your missing wife.'

He nodded again, accepting what she had said. He stood to leave.

'My husband died six months later,' she continued. 'Of cancer. But I'm sure Ruth's death had an effect on him.'

'I'm sure it did,' Matt said softly. 'I'm so sorry for your loss.'

He turned to leave. He had an answer to his question, although not an answer he could ever have expected.

'I'll show you out,' she said, getting up from her chair. He followed her to the front door.

'If I could ask you one more question…' he said as they got to the door. 'You might think it a strange thing to ask, and I certainly don't mean any disrespect.'

She smiled up at him. A sad smile. 'Ask away.'

'Was she your daughter? Your natural daughter, I mean?'

'You mean was she adopted and did she have a twin sister whom you met?' she asked.

'I – I'm not sure what I…'

'She was our natural daughter. I was her birth mother, to use that horrible modern parlance. She was not adopted, and no: she did not have a twin sister. She was an only child.'

Matt nodded again, again not knowing what to say

to her.

'Could I see your wife's photograph again?' she asked.

'Surely.' He took out the picture once more.

'Yes, I can see a similarity,' she said. 'But that's not my daughter. I am sorry you've had a wasted journey.'

'Not wasted,' Matt said resignedly. 'Just crossing off one possibility, that's all.'

'Have you been to the police?' she asked. 'About your wife, I mean.'

'I have. But I have to look for myself, too. Have to be doing something.'

'I understand.'

Matt smiled at her. 'I'll leave you in peace now. Thank you for your time. And once again: I'm so sorry for your loss. And that of your husband.'

'I hope you find your wife,' she said, slowly closing the door.

Matt turned and walked back to his car. Put the key in the ignition, then stopped before turning the key. He looked over at the Dubois house. Through the window of what was her lounge Matt could see the outline of the rear lounge window. He thought he could see the silhouette of Mrs Dubois watching him. He started the engine and drove off. Turned the corner of the first cross street and pulled over again. He turned off the engine and leaned back in the seat.

He looked back at the street he had left. It was time to go home now: he could see no reason to prolong his visit. He reached for his cell phone and called his parents' house. His father answered.

'Hello, Dad, it's me.'

'Hello there, son; how's the trip going?'

Matt could not be sure how much his mother had

told his father.

'Just winding things up, that's all.'

'I'll just get your mother.'

Matt gave a wry smile as he waited.

'Hello Matt; how are you?' Estelle asked.

'Fine; about to set off for home.'

'Good; nice and early. How did it go?'

'Well, I managed to see -'

'Hold on for a second.'

Matt paused for a moment and then his mother said, 'Carry on. Your father just came in. I haven't told him why you went down there. Not the full picture anyway.'

Matt then proceeded to tell her about his conversation with Elisabeth Dubois. His mother said very little, just the occasional 'u-huh' and a gasp when he told her about the car crash.

'Well, come on back now if you've finished there,' she said. 'We can have a better conversation when you are here.'

'I will. Is Nathan around?'

'Yes, but he's asleep.'

'Asleep?'

'Yes. He and your father were having a game of basketball in the yard and he fell asleep on the couch not ten minutes ago. I think his Grandpa will be doing the same thing soon,' she added.

'See you around seven I expect.'

'You two going to stop over?'

'Probably not. I'm supposed to be back at work tomorrow. See what time I get to yours. Another hour in the car shouldn't make much difference.'

'Look, Matt; if you have things to sort out, why not let Nathan stay here a couple of days? Would be a break for him. Surely it won't matter if he misses a couple of days at kindergarten.'

Matt thought. Although he was desperate to see his son again, he did have a lot of things he needed to do, and it would make it easier if Nathan was with his parents.

'Yeah, but what about clothes and stuff?'

'Don't worry. We can sort things out.'

'All right; guess you're right. Look – it's Wednesday. What about I come down Saturday and pick him up? Maybe we could drive home Sunday.'

'That sounds perfect to me. The two of you are always welcome; you know that.'

'Okay. I'll head straight home then. Give you a call when I get back. Speak to Nathan then. If he's happy about staying till the weekend, then that's what we'll do.'

'I can't see him having a problem with that. But I'll ask him anyway.'

'No, I'm sure he won't. Tell him I love him and I'll call tonight.'

Matt hung up and started the car. It was going to be a long day and he wanted to get home. He needed the peace and quiet of his own house to think things through; he needed to be in Boston tonight.

He made good progress east along the New York State Thruway, and around two thirty pulled over to fuel up, use the bathroom and get something to eat. There was a self-service cafeteria at the service area. He stood in line with his tray, and ordered a club sandwich and fries and a cola.

For the second time that day, he picked a window booth and sat eating his late lunch. Whilst eating, he could not help but ponder his visit to Elisabeth Dubois.

He had some answers now, but not the ones he

was expecting. He was unsure whether to feel guilty for calling on her and raking up painful memories, or whether she had told him the whole truth. There was an uncanny similarity between her daughter and his wife; the dates of birth were the same, and they shared the same name. But her daughter had been dead nearly three years. And what reason would she have for telling him anything other than the truth? What she told him was clearly upsetting her.

So: Ruth Dubois and Ruth Levene Gibbons shared the same birthday, but were two different people, both only children. Ruth Dubois died three years ago. Ruth Levene Gibbons was alive, so Matt hoped and prayed. Different people. The theory that Matt had dreamt up about them being twins separated at birth could be discounted.

But now Matt had another question: why did his Ruth have the other woman's birth certificate hidden away?

Chapter Twenty-Nine

ONCE HE KNEW that Nathan would be staying at his parents' house, Matt took the drive back more easily. No need to rush. He was not exactly reluctant to get home, but it would not be the same without Nathan. It was not the same without Ruth, but not having his son around would be worse. He tried to recall the last time he had spent the night at home without Nathan: he was sure it had happened before, but could not recall when. The house would seem really empty tonight. He suddenly felt lonely.

Needing to focus on something else, he deliberated over today's events and his next steps. He needed to speak to Lieutenant Weber: to check on any progress with Ruth, and to update him on what he had turned up. On the birth certificate for Ruth Dubois and his visit to Rochester for a start; find out what the police were told at Cambridge Pharmaceuticals; and tell him about: what was her name? Aki Watanabe. Did the police know she was Danny Clark's girlfriend? They probably did, but it might be important.

He needed to speak to Gail as well. Gail was Ruth's best friend, and had known her longer than he had. He needed to speak with her about the birth certificate, and the Rochester connection. Once he had got home, he would call her.

As the turnpike passed the CSX Beacon Park Rail Yard, Matt checked the time. It was still relatively early in the evening. Time then to turn off at the next exit and go up to Gail and Ryan's this evening.

Would be better than calling her. He negotiated a number of intersections and was soon heading north up the Mystic Avenue. A touch of *déjà vue*, he thought, as he turned into the little parking lot at Gail's building. He had not been here for some months, then twice in a week or so.

He climbed the stairs to their floor and knocked on the door. A few seconds later, the door opened slightly. Gail peered round over the chain.

'Sorry to call unannounced,' Matt said, cheerily but wearily.

'Hey there,' she said, sounding surprised. She closed the door so she could release the chain, and then opened it to let him in.

'How you doing?' she asked, reaching up to kiss him.

'I'm doing okay,' he said. 'In the circumstances.'

'Has there been any news?' she asked.

'There've been a few – er, developments,' Matt said.

She walked over to the breakfast bar which separated their kitchen from the living room and lit a cigarette. Matt noticed she was not fully dressed: she was wearing a dressing gown, black with a dragon emblem on the back.

'I see,' she said, taking a drag. 'Developments. That sounds mysterious.'

'Well,' Matt said, taking his coat off. 'Stuff that's a mystery to me. Might not be to you.'

'Oh, how so?' she asked.

'It's just that you've known Ruth longer than I have.'

She took another puff. 'Oh, I see. Sorry, Matt; do you want a drink or something?'

'Well, I wouldn't say no to a coffee. It's been a

long day.'

'All right. You take it black, don't you? Sit down; it won't take long.'

'Do you mind if I use the bathroom first?' Matt left her in the kitchen. After a long drive Matt needed to pee, desperately. A couple of minutes later, much relieved, he joined Gail outside. 'Thanks,' he said as she passed him the coffee. He sat on one of the breakfast bar stools. Gail remained in the kitchen.

'Do you mind if I carry on?' she asked, as she moved foil boxes from the refrigerator to the oven. 'Ryan's due home soon, and we've not eaten yet.'

Matt had always had a lot of time for Ryan. He had known Gail for almost as long as he had known Ruth, and while he liked her, there was just something about her that made him glad she was Ruth's friend, not his. Something he could never quite put his finger on. Ryan on the other hand was a guy Matt warmed to as soon as they met. Although not friends themselves – they moved in different social circles – they would always find themselves on the same wavelength. Whenever they met up as a foursome, he would always enjoy Ryan's company more than Gail's, and always found him easier to talk to. On the occasions that Gail and Ryan visited Matt and Ruth at their house, he got the impression that Gail looked down her nose at their home. Maybe it was the continual mess the place was in, thanks to Nathan. Sure, it was not the luxury condominium she and Ryan had, but it was their home nevertheless. Ryan on the other hand was the perfect guest, even though he was probably earning five times what he and Ruth were. And there was the way they were with Nathan: Gail tended to be rather aloof at times, happy for him to be doing his own thing; Ryan, however, had no problem getting on the floor and playing dinosaurs with him.

'Where's Nathan, by the way?' she asked.

'Down with his grandparents until the weekend. Gives me time to do stuff.'

She nodded. 'Right.'

'Is Ryan not in then?' Matt asked, looking around, expecting him to be in one of the other rooms.

'No,' she said. 'Still on his way home. Due in about half an hour.'

Matt seemed surprised; he had a feeling Ryan was at home. He nodded and drank some coffee. 'Okay.'

'So…,' Gail said. 'These developments?'

Matt got off the stool and walked over to the chair where he had left his overcoat. He reached in and took out the envelope. 'How long have you known Ruth?' he asked, returning to the stool.

Gail stopped whatever she was doing in the kitchen and mentally counted. 'Quite a few years,' she said, half laughing.

'More years than I have.'

She nodded. 'A few, yeah. Why?'

'What was her maiden name?'

'Levene. You know that.'

'Right. Levene.' He opened the envelope. 'Look at this,' he said, passing the birth certificate over to her.

She read it a couple of times, and then looked up at Matt.

'It's Ruth's -'

'Look at it again. Look at the surname.'

She looked again. 'I didn't notice. Dubois. This isn't Ruth's, then.'

'Did you know her parents?'

She passed the certificate back. 'No. They were

already dead when we first met.'

'You don't know what their names were.'

She shook her head.

'I found this certificate hidden in a box in the attic. *I* didn't put it there. But look at the date of birth on it: exactly the same as Ruth's, isn't it?' He showed it to her again. 'And the name. Apart from the surname, it could be Ruth's. There was nothing she ever said to you – even years ago – that could explain this?'

'No; nothing.'

Matt tutted and slid the certificate back in the envelope.

'Don't forget, Matt: Ruth had always been a private person. If there was stuff she didn't tell you, she wouldn't have told me.'

He shrugged. 'Maybe I thought you two had woman to woman conversations.'

'We did. But not about that. I've never heard of a Ruth Dubois. And her parents were always dead.' She shook her head. 'You know what I mean.'

'Elisabeth Dubois is still alive,' Matt said.

'Oh?' Gail asked. 'You've spoken to her?'

'That's where I've just come back from. That's why Nathan's at my folks' place. I did some online searching for the surname of Dubois in Rochester, and found her. I spoke to her today.'

'Oh?' said Gail, finishing her cigarette. 'What did she tell you?'

'Not much. Not much I *think*. She was married to an Ira Dubois – he died a few years back, apparently. Their ages are right for Ruth's parents. But she told me that the Ruth Dubois on the certificate was her only daughter. Only child. But she died in an auto accident couple of years back.'

'I see.'

'So,' Matt went on, 'this obviously isn't Ruth's certificate. But it doesn't explain why Ruth had it. And there's this.' He took out one of the photographs and held it up for Gail to see. 'That's a picture apparently of her daughter. Can you see the similarity?'

Gail looked closer. She crinkled her nose slightly. 'Could be. But obviously isn't.'

The door opened and Ryan stepped in.

'Sweetie, I'm – hey there, Matt, fancy you being here. This is a surprise. Any news?' he asked as they shook hands.

'She hasn't shown up,' said Matt. 'But I'm following a few lines of enquiry.'

'Don't the police do that?' Ryan asked as he took off his coat and hung it in a wall closet next to the door. He went over to Gail and embraced her. 'Mm,' he said. 'You smell good.' He swished her robe cord. 'What's this? Don't tell me: you had plans for me tonight, but Matt came in and spoilt it?'

'Not exactly,' said Gail. 'I got home a bit earlier than usual. Just climbed out of the bath.'

Ryan laughed. 'Okay,' he said, raising his palms in mock surrender. 'Let me go freshen up.'

He kissed Gail again and went into their bedroom, putting his hand on Matt's shoulder as he went past.

'What are you going to do now?' Gail asked, when Ryan had gone.

'No idea, to be honest. I'll probably get hold of that police Lieutenant who came to see me. See what he thinks. Hey,' he said, changing the subject, 'did you see the TV news last night?'

'Er, may have done. Why? Was there something about Ruth?'

‘No, no. It was about a suspicious death. A woman up in the Winchester area.’

Gail shook her head.

‘It was a woman called Watanabe. Aki Watanabe. Found dead in her bath. But the thing is: you know I told you I went down to Cambridge Pharmaceuticals to see if Ruth was there.’

‘Ah, yes; I think you did.’

‘Well, the manager there told me he’d never heard of her. I knew it was bullshit, so I waited outside to see if I could catch her leaving for lunch.’

‘Okay. Yes.’

‘I saw him – this manager – walking down the street with someone I thought was Ruth. I followed them to a bar on Washington. But it wasn’t Ruth he was with; it was this woman.’

‘The dead one?’

‘I’m pretty sure, yes.’

‘Are you going to tell the police that, also?’

‘Yes; absolutely.’

Ryan burst out of the bathroom. ‘Well, I’m ready to eat. You staying, Matt?’

‘No, I have to go. Thanks all the same.’

‘Go on, stay. There’s enough, right, Gail?’

Gail opened her mouth to speak, but Matt answered for her.

‘No, honestly. Thanks all the same. Another time, perhaps.’

‘Sure. Come over any time. Bring Nathan of course. Where is the little guy, by the way?’

‘He’s at his grandparents for a few days.’

‘Cool. He always enjoys it down there, doesn’t he?’

‘He does, yes.’

‘Must be the sea air. Fresher than the city. Tell

him I said hi.'

'I will, yes.'

'What about his kindergarten?' asked Gail.

'I don't think missing a couple of days would be a problem for him,' said Matt.

'He's back Monday, then?' she asked.

Matt nodded. 'Yeah. Should be.' He put on his coat. 'I'll let you two eat in peace.'

'I'll see you out.' Ryan took him to the door.

'Let us know if there's any other news,' Gail called out.

'Yes,' added Ryan. 'You know if there's anything…'

'I know,' said Matt. 'And I will.'

He shook Ryan's hand and left.

Sitting in the Hyundai a few minutes later, he looked up at the building. He could see one of Gail's windows, the kitchen he thought. A light went on two windows down. He stretched and rubbed his eyes. There was something odd up there. It was to do with the bathroom. If Ryan was not yet home from work, why was the toilet seat up? And if she had just had a bath, why wasn't the bathroom even a little steamed up and damp? Or was his imagination running wild? He was so tired now. He started the car and pulled into the street. As he waited at a stop light he remembered they had an *en suite* bathroom in their bedroom. Nothing less for Gail. It was time he went home and slept.

As he arrived home forty minutes later he noticed half a dozen cars parked in the darkened streets. He was too tired to use his own garage, so he parked on the street also, albeit two doors away from his own house. As he turned the key in his door, he heard a familiar voice.

‘Mr Gibbons. Do you have a few minutes?’

He turned round and groaned inwardly as he made out the form of Lieutenant Weber approaching. He nodded and Weber followed him inside.

‘Don’t you sleep, Lieutenant?’ he asked.

‘I finished my shift an hour ago. I was just passing.’

‘So this is an unofficial visit?’

‘Kind of. I needed to give you some news.’

‘News of Ruth? You’ve found her?’

Weber shook his head. ‘No, I’m afraid not. But your car’s been found.’

Chapter Thirty

'WHERE DID YOU find it?' Matt asked as he closed the front door.

'I didn't find it,' said Weber as he followed Matt through to the kitchen. The NYPD found it.'

'New York? What the hell's it doing up there?'

'Waiting to be picked up, I guess.'

Matt turned round and faced Weber across the kitchen table. 'In Manhattan?'

'No, in Brooklyn.'

'Brooklyn?'

'U-huh. It was found in a parking garage on,' - he took out a small note book and consulted it - 'Schermerhorn Street, Brooklyn.'

Matt shook his head. 'I don't know anyone who... Never been...'

'Neither had I.'

'How long had it been there for?'

'A few days. The garage is one of those open twenty-four hour joints. Whoever had left it there had paid twenty-five bucks or whatever it is and never came back for it. It was parked on the bottom level; it's an underground garage. The super noticed it after a couple of days and called to get it towed.'

'Was there any sign of anything in the car?'

'Sign of what?'

'I was just wondering if this had anything to do with Ruth's disappearance.'

'I don't think it was. Just crap timing, that's all. Do you know how many vehicles are stolen in the City of Boston each day?'

'A lot, I guess.'

'You guess correct. But to answer your question: no, there was no indication as to who took it, or why.'

'What's special about Schmerhorn…?'

'Schermerhorn Street. Nothing special, as far as I know. I don't know that part of the city that well. Okay on Manhattan, but not any of the other boroughs.'

'So where's the car now?'

'It got taken to a pound in Brooklyn, where they take cars that are towed for illegal parking, that sort of thing. When it arrived, they did the standard check on the plate, and it got flagged up as stolen.'

'Can I go and pick it up?'

'I'd leave it until the morning, if I were you.'

'I was thinking about Saturday morning. Will it still be there?'

'It'll be there for a few weeks. Then it and any unclaimed vehicles get auctioned. Just take your ID and registration documents. You got any wheels?'

'Rental car.'

'I guess you could call the rental office and arrange to return it to the New York depot. Then take the subway to the pound. It's on Sands and Navy. Ironically, just a couple of blocks from where it was found.'

'Okay, thanks. I'll go Saturday.'

'Fine. Well, I'll let you get on.' Weber made to leave.

'I was going to call you, actually.'

'Oh, about what?'

'About a couple of things. First of all I found in Ruth's stuff a birth certificate for a Ruth Dubois, who was born in Rochester the same day as my Ruth was born.'

‘I take it Dubois wasn’t your wife’s maiden name?’

‘No, it was Levene.’

‘Hold on, that was the name she used before you two got married, yes? It doesn’t mean it wasn’t her maiden name.’

‘You mean like she was married before?’

Weber shrugged. ‘Or just used a different name. For any reason.’

‘Good point. I hadn’t considered that.’ He paused. ‘Well, I did an online search and found an Elisabeth Dubois – the mother’s name on the certificate – still living in Rochester. Her age would have been about right.’

‘Is that where you’ve been today?’

‘That’s right. I spoke to her, but she told me her daughter was killed in a car crash almost three years ago.’

‘So she wasn’t your Ruth?’

‘No. But look at this photograph.’ He reached over to the brown envelope he had found in the attic. ‘I found this old photo with the birth certificate, and this girl here looks like a younger version of Ruth.’

Weber studied the photographs. ‘I’m not saying you’re right, but are you happy for me to pass these to the Missing Persons Unit? They may or may not find them useful. I’ll have them take copies and return them.’

‘That would be great. Thanks.’ Matt passed the envelope over.

‘You were going to call me about a couple of things, you said.’

‘Yes, I did. While I was in Rochester, I saw a news item from here about a suspicious death.’

Weber’s ears pricked up. ‘Oh yes?’

‘A woman by the name of Akira Watanabe. Is that right?’

Weber nodded. ‘Did you know her?’

‘No, but the day I went down to Cambridge Pharmaceuticals and spoke to the office manager, Danny Clark. The guy who told me he’d never heard of Ruth.’

‘Go on,’ said Weber.

‘Later on, I saw Clark go into an Irish pub on Washington.’

‘You were following him?’

‘Kind of. The person he was with looked like Ruth from behind. I thought – well, you know…’

‘Go on,’ said Weber again.

‘I followed them into the pub and he was sitting there with this woman.’

‘With Ms Watanabe?’

‘Yes, that’s right. He introduced her to me as his girlfriend Aki. Made a big deal about her not being Ruth.’

‘His girlfriend. I see. Mr Gibbons, I know you don’t have a high opinion of this Mr Clark: neither do I, as it happens, off the record; but are you sure about all this? I wouldn’t like to think you’re trying to make things difficult for him. There was no trace of any boyfriend, Mr Clark or anybody else, in her apartment. She was unattached. But I’ll make a note of what you’ve told me.’

‘You’re dealing with her case?’ Matt asked.

‘That’s right. As I say, I’ll note your comments. If we need any clarifications, we’ll be in contact.’ Weber adjusted his overcoat and stepped over to the door. Matt followed him, and held the door open while the Lieutenant left. After saying goodbye, he double locked the door, and went into the living room, where he collapsed into a chair.

He was woken up by the sound of his cell phone ringing. He looked at the display and saw it was his mother's number.

'Shit,' he said aloud. He had forgotten to call them as he had promised. 'Hello Mom,' he said, answering the call. 'Sorry, I forgot to ring, didn't I?'

'You did. We were all worried about you.'

'Where's Nathan?'

'He went to sleep an hour ago. He was waiting for you to call. Did you get held up in traffic?'

'No, the opposite in fact. I decided to make an impromptu call on Ruth's friend Gail. You know, to see if she knew anything about the Dubois connection.'

'And did she?'

'No. Then just as I got home, the police arrived.'

'The police? Did they have any news?'

'Not about Ruth. The Lieutenant came to tell me my car had been found.'

'Well at least that's something. Where was it found?'

'Some all night parking garage in Brooklyn. It's at the police pound now. I'm going to go over to collect it Saturday morning. Then I'll go straight over to you.'

'Some good news at least. I'll tell Nathan you'll call him in the morning?' The last sentence was more of an instruction than a question.

'I will, yes. Good night then, Mom.'

'Good night Matt.'

He disconnected, stood up and stretched. Time for bed. No – one more thing first. He booted up his laptop and logged on. Went onto Google Maps and found the parking garage in Schermerhorn Street. There it was, just as the Lieutenant had said. He moved the cursor up slightly and found the Hoyt-Schermerhorn subway station. Yes, only a couple of blocks apart. Then clicked on a link to the New York MTA. Then on to Subway Maps. Weber was right: the A, C, and G lines ran through here. The G ran from Smith and 9th to Court Square, Queens. The A and the C ran way Uptown.

He sat back in the chair, rubbing his eyes. It had been a very long day, and he was fatigued by the amount of driving he had done over the past forty-eight hours. He was not sure if his mind was not being over-active, as it was earlier when he was analysing why Gail's toilet seat was up. There must have been a reason why whoever had parked his car chose that location to leave it. Close to the subway station. The A and C lines were busy commuter routes into Lower Manhattan. Was this their final destination?

Chapter Thirty-One

THURSDAY MORNING AND Matt arrived at work at eight fifteen, a good twenty minutes or so before his normal arrival time. Not having to make Nathan's breakfast and journey to kindergarten helped the time-keeping, and the call to his parents to talk to his son only took ten minutes. As he paused to double lock the Hyundai, he heard a horn sound the other side of the office parking lot. He waved at Larry Mason as his colleague parked his car.

'Morning Matt,' Larry asked as he joined him at the foot of the steps leading up to the rear door. 'How's it goin'?'

'Morning. Going okay. As okay as expected.'

'Any news? Did you get much done on your days off?'

'No news from Ruth,' Matt said as Larry unlocked the door and they walked in. 'The days weren't entirely unproductive, though.'

'Oh, how so?'

After they had taken off their overcoats, they made their way to the staff room for the first cup of coffee of the day. On the way, Larry called out a greeting across the banking hall to the Chief Cashier, who was setting up the tills.

As they poured themselves a coffee, Matt related to Larry the saga of the Ruth Dubois birth certificate, the photographs and his visit to Rochester. Larry stood listening, open mouthed, occasionally taking a sip of his coffee.

'Jeez,' he said. 'You've had a busy time away

from here.'

'That's not all,' said Matt, as he added the detail about Akira Watanabe.

'Jeez,' repeated Larry. 'Are you sure it's the same person?'

'Ninety-five percent sure.'

'Have you told the police?'

'I told them last night. That Lieutenant Weber called round last night.'

'What did he say?'

'Well,' Matt said, pouring more coffee, 'I get the impression they feel she was single; you know, no significant other. I think he said there was no trace of any boyfriend or partner in her apartment. He said he's going to take it under advisement. I think he feels I've got it in for this Clark guy because he's such as asshole.'

'Why did he call round last night?'

'Morning guys.' They were interrupted by José Vasquez, who had just arrived. 'Hey there, Matt. Any news?'

Still looking at Matt, Larry raised his eyebrows and inclined his head over to José, as if to say *can I tell him?* Matt nodded.

'Matt's had a busy few days,' Larry said.

Matt proceeded to repeat the story to José.

'Man,' said José. 'That's really weird.'

'Tell me about it.'

'And there's still no word about your wife?'

'No.'

'You were saying why the police called round last night,' said Larry.

'Oh yes, that's another thing: my car's been found.'

'Really? Where?' asked Larry.

'It's turned up in a parking garage in Brooklyn.'

'Brooklyn?' the two others exclaimed in unison.

'That's right. It had been left there a few days. Then they called the police and got it towed.'

'So where's it now?'

'At a pound in Brooklyn. A few blocks away from there it was found, according to the police. I'm going to pick it up on Saturday.'

'Why Saturday?' Larry asked. 'Why not go today?'

'I can't. I have to work, don't I? I can't keep taking time off. Queen Bitch has been searching for a chance to get rid of me.'

'You've got no appointments the next couple of days,' said José. 'And in any case, don't worry about her.'

'Don't worry about her? You've got to be kidding.'

'For a start,' said José, 'she tries to make us all feel like that. Never in public; only on a one to one basis. Secondly: I hope you don't mind, but she and I had a conversation about you yesterday.'

'Oh yes?' Matt looked over at Larry, who shrugged, put his cup in the sink, and left.

'She's still off with the flu, but yesterday she called and demanded a conference call with us all. Said she expected to be back next Monday, and what were all of our sales figures so far this week. When it came to yours, Larry said you had to take two or three days out. She went *loco*. As much as you can when you have the flu. Said as soon as she got back she would be speaking to the Bank President about having you fired, as your personal problems were not ours.'

'Bitch.'

‘Well, we know that, don’t we? Anyway, I reminded her that you were taking personal time, unpaid time. Your car had been stolen, you were virtually a single parent, your wife had gone without a trace, and if the press got to hear how the Bank had fired an employee for taking unpaid time with all that going on, it would mean a lot of bad publicity, which the Bank President wouldn’t appreciate.’

‘Wow, José; way to go.’

‘I finished by saying that if the bank fired everyone who took unavoidable time off, they’d have no workers left. She kind of calmed down then; said she hoped you would be back in on Monday.’

‘Wow,’ Matt repeated.

‘I mean, at the end of the day, I think she’s taken more time off with this flu thing than you’ve taken.’

‘Well, thanks,’ said Matt, squeezing José’s shoulder. ‘I owe you one.’

‘No worries. So, get the hell out of here and go get your car. See you Monday, I hope.’

‘Thanks again,’ said Matt as he put his cup in the sink with Larry’s and picked up his overcoat to go. ‘One thing, though,’ he said, resting his hand on the door handle. ‘How would the press get to hear of it if she had fired me?’

‘Simple,’ grinned José. ‘I would have called them. Anonymously, of course.’

Matt returned the grin and left the staff room. On his way out he stopped at Larry’s desk.

‘José’s talked me into taking the rest of the week off. Try to get everything sorted out this week. Off to New York now to get the car.’

Larry was in the process of sending a text message. He stopped and looked up at Matt. ‘Okay. When will you be back?’

'Hope to be back here Monday. Unless…'

'You stopping over there? What about Nathan?'

'No, it'll take four or five hours, I guess; so I'll try to make a round trip. Nathan's staying with my folks, anyway.'

'Down at the Cape?'

'That's right.'

'I was just wondering,' Larry said. 'Did I hear you right? That cop called round personally at night to tell you your car had been found? That's unusual personal service.'

'Yes, he did. I've thought that, as well. He said he was on his way home after finishing his shift. He seems to be taking a personal interest in my case.'

Larry shrugged. 'Anyway, good luck, buddy. See you Monday.'

'See you.'

Matt stopped momentarily at his bank's ATM and withdrew some cash. Then went to the car. He called Avis and got confirmation that he could return the car to a New York office. They gave him the address as 220 West 31st Street. He typed the zip code into the GPS and set off.

He turned into State Street and the first set of lights, just past the bank, he got a red. While waiting he happened to glance in his fender mirror. He had a good view of the main door to his bank, and saw Larry Mason exit the building and hurry round the corner. Larry's cigarette breaks get earlier and earlier, he thought.

The light turned green, but such was the level of traffic he only moved a few yards before the light turned red and Matt had to stop again. He started to think about what Larry had said about Lieutenant Weber. He was right.

Matt did seem to be getting the personal service.

Chapter Thirty-Two

THE GPS TOOK Matt immediately onto the Interstate route 90, then at Sturbridge, a few miles from the state line into Connecticut, he joined the I-84. He had a half hour break just outside Hartford to fill up with gas, get something to eat and take a comfort break, then set off again in a south westerly direction. Fifty or so miles later, he merged onto the I-684, past the direction signs for New York City. He was eventually driving down the elevated Henry Hudson Parkway, the Hudson River to his right, the Riverside Park to his left.

He turned left off the 9A onto West 42nd Street just before the Javits Center. 'Great,' he said out loud as he joined a line of traffic headed for Times Square. He was following the GPS blindly; surely he could have turned down a quieter street, such as Tenth or Ninth Avenues? Too late now.

At Times Square, he turned right into Seventh Avenue; right again at 31st Street. On his left, opposite Penn Plaza and the rear of Madison Square Garden and sandwiched between the Capuchin Monastery of the Church of St John and an anonymous grey building was a six floor Park N' Lock garage. A small Avis office was next to the garage, and there was a sign at the entrance to the parking garage that Avis returns should proceed to the second floor.

On the second floor there was a small booth dedicated to Avis. Matt parked the car, and a young man in a uniform with a discrete red and white badge sauntered over. He and Matt checked the Hyundai for any scratches or bumps, of which there were none, and Matt counter-signed the paperwork. The young man advised him he had had the car one day longer than the original rental agreement, so the additional day's charge would be taken from his credit card. Matt acknowledged this, handed over the keys and took the payment slip. Then took the elevator down to street level.

As he got onto 31st Street, he looked around. There was some building work being carried out on Madison Square Garden, so the sidewalk that side of the street was blocked off. There was the loud noise of traffic and construction work. A large truck filled with spoil pulled out onto the street and headed west.

Matt checked his watch: it was now three o'clock. No way could he get over to Brooklyn, pick up his car, and drive back to Boston tonight. Fortunately, Nathan was with his parents.

He decided to go pick up the car, then find somewhere to stay, probably in Brooklyn, and then make the journey back to Boston in the morning. He knew he was not far from Penn Station, so he could catch a subway to Brooklyn from there.

At Penn Station, he paid $10 for a MetroCard, and checked a subway map on a wall. From here he could catch a 2 or 3 train over to Brooklyn. He was about to insert his card into the turnstile, when he had another thought. He could easily leave the car at the police pound another day; after all, he had told Weber he was going to pick it up on Saturday. If he picked it up now, he may have to pay for another day's parking himself.

To avoid the noise from the street, he stepped into a Café 31 across the street and bought a coffee and pastry. While he ate and drank, he called a central Holiday Inn number and made a booking for that night at a hotel in Union Street, Brooklyn. He had no idea how far away from the pound this was, but he remembered seeing a Union Street station when he was consulting the map last night.

Now three thirty. He decided to make a brief detour. He finished his coffee, then walked east along 34th Street to Herald Square.

At Herald Square, on the corner of 34th and Broadway, sits Macy's department store. One of Ruth's all time favourite movies was *Miracle on 34th Street* – the 1947 version with Edmund Gwenn – and every Christmas she, Matt and Nathan would sit together to watch it. Last Christmas was no exception.

Matt stepped over to the small piece of sidewalk which separated Broadway from Avenue of the Americas. In this V-shaped section were two metal seats. One was fully occupied, one was empty. He sat on the empty one and looked up at Macy's storefront.

And thought of Ruth, and their times snuggled together watching the movie.

Then suddenly, amongst the noise and bustle and traffic and people rushing past, Matt began to cry.

Chapter Thirty-Three

IT WAS GETTING dark, and colder. Matt wiped his face and blew his nose. Looked around; none of the passers-by rushing past had taken a blind bit of notice of him. He checked the time: almost four. Time, he thought, to find this hotel.

He walked back along 34th Street and into the 34th Street-Penn Station subway station. Five minutes later, he was riding on a 3 train through Lower Manhattan towards Brooklyn. His plan was to alight at Atlantic Avenue station, where he would change to the R line for Union Street. However, he checked a street map at Atlantic Avenue and learned that the hotel was only a few blocks down Fourth Avenue. It was now dark, bitterly cold and with the hint of snow in the air, but Matt had spent most of the last forty-eight hours driving, and he felt he needed a brisk walk.

He arrived at the hotel around 5:15; checking in, he received a strange look from the receptionist when she saw he had no luggage.

'Short notice stay,' he muttered to explain.

She smiled to acknowledge this, and handed him his key card. He noticed there was a Duane Reade store across from the hotel, so ran across the street and purchased shower gel, some disposable razors, toothpaste and a toothbrush. Once he got to his room, he took a shower and lay on the bed in his towel. He turned on the television, and muted the volume while he rang his parents. His father answered.

'Hold on, son; I'll just get your mother.'

Matt laughed and shook his head as he waited for his mother. She could hear her in the background calling Nathan.

'Hello Matt; Nathan's in the bathroom. Where are you?'

'New York.'

'New York? I thought you were going to do that Saturday?'

'I was, but I was able to get the rest of the week off work. Personal reasons.'

'So are you staying there tonight?'

'In a Holiday Inn Express in Brooklyn. I'm going to pick up the car and drive back tomorrow.'

'Oh that's good. I was worried about you making such a long round trip in one day. Are work okay about it, then?'

'They're fine. I think I'll drive straight down to you tomorrow afternoon, if that's okay with you.'

'Of course it is. You don't have to ask. Oh, here's Nathan.'

'Hello Daddy!'

'Hey there, buddy. What have you been up to today?'

'I've been helping Grandpa in the den. Making things with wood.'

'With wood? Are you being a good boy for Grandma and Grandpa?'

There was a moment's silence, then Matt could hear his mother's voice whisper, 'Yes, you have.'

'Yes, I have,' said Nathan. 'When are you coming home, Daddy?'

'Tomorrow.'

'Cool! Is Mommy coming home too?'

'No, not yet. She...she's still not very well.'

Nathan said nothing.

'You still there, sport?' asked Matt.

Still no answer.

'Nathan?'

'I'm here, Daddy.'

'I'll see you tomorrow afternoon, okay?'

'Okay, Daddy. Can I go and play with Grandpa again now?'

'Sure. See you tomorrow. Love you.'

'Love you too. Bye.'

Matt heard the phone being laid on a hard surface and Nathan's footsteps running off. Estelle returned to the phone.

'Is he okay?' asked Matt.

'I think so. He kept asking about Ruth today. He needs you, Matt.'

'I know. I'll see him tomorrow. Promise.' He started to fill up. 'What's all this about making things with wood?' he asked, changing the subject.

'Oh, your dad went down into town and bought one of those child's carpentry sets. It's quite safe. He loves messing about in the den with your father.'

'Okay. Well, I'll call you in the morning.'

'All right, Matt. See you.'

Matt hung up and ran his hand through his now almost dry hair. He was getting hungry. He reached across the bed and got the hotel guide. They only served breakfast here, and he was right: if he had the car, he would have had to pay for parking it.

He finished drying himself, got dressed, and consulted the guide again. There was a section for local places to eat. There was a restaurant two blocks away on Fourth Avenue. He put on his coat, and walked round.

It was a small establishment, probably family run, with a limited menu. He settled for an all-day breakfast: two eggs, bacon, sausages, and potatoes, and coffee. Unhealthy maybe, but it tasted delicious. All for $7.50.

As he sat back awaiting the check, he looked around the place. The walls were filled with framed photographs of what looked like famous sportsmen – basketball players, probably – sitting in the restaurant. Some of the pictures looked like they were taken in the 1950s, and the décor looked as if it had not changed since. In one corner was a picture of Muhammad Ali in his Cassius Clay days posing with a man in a chef's outfit. To the left of the picture was a small CCTV camera, its red light blinking. Matt looked around: there was another camera in the opposite corner. Sign of the times, Matt guessed: décor from the mid twentieth century, with technology from the early twenty-first.

The waiter brought over the bill: Matt gave him $10 and said, 'No change.' The waiter thanked him and returned to the back of the restaurant. He came back to Matt with a coffee pot and gave him another refill. Matt was staring at the cameras again.

'Can I take that to go?' he asked the waiter. The waiter nodded and fetched a paper cup of coffee. Matt thanked him and left the restaurant.

He ran back to the Union Street subway station and consulted one of the wall maps. To get to Hoyt St-Schermerhorn Street would mean one change: an R to Jay Street, then an A to Hoyt. The journey took only twenty minutes and Matt burst onto the street looking for the parking garage where the Toyota had been found.

He found the garage and walked up a short ramp to a booth. The woman in the booth looked at him suspiciously.

'Yes?'

'Is the super here right now?' he asked.

She looked around, chewing. 'You wanna see him?'

'Yes please. It's important.'

She shrugged, muttered something unintelligible, and picked up the phone. Moments later, a large African American man, well over six feet tall, came through a door. He leaned over to speak into the hole in the booth glass. 'Yes?'

'You the super?'

'Yeah.'

'A few days back, you reported a Toyota left here to the police.'

He thought for a moment. 'Yeah. The police took it away.'

'Did you see who left it?'

'No.'

'I'm the owner, and -'

'The police took the car away.'

Matt was getting nowhere. He pointed up to a camera high on the wall opposite. 'You have cameras on every level?'

The man sniffed. 'So?'

Matt reached into his back pocket and pulled out five $20 bills. He fingered them. 'The car was left on the bottom level. I wonder if I could have a look at the footage of the day it was left.'

The super looked at the hundred dollars and back to the woman. She was talking to a man who was paying for a ticket. 'Wait here,' he said. He left the booth and moments later appeared through a door halfway down the ramp. Matt hadn't even noticed the door. 'Come up here,' the super said.

Matt followed him up a dingy flight of stairs to a

second floor office. The super sat on the dirty, cluttered desk. 'It was left here last Saturday,' he said, holding out his palm.

'That was the day after it was stolen. Can I see the footage?' Matt asked, passing him two bills.

He looked down and took the money. Sat down behind the desk and swivelled his tattered leather chair to face a grubby computer. He stabbed at a few keys and got a drop down menu of dates. He highlighted the previous Saturday; then another menu of drop downs, each numbered. Matt presumed they referred to floor levels.

'Here,' the super grunted. 'Bottom level.' He held out his palm again and Matt gave him the other three bills. He stood up and motioned Matt to sit in the chair.

'Did the police ask for this?' Matt asked, sitting down.

'No. Just took the car.'

'Where was the car parked?' Matt asked.

'That corner. There.' The super stabbed at the screen with a dirty fingernail.

Matt was able to fast forward the images using the mouse. Cars whizzed in and out, drivers and passengers rushed to and fro. Matt kept his eye on the spot where the Toyota was found. An SUV arrived during the day. Matt frowned: had they got the right day, or the right floor? After a while, the driver returned and the SUV left. A few moments later, another car arrived. Matt slowed the footage down to normal speed and sat up to watch as his Toyota backed into the space. The driver got out, locked the car, and looked around. Then walked out of view. Matt wound backwards a few seconds then froze the screen with the image of the driver standing by the car.

He sat back in the leather chair. He could feel his face flush; his mouth dried up, and his heart was now beating faster.

It was Ruth.

Chapter Thirty-Four

'HEY, SLOW DOWN a minute.'

Squinting in the late afternoon sun, Lieutenant Weber looked down the alleyway they were passing.

'No, stop here.'

Mancini pulled up and applied the brake. 'What is it?'

'There's someone down there,' he said. 'Behind the trash. Wearing a hood.'

They both got out of the car and walked to the alley entrance. An elderly woman with a supermarket cart filled with newspapers hurried on by, giving them a curious look. Silently, Weber cocked his head in the direction of the alley and they both slowly walked down. Both had a hand on their weapon.

The alley was about fifty yards long. At the end was a chain link fence, around ten to twelve feet high. On the other side there was a small parking lot. On both sides were the rear entrances for the buildings either side, business properties on the left and a night club on the right. Weber reflected how out of place premises like this look in the daytime, the neon signs which would be colourfully lighting up the street in a few hours looked dull and derelict. Like Christmas decorations in a sunny daytime. Outside each door was a dumpster, maybe two, some overflowing with plastic garbage bags.

They heard a sound from behind a large blue dumpster at the end of the alley. The two police officers looked at each other, silently nodded, and pulled out their weapons. They were about to cry out to identify themselves when a figure shot out from behind the dumpster, knocking Mancini to the ground.

'Police, stop!' Weber called out as the figure ran towards the open street. Mancini stood up.

'Stop, or I shoot!' he called out again. The figure stopped and turned round, both arms raised. Still covering him, Weber and Mancini caught up. Weber pulled the hood down. The figure was a white male, early twenties, around six feet, shoulder length red hair, and wearing grubby sneakers, jeans and a red sweatshirt.

'Okay, assume the position.' Roughly, Mancini took his arm and swung him round and leaned him against the wall. Weber watched while she patted him down. 'He's clean,' she called out.

'Right,' she said, swinging him round to face her. 'We'll get round to assaulting a police officer later. For now, you want to tell me what's going on?'

'Uh?' the man grunted.

Weber walked over and put his face six inches away from the young man's face.

'She's asking what you were doing here, and why you -'

'Sam, there's another,' Mancini called. They both swung round as a second figure, smaller this time started climbing the fencing.

'I'll get him,' Weber said.

Mancini looked down at Weber's stomach. 'You gotta be kidding,' she called out, already running off.

Weber took a set of handcuffs off his belt and secured the young man, watching Mancini.

'Police, stop!' Mancini called out as the figure got further up the fence. She put her revolver back in its holster and began to climb the fence. The figure had almost reached the top when Mancini grabbed its leg, and started to pull down. The leg kicked about a few times, then the figure stopped climbing.

'Down, now,' Mancini said, tugging at the leg. The figure began to slowly climb down. 'Take the hood off,' Mancini ordered when they were both on the ground.

The figure did so. She was a girl, maybe late teens. Pale skin, black hair in an untidy cut, lipstick the same colour. She had a ring through her left nostril, and was chewing. Her sweatshirt was a dark grey and had a logo which Mancini didn't recognise on the right breast.

'Assume the position,' Mancini repeated, and checked the girl. Weber had already brought the young man over.

'So,' Weber said to the young man. 'I'll ask you again: what are you two doing back here? Making out or something?'

'Yeah, that's right,' the young man smirked. 'We were making out.'

While Mancini cuffed the girl, Weber looked around the side of the dumpster they were behind. There were a couple of opened soda cans, a cigarette end and a sweater. Weber picked the sweater up. It looked almost new.

'That's mine,' the young man said.

'Sure,' said Weber and continued to look around, poking around with his foot. He looked up at the dumpster. It was nearly full, mainly of black trash bags. On the top, however, wedged in the side of the dumpster was a smaller plastic bag, which probably originated from a store. 'What's this?' he said.

Mancini watched the couple's faces during Weber's search: they showed no reaction.

Weber pulled out the bag and looked inside. 'Jesus,' he said, slightly recoiling.

'What is it?' Mancini asked. Weber passed her the bag.

Mancini recoiled as well as she looked in the bag and saw the contents: a half eaten burger and a used condom. The ketchup from the burger had spread inside the bag and gotten mixed with the semen on the condom. 'Ugh,' she said, closing the bag and passing it back. 'That's gross.'

'Yours?' Weber asked, holding it out to the young man. He shrugged and looked away.

Weber tossed the bag back onto the dumpster and continued to ferret about. There were two small upside down wooden crates up against the wall, presumably where they had been sitting. As Weber's foot touched one of the crates, Mancini noticed a flicker of reaction in the girl's face.

'Sam, check the crates.'

Weber squatted and moved the boxes.

'Well, looky here,' he said as he lifted the box up. The young man and woman looked over at each other. Under the crate was a small black backpack. Weber lifted the other box: there was nothing underneath that one. 'What have we here?' he asked, undoing the bag. He looked inside: there were three men's wallets, two women's purses and two wrist watches. Weber held the open backpack out so Mancini could see inside.

'I suppose this isn't yours?' he asked, holding the backpack out.

The man sniffed. 'Never seen it before.'

The girl said nothing, just looked at the man.

'So your fingerprints won't be on them?' Mancini asked, her question directed more at the girl.

'We didn't take them,' the girl blurted out.

'Oh,' said Weber. 'Who did, then?'

No response.

'I'll ask you one more time,' Weber said as he again put his face up against the young man's. 'Where did they come from?'

Still no answer.

'That's such a pity,' Weber said, brushing the dust off the young man's sweatshirt. 'Because you see – if you don't tell us where they came from we'll have to assume you took them. And you'll spend more time away for robbery than for just receipt of stolen goods. So when your girlfriend here,' – he looked over at the girl, who was staring down at the ground – 'is released, she'll be well into middle age.'

'You can't prove nothing,' the young man said petulantly.

'Well into middle age,' Weber repeated looking at the girl.

'It was Jay. We -'

'Shut up, you stupid skank. They can't prove nothing!'

'You shut up,' the girl said. 'I'm not going down just because you're too -'

'She's full of shit. She doesn't know anything.'

'We're getting nowhere here,' Weber sighed. 'Let's take these two cupcakes back and talk to them there.'

Mancini took the girl by the arm and started to lead her back to the car. Weber did the same with the man.

'So who's Jay, then?' Mancini asked as they walked back.

'Don't say anything,' the man called out.

'Quiet.' Weber held tighter into his arm as they

walked back to the street.

'Jay – I don't know his other name. We got the stuff from him. To sell. We have to give him most of what we get for them.'

'So this Jay steals the stuff?' asked Mancini as Weber bundled the man into the back of the car. 'Where can we find him?'

'He's probably at the Galleria at CambridgeSide,' she said, her eyes darting back to where the man was sitting.

'What do you think?' Mancini asked Weber. 'This guy Jay could be…'

'I know. Let's get down there. We can call for a blue and white to meet us down there. She can identify this guy, then we can get them all booked.'

Mancini pulled into traffic and hit the siren. Weber fastened the red light to the roof as they sped over to the CambridgeSide mall.

Chapter Thirty-Five

WEBER AND MANCINI pulled up outside the Galleria twenty minutes later. A patrol car was already outside the main entrance on CambridgeSide Place and Mancini pulled up alongside it. Two uniformed officers got out.

'Keep an eye on this one,' Weber said. 'We're taking her inside to see if she can spot their accomplice.'

As they stood in the doorway, Weber unlocked the girl's handcuffs. 'Don't get any ideas,' he said. 'If you try anything, we'll catch you, you know that.'

Still chewing, the girl nodded. The three of them stood in the doorway, looking around.

'Well?' Weber asked. 'Where's he likely to be?'

'Most likely at one of the department stores.'

'Wandering around?' asked Mancini.

'Maybe. Or maybe sitting around outside. Waiting for the most likely person.'

'You mean someone who looks vulnerable. A little old lady loaded with shopping?' said Weber angrily. 'Son of a bitch.'

'Do you have his cell phone number?' Mancini asked. 'Call him, see where he is.'

'Don't have his number. He just calls Robby when he has stuff to sell.' She inclined her head back to the car outside.

'Okay.' Mancini looked around. 'What's your name, by the way?'

'Abby,' Abby grunted.

'Robby and Abby,' Weber muttered. 'Not exactly

Bonnie and Clyde, are you?'

Mancini picked up a guide from the nearby stand. 'There's a Best Buy up on Level 2. And a Sears and a Macy's on 2 and 3.'

'Let's go up to Level 2 first,' said Weber. 'And don't forget, Abby: no tricks. It would help you considerably with the DA if you identify him.' He took Abby's arm and they led her up the escalator to Level 2.

When they reached the second level, Weber and Mancini looked around. Still holding her arm, Weber turned her around to get a 360 degree view. Macy's was on the right as they stood at the top of the escalator. A store called Love Culture was behind them, and on their right a one hour photo shop sandwiched between Victoria's Secret and Ann Taylor's. Ahead of them, along the mall, were seats, not heavily used. Mainly fathers with strollers waiting for their wives.

'Look around, Abby,' said Mancini. 'Any sign of him?'

Abby looked and shook her head.

'Should we go into Macy's first?' Mancini asked Weber.

Weber looked around and shook his head. 'No, I think we might be better off outside here. If he catches sight of her with us, he's going to run. And we could easily lose him inside there.'

'What about getting her boyfriend to go round with you, and I'll take her?' asked Mancini.

'Could do,' he nodded.

'He might be eating,' Abby muttered.

Mancini looked at Weber and nodded. 'Could be right. Late afternoon.'

'Right. Is there a food hall here?'

Mancini consulted her guide. 'Downstairs. At the back.'

'Shit. Okay, let's take her back downstairs.'

They stepped over to the down escalator and led her back down to Level 1. Then made a 180.

'There. It's down there,' Mancini said.

As cautiously as before they slowly led Abby down to the food court. There were the usual establishments there: Burger King, Dunkin Donuts, Master Wok, Taco Bell, and various other eateries.

'What does he look like?' Weber asked, looking around.

'Similar to Robby. He's his brother.'

'Jesus Christ,' Weber said through gritted teeth. 'Talk about keeping it in the family.'

'Abby, focus.' Mancini squeezed her arm. 'Is he here? You owe him no favours, remember.'

Abby looked around. 'No; can't see him.'

Weber shook his head. He reached out to Abby's arm to guide her out of the food court when he caught a flash of recognition on her face. He spun round and saw a young man, very similar to Robby coming out of the Sarku Japan Sushi Bar. It looked as if he was carrying a kind of wrap. He immediately recognised Abby, and it registered on his face whom she was with. He flung the wrap on the floor, scattering fish, vegetables and rice on the floor, and ran across the court towards a fire exit door. Mancini held onto Abby while Weber gave chase.

'Stop, police!' he called out, unable to draw his service revolver due to the people eating. Jay ignored this and ran to the fire exit. He pulled at the bar and opened the door. Weber followed him out the door and along a short white washed brick corridor which led to a door to outside. Away from the food court, he drew his weapon. At the sound of the gun being cocked, Jay stopped and turned round. He had the same expression on his face as his brother had earlier.

'Right. Against the wall,' Weber ordered. He reached out for Jay's arm and just as he was about to manoeuvre him to face the wall, Jay swung round and kicked Weber hard in the groin. Weber dropped the gun and with a groan, collapsed on top of it. Jay was about to push the door handle, but had second thoughts. He leapt over Weber's prone body and ran back towards the food court. However, instead of returning to the mall, he began to climb up the stairs which led, Weber presumed, to the upper levels. At that moment, Mancini burst through the doors.

'Sam! You okay?'

'I guess,' Weber gasped standing up and picking up his gun. 'The bastard kicked me in the nuts. Where's the girl?'

'When he ran in here I called the guys outside. One of them came in and took her out. She's in the car with her boyfriend. Where did he go?' She could see the fire exit door was still closed.

'He's gone up there,' Weber said as he started to climb the stairs. 'God knows why; he can't get away there.'

'Yes he can,' said Mancini. 'There are parking garages on all three levels. He can get out there.'

'Shit,' gasped Weber. 'Look, I'll follow him up here. You call for more back up and see if you can get him on the other levels. Use the escalators.'

Mancini was about to argue with her partner, but he was already almost at the first landing. As he reached Level 2, he noticed that one of the row of five doors which led to the mall was not shut properly. He pushed it open and found himself on Level 2, opposite the entrance to Sears. He looked around: the mall was beginning to get busier. It was early evening now, dark outside, and many nine to five workers were beginning to arrive. He stepped forward a few paces, and looked around again. To his left was an H&M store. In the window of the store, he thought he could see Jay loitering around inside, looking out. Weber took a deep breath and ran over. Just as he got to the entrance, the man came out, and greeted an older woman. Weber turned and swore. He walked over to the railing and looked around: along this level, down at ground level, and up at Level 3. Level 3 was where he saw him, nonchalantly walking along the upper level.

There was a stairway further along this balcony. Weber ran over to and up the stairs, three at a time. He had to push past several people who were in no hurry to go up or down. Once up on Level 3, he looked around again. There: over the other side, outside White House Black Market, Jay was walking along. Weber hurried along on his side, almost parallel with Jay, hoping to catch him at the end. Both had almost reached the end when Jay spotted him. With a look of shock on his face, he turned and ran. Breathlessly, Weber called out, 'Stop! Police!' but this had no effect. Weber rounded the end of the mall and chased Jay down his side. He could see him at the end, hesitating, not certain which way to go. Still, it was too busy for Weber to draw his weapon.

Jay leapt to his right, and disappeared from view. When Weber had reached that spot, he could see that Jay had run down a corridor leading to the restrooms. A man passed Weber as he made his way slowly down the corridor. There was one door either side half way down: one was marked *Stores*, and the other

Baby Change. He tried both handles: the store room was locked and the baby change room was empty. At the end of the corridor were the men's room, and the women's. Weber hesitated for a second as he decided which to take first.

Training and experience had taught Weber that in a situation like this, the person being chased will invariably take the most conventional option. Despite being chased by the police, and knowing he could face a lengthy jail term, something inside the suspect will always click and he will do what comes most naturally, and head for the men's room. Not the women's. Most of the time.

Weber pushed open the door, this time with one hand on his gun. Inside the men's room, one man was just finishing at a urinal. He looked round, flushed it, and stepped over to the wash basin. He looked in the mirror and saw Weber's reflection. He noticed where Weber's hand was, and quickly dried his hands and left. He looked around: there were five stalls, three of which were unoccupied with their doors open. He heard the sound of flushing coming from one of them and an elderly man came out, giving him a surprised look. Weber nodded and went over to the other door. He pushed at it gently and it swung open. Empty!

Weber swore and ran out to the women's. 'Sorry, police,' he said to two women who were leaving. Once inside, he paused for a second as he realised there would be no urinals here: just two rows of stalls beyond the wash basins. Two doors were shut; behind one, he could hear banging and rustling. He walked down to the stalls and looked up. There was a row of windows above the stalls, and Jay was halfway out one of them. Weber kicked open the door and climbed up onto the pedestal. By now, Jay was out of the window. Weber heaved himself up onto the window shelf and looked out. The window led to a flat roof, presumably over one of the stores, and Jay was running across towards a door on the other side. The space was about two feet square, only just enough room for him to squeeze through. He took off his overcoat, flung it on the floor and climbed through. He could hear some female consternation behind, and the sound of his own heavy breathing.

Puffing, and with a pain in his side, he chased Jay across the roof. The younger man was trying the handle of the door, but it was locked. Weber took out his gun and pointed it at Jay. 'Face down on the deck, you son of a bitch,' he said breathlessly. Jay had no choice now but to comply. Weber sat on an air conditioning unit covering Jay and breathing heavily.

'You idiot,' Mancini yelled at Weber when she reached the roof. The door which Jay was trying to open was at the top of an emergency stairway to the roof, designed for use by maintenance engineers needing access to the elevator gear and air conditioning. Weber had called her from the roof and ten minutes later she arrived with two uniformed officers to take Jay away with his brother and Abby. 'Why didn't you call for back-up?'

Weber shook his head. 'There wasn't time. I didn't want to lose him. Have the others said anything else yet?'

'Nah. But I'm sure they will when we get them downtown. I spoke to O'Riordan and he's pretty sure they are the guys we've been after.'

'How can he know that already?'

'Some of the stuff in that backpack matched items on the stolen goods list. You okay, Sam?'

'I'm fine,' said Weber, standing up. 'Just out of breath, that's all. Let's get downstairs.'

'By the way,' said Mancini, as they went down the stairs, 'O'Riordan says you're an idiot, too. Says a man your age and size shouldn't be running about like a twenty-something.'

'I told you: he's full of shit. Always was, always will be. He might have a point about the size. Must get Mrs W to make me more salads.'

They eventually reached Level 1 and began to make their way to the car. Weber struggled to keep up with Mancini.

She turned round. 'You sure you're okay, Sam? You look real -'

Weber staggered a few steps and leaned against their car. He could feel a heavy, crushing, squeezing pain in the middle of his chest. He clutched it with both hands. He could hear Mancini calling to him but her voice was so echoic he was unable to make out what she was saying. He fell to the ground, rolling over. He could still see Mancini, but she was blurred, and then she was gone.

Chapter Thirty-Six

MATT STARED AT the screen, wondering for a moment if his heart was ruling his head; if, because he wanted Ruth back so badly, this was a case of auto-suggestion or something. He blinked; looked again. Yes, it was her. With his Toyota. With *their* Toyota.

He checked the date on the bottom right corner of the screen. Did a quick calculation in his head. Yes, it was the date the Toyota disappeared from the bank parking lot. The time: almost five-thirty. Another calculation: the last time he saw the car was when he parked it just before nine that morning. Depending on when it was taken, there would have been plenty of time to drive it here.

He sat back, rubbing his eyes: he was tired. Then he tried to figure out how she had gotten hold of the car. He had the main set of keys, kept on the same key ring as the front door keys. Instinctively, he felt his pockets for them. But the spare set: he frowned as he thought through what might have happened to them. The first day Ruth disappeared, he checked the keys and they were upstairs. He was sure of that. But after the car had gone, when those two police officers called round, the keys had gone. At first he assumed he had been mistaken, but the more he thought about it, the more positive he got. The keys had definitely been taken between those two days. He shook his head: it must have been Ruth. She must have gone somewhere the night she failed to come home, and the next few nights; returned home during the day when she knew he would be out and taken the keys. What the hell was she playing at? And where had she gone those first nights? If they had had a fight, and not come home, then Gail's place would have been the obvious choice. But they had not had a fight; in any case, this was a different situation, and Gail didn't know where Ruth was either. So she maintained.

Gail. Ruth's closest friend. If Ruth was up to something, Gail would know and deny all knowledge to him if Ruth asked her to. And - Matt began to nod his head as he thought this scenario through – when Gail called round the other night, she went to the bathroom before she left. She could have taken the keys then, if Ruth had told her where they were.

'Jesus, pull yourself together,' he said aloud, realising how paranoid he was becoming. He leaned forward in the chair and clicked on the play/pause box again. Ruth walked away from the car, stopped and looked around the parking garage, briefly looked back at the car, then walked out of the picture. Matt clicked on the fast forward button and watched the next couple of minutes, but Ruth did not return to the car.

'Did you find what you were looking for?' Matt jumped as the super returned to the office.

'Er - yes,' he said, glancing over his shoulder. He did consider asking if he could take a copy, but decided there would be little point. 'How long are these pictures kept for?' he asked. 'Do you erase them after a while?'

'After a month,' the super replied. 'Why?'

Matt shook his head. 'No reason. Just wondered.' He needed to get back to the police with this, so a month would give them plenty of time to investigate.

The super gave him an *about time you left* look; Matt got the hint.

'Well, thanks very much,' he said, getting up. 'I do appreciate it.'

'Right.' The super shuffled over to his chair. He looked down at the screen, moved the mouse and the image of the Toyota was replaced by the screensaver, a picture of a topless brunette. 'You can find your way out, can't you?'

'Sure, no problem.' Matt did up his coat, left the super in his office, and walked back down to street level. He looked up at the sky once he was back on the sidewalk. Through the light from the streetlamps, he could see the night sky was heavy with cloud. Snow was beginning to fall and it was now bitterly cold. He began the walk back to the hotel. He contemplated calling his parents or even Lieutenant Weber to tell them, but decided it was late, he was cold and tired, and he would wait until morning. After breakfast he would pick up the Toyota from the police pound, and drive over to the Cape.

In the hotel reception, he exchanged smiles with the receptionist and headed for the elevator. As he waited for it, he looked around. There was the sound of men's laughter coming from the bar. He paused a moment; as the elevator doors opened with a ping, he decided to visit the bar before going up to his room.

The hotel bar was not small, but not the largest he had seen. Three suited men, clearly in New York on business, were standing at the bar laughing. It was two of these men he had heard just before. Another businessman was sitting at a table over in the far corner of the bar, engaged in quiet conversation with a girl half his age. He had his hand over her shoulder; she had a hand on his knee. *PA or hooker?* Matt speculated. A middle aged man was sitting alone at another table, reading a newspaper. Matt bought a whisky and soda and sat down at an empty table. A large screen television was on the wall just across from Matt. He took a mouthful of his drink and looked up. Playing on mute, it was a football match: the New York Giants against the San Francisco 49ers. Although not a follower, Matt assumed this must be a rerun: he was pretty sure the SuperBowl was due anytime, and this looked like an ordinary game.

Matt took another look at the furtive couple in the corner, and decided she was a PA; a hooker would be dressed differently. He looked around for an old newspaper or something to read. He noticed at the other end of the bar there was a small alcove in which were situated two computer screens. There was a small sign above them, advertising internet access. He took his drink over. Underneath the sign was a smaller notice stating that the charge was five dollars for fifteen minutes. He could purchase time at reception. He wandered over to the desk, waited until the receptionist had finished dealing with a couple who were checking in, and then paid ten dollars for half an hour access. She gave him a receipt with a code number. Sitting down at one of the screens, he typed in the code when prompted and got access. A small countdown clock at the foot of the screen told Matt he had 25 minutes left. Matt snorted; somebody can't count, he thought.

He searched for his own ISP and got into his email account. It had been a few days since he had last checked his mails, and there were ten, eight of which he was able to delete immediately. The ninth was from Nathan's kindergarten about forthcoming fund raising events, and the tenth was from his insurance company, reminding him that his house insurance was due for renewal on 1st March.

He then signed into his online banking account, and checked the transactions on his account. Maybe if Ruth was still in New York, she would have used an ATM….

Slightly disappointed, he saw his balance was the same as when he had last checked. He checked his wallet; he would need to visit an ATM himself in the morning.

Then he logged onto the Boston Globe's online pages, not looking for anything in particular. He had long stopped checking here for news of Ruth, although he was due an update from the Missing Persons Unit.

Nothing in the news headlines section caught his interest. He went back a couple of days; he thought he would check for anything here about the Watanabe woman. Despite Lieutenant Weber's indifference, he was still certain she was the person he saw in the pub with Ruth's boss, but could never prove anything.

He spent the next ten minutes idly browsing, until the little timer showed 3 minutes left. He logged off, finished his drink, and went back to the elevator. Once in his room, he got ready for bed, and, in contrast to the previous nights, went straight to sleep.

Also in contrast to previous nights, he slept until seven forty-five the next morning. Surprised he had slept in so late, he leapt out of bed and into the shower. Once out of the shower, he called room service to order breakfast, only to be told he needed to have called by midnight, so would have to take breakfast in the bar. Slightly annoyed, he dressed and called his parents. His father answered.

'Morning, Dad. It's Matt.'

'Morning, son. How are things?'

'Listen Dad, I've got some news.'

'Hold on, I'll just get your mother.'

'Okay.' Matt raised his eyes to the ceiling.

A moment later his father came back.

'Matt? Your mother's gone out. Taken Nathan somewhere I'll bet. Shall I tell her you called?'

'Yeah, okay,' Matt said resignedly. 'Tell her I'll call again later.'

He hung up and went downstairs to breakfast. Afterwards, he packed what personal effects he had into the Duane Reade bag and went back downstairs to check out. Stepping out onto the street, he took his bearings, and decided to take a brisk walk up to the car pound. The snow he noticed as he left the parking garage had left about an inch on the sidewalks. Already the road was clear, and some premises had already cleared the snow from outside their frontage.

A couple of blocks later, he stopped outside an HSBC branch. There was an ATM on the corner. Matt felt he kept a pretty close eye on his account balance, but always double checked the balance before he had an ATM withdrawal. As he checked the balance this morning, he gasped as he saw the account was two hundred dollars down on the night before. He looked around, as if one of the passers-by had taken the money. He withdrew his intended amount of one hundred, put the cash and card into his wallet, and looked around. Then half ran, half walked back to the hotel, where he bought another fifteen minutes internet time. Logged into his online banking account and checked the transactions. Sure enough, there had been a $200 withdrawal at 07:58

that morning. He began to breathe heavily and rubbed his forehead. It must have been Ruth. He had his card; unless her card had been stolen, in which case surely the thief would have taken the $500 maximum from the ATM, it must have been her. A few days back, he had considered stopping her card as a way of smoking her out, but never gotten round to it. In any case, he was not sure if the bank would agree to it, as it was a joint account after all.

There was a reference number by the withdrawal, in blue and underlined. Matt clicked on the link and saw where the withdrawal had taken place.

It was Banco Santander S.A., 45 East 53rd Street.

Matt sat back in the chair. His heart was beating fast again. So –

Ruth *was* in New York.

Chapter Thirty-Seven

MATT SAT BACK in his chair. He was not sure how he should feel right now. A sense of relief that she was still alive, apparently. Relief on Nathan's behalf, too. Anger at her because of what she had done to him and their son. Curiosity as to what was going on, and why. Curiosity about Ruth Dubois and her connection with his wife. And a determination to get to the bottom of it all. Should he drive back to Boston, go see Lieutenant Weber and hand over everything, leave it all to them? Go home and wait by the phone? No way.

The little clock showed he had seven minutes left, so he went to Google Maps and entered the address. He found the location: on 53rd, between Madison and Park. He checked the street view: nothing out of the ordinary, just a run of the mill New York street. He contemplated getting a subway up there, but decided there was little value doing this. No way was he going to just bump into her there.

He went to Reception and bought another thirty minutes of internet use. He searched for newspapers in Rochester, NY, and found three. Merely because it was the first entry, he went to the *Rochester Democrat and Chronicle*. At the foot of the Home page he clicked on Paid Archive. In the search screen, he typed in Ruth Dubois, and in the date range the last three years. Five entries came up on the screen, one of which referred to a fatal highway accident. Next to this summary there were two files for Matt to click on. One was to obtain a free summary; the other was for the entire article, for which there was a fee. Matt clicked on the paid article file, and got another screen requesting a $3.95 fee for the whole piece. Matt entered his credit card details, and momentarily the entire article filled the screen.

The circumstances of the crash were virtually as Elisabeth Dubois had related: it was raining heavily, and there was construction work going on at the time. The driver of the car, a Ford Mustang, somehow lost control, skidded off the road and careered straight into the wall of an overpass. The speed limit on that stretch of highway was twenty-five at that time, but the police spokesman said the estimated speed was at least fifty. On impact with the overpass, the fuel tank ruptured and the car exploded. The spokesman said it was a miracle no other vehicle was involved.

Matt sat back and took in what he had read. He found his eyes were welling up. There was no reason for him to be upset; after all, he knew that this was not his wife he was reading about. Nevertheless…

He wiped his eyes and read further down the article. It was his understanding, from newspaper articles, television and the movies, that in situations such as this, a victim was generally identified by their dental records. Not so in this case. The heat caused by the explosion was so great that the entire body was burnt to a crisp. The police had estimated that the temperature of the blaze was in excess of 600 centigrade, or 1100F. The article went on to say that DNA is destroyed at 400 degrees, so identification could not be made that way. However, by some strange twist of fate, her purse had been thrown from the car in the explosion. The bag had been badly burnt; all the personal items destroyed, except for the drivers licence, which, although badly damaged, had only been partially destroyed. It was a New York State licence, and the piece of the licence containing the ID number had survived. At least, most of the number. The top right corner of the photograph had survived. With this surviving information, the police were able to identify the victim as Ruth Dubois. The Mustang was registered to an Ira Dubois, who was identified as the victim's father.

Matt glanced at the foot of the screen. His time was almost up. He logged off and walked back out to the street. So what Elisabeth Dubois had told him was confirmed. Time to go to the car pound and drive back home. As he walked back up Fourth Avenue, he called his parents again. No answer. His mother and Nathan must still be out, and his father must be occupied.

After forty-five minutes of brisk walking, he arrived at the pound. He went through a wire gate, then pressed an intercom at the door to a single storey building.

'Can I help you?' a woman's voice rasped from the speaker.

'My name's Matthew Gibbons. You're holding a car of mine which was recovered. A Toyota.'

There was a loud buzz and a click as the door was unlocked. Matt pushed it open and went inside. Just beyond the door was a high counter, not dissimilar to the ones at his office. A uniformed policewoman was sitting on a high chair behind the counter.

'Help you?' she asked casually.

'Yes,' said Matt. 'You're holding a car of mine. It was stolen a few days back and was found in a parking garage here.'

'Licence number?'

Matt gave her the number and she checked her

computer screen.

'Drivers licence, please, and registration documents?'

Shit, Matt thought. 'Sorry, I only have my drivers licence.'

'No, I can only… Hold on.' She read something on the screen. 'Oh, there's a note here confirming your ownership.'

'Is there?' Matt asked, surprised.

'Yeah, a Lieutenant Weber from Boston PD called. Spoke to my Sergeant. Said you'd be coming. You know the Lieutenant?'

'In a way. He's dealing…. He's my guardian angel, you might say.'

Ignoring his quip, she called out, 'Harry!'

A male officer came out through a door, holding a paper cup of coffee. She turned round to him. 'Bay 5C. The Toyota.'

'Come this way, please, sir.' The officer led Matt outside. He took him along two rows of various vehicles until they came to his Toyota, parked between a Mazda and a vehicle Matt didn't recognize.

'Here we are, sir,' the officer said, looking the car over. 'You're lucky. It was found undamaged.'

Matt felt in his pocket and took out his keys.

'Don't bother,' the officer said. 'It was found with the keys still in the ignition.'

'That's weird,' said Matt.

'Happens sometimes. When cars are just abandoned.'

Matt climbed in and started the ignition. The tank was almost empty. He wound down the window and asked the officer where the nearest gas station was. The officer gave him the directions and walked back to the building. Matt drove out of bay 5C and stopped at the barrier by the exit. Momentarily there was a buzzing sound and a section of the chain link fence slid open. It slid shut after Matt passed.

The nearest gas station was an Exxon Mobil outlet on Flatbush. Matt filled up, and after paying, pulled over next to the air tower. Switched off the engine and dialled his parents' number. His father answered.

'Oh, Matt it's you. Where are you, son?'

'I'm still in New York. I've just picked up the car, and I'm about to -'

'Matt, I, er - look, speak to your mother, will you?'

His father left him holding. Matt frowned: his father sounded different this morning.

'Matt, where are you?' asked his mother. Her voice sounded shaky.

'I'm still in New York, just about to start the journey back. Mom, I've found out that -'

'Matt, listen. Something's happened. It's Nathan.'

Matt sat up. 'Nathan? Why? What's happened?'

'We'd been into town. We got back an hour or so. I left him playing in the yard.'

'Mom, what's happened?'

His mother's voice started to quiver as she spoke.

'We can't find him anywhere.'

Chapter Thirty-Eight

AS INTERSTATE 84 heads east out of Hartford CT, the speed limit is 65 miles per hour. Matt paid little attention to this as he took the Toyota further and further east. At the intersection with the 190 at Morey Pond, the speedometer showed eighty-five. The occasional vehicle he passed showed their annoyance by flashing their lights. He would flash his own when a slower moving vehicle was in front, and they all changed lanes without any delay. All throughout the journey he was expecting to come across a police car and get pulled over; now and again he saw a sign stating that speeds were being tracked by radar. He accepted that his licence number would be taken by a camera and he would incur a penalty, but he was prepared to accept that.

As he headed to the Cape, his mother's words kept ringing in his ears.

'Matt, listen. Something's happened. It's Nathan.'

Matt sat up. 'Nathan? Why? What's happened?'

'We'd been into town. We got back an hour or so. I left him playing in the yard.'

'Mom, what's happened?'

His mother's voice started to quiver as she spoke.

'We can't find him anywhere.'

'What do you mean, you can't find him?' There was panic in his voice.

His mother tried to speak calmly: Matt could hear her controlling her voice. 'I took him into town. Just after breakfast. He wanted to go to that little bookstore and see if there were any books on dinosaurs there. We got back here a little after ten. It was a nice morning. He asked if he could play in the yard a while. He still had his coat on, so I didn't see any harm.'

'Did you shut the gate?'

She sniffed. 'Of course I did. And I left the front door open. He was playing with that large inflatable brontosaurus thing he has. I could hear him running about, making all the dinosaur noises. Then I realised I hadn't heard him for a while. I called your father, and he -'

'Mom, I'm coming back now. Tell me all this when I get back. I'll be as quick as I can. In the meantime, call the police.'

'I will. How long do you think you'll be?'

'Five, maybe six hours. I'll be as quick as I can.'

'Drive safely, Matt.'

'I will.'

Four hours and one very brief comfort stop later, the Toyota's wheels squealed as the car leapt over the Sagamore Bridge. Five minutes later, he sounded the horn outside his parents' house. His father was out front, and opened the gate for him to drive in. His face was lined with worry.

'Matt, I don't -' he said as Matt leapt out of the car.

'It's okay; where's Mom?'

'She – she's in the house.'

Matt ran up the driveway and met his mother on the porch. She held out her arms and hugged him. Her eyes were red.

'Matt, I'm so sorry. I -'

'It's okay, Mom.' He sat her down in the porch. His father joined them. 'Is there any more news?' he asked them.

His father shook his head and opened his mouth to speak but his mother answered first.

'No. We called the police. Glen Miller, the Sheriff, has been over. He took a description and said he would drive around and get back to us. We've heard nothing yet. Old Harry Dobbs took your father round also in his station wagon -'

'Nothing. No sightings,' said his father.

'I stayed here, just in case he wandered off and found his way back.' She sniffed again, and blew her nose. Matt nodded and rested his hand on her arm.

He looked up at his father. 'Have you tried the neighbours?'

'The two this side,' – his father nodded over to the right – 'are away on vacation. They left us a key in case of emergencies. I went in and had a look around, in the house and in the yard and garage. No sign there. The two – the two guys the other side are in, and they looked round their place as well.'

'And here?' Matt asked. 'You've checked both floors, the attic, the basement?'

His father nodded. 'All the closets and rooms. And the garage and den.'

Matt stood up. 'Come with me as I drive around,' he said to his father.

'Right you are,' Matthew Senior said, and followed his son down the steps to the Toyota.

'I'll have my cell phone right here,' he called out to his mother as he climbed into the car. 'Call me if anything…you know.'

Estelle swallowed and wiped her nose. She nodded and stood up as Matt reversed onto the street.

'What was he wearing?' Matt asked as they headed towards town.

'A - a grey overcoat with a hood.'

‘Yes,’ said Matt grimly. ‘I know the one.’

Matt drove slowly along Route 6A, continually checking his side of the road. His father checked the other. Normally Matt hated driving with his father, as he would always remind Matt how long he had been driving, and point out the things Matt was doing wrong: going too fast, going too slow, too near the centre line, watch out for the truck fifty feet ahead. This time he was silent, a sure sign how worried he was.

‘I’ll go as far as Main Street,’ Matt said. ‘No way could he have gotten even that far. Then I’ll do the same in the other direction.’

In town, he turned right onto Liberty Street, right again onto Main, then took Tupper Road back up to the 6A. As they approached his parents’ house, they saw a police car parked outside. His mother was talking to a figure in uniform.

‘That’s Glen, the sheriff,’ said his father.

‘Glen Miller?’ asked Matt.

‘U-huh.’ Any other time, his father would have cracked a joke.

As Matt drew up, the sheriff’s car pulled away. He wound down the window. ‘Any news?’ he asked his mother.

Arms folded, she shook her head. ‘He said there’ve been no sightings. His department are continuing to look, and it’s been reported to the State Police Missing Persons -’

‘Missing Persons Unit,’ Matt finished her sentence. ‘Seems I know the drill. Look, we’re going to take a ride in the other direction.’

‘Okay,’ she mouthed, and shivered.

Matt released the brake and pulled away. As he waited to cross the eastbound lane, a bright red SUV turned into the next door driveway. The driver waved and stopped.

'That's Jerry Looper,' Matthew Senior muttered. 'One of the – the guys next door.'

Jerry wound down his window. 'What's going on, Matt?' he asked Matthew Senior. 'I saw all the police here just now.'

Senior looked over at his son, then back to Jerry. 'You were out when I called earlier. Marty checked the house for me. Nathan, our grandson, Matt's boy,' - he indicated over to Matt – 'has gone missing. Has been gone – well, almost six hours.'

'Damn,' said Jerry. 'I saw him around that time ago.'

Matt got out of the car and spoke to Jerry over the Toyota roof. 'When? Where?'

'He was talking to a woman -'

'A woman? What did she look like?'

'I don't know – thirties, tallish, I guess. Black hair, long, I think. The boy seemed to know her well.'

'How so?'

'Well, they were talking a lot out here. She was playing with that big blow-up thing he had. A dinosaur, was it? Then he got into the car with her. Dinosaur as well.'

'What was the car?'

'It was like this – a Chrysler. A convertible. May have been a Crossfire. Silver.'

Matt slammed his fist down on the Toyota roof. 'I knew it! The fucking bitch!'

'Matt – what is it?' his mother asked as she approached.

Matt leaned in the car. 'Dad, get out. I have to go.'

'What do you mean? To go where?'

'To get my son back. I know whose car that is.'

Chapter Thirty-Nine

THE PREVIOUS NIGHT, Ryan Wilson manoeuvred the metallic blue Audi R8 GT Spyder off the Interstate and onto the final leg of the journey home. Even for a mid-week night, the traffic was lighter than normal, and the journey from his workplace at Logan had taken just under an hour. If only it had been like that last Friday, he reflected: at the end of the week, it had for some time been his and Gail's tradition to unwind with a candlelit meal at home, plenty of wine, both at the table and in bed where they would finish the bottle watching a movie. It was their practice to alternate whose choice of movie they watched; the first week Gail would choose a romcom maybe, or some kind of chick flick, the next week Ryan would choose. Then the night would become less restful: it was not uncommon for their session to last past three o'clock Saturday morning. Last Friday was different. Last Friday it was Ryan's turn to choose the movie. He was a fan of classic black and white movies, and that week they watched *The Third Man*. Not Gail's type of picture; in fact during the scene where Harry Lime played by Orson Welles is hiding from Joseph Cotten's Holly Martin and his hiding place is given away by Lime's cat, Ryan nudged Gail to watch the image of the cat nudging Lime's shoe. Getting no response, he looked down and saw Gail flat on her back sound asleep. He completed the rest of the movie alone, and then fell asleep himself.

Still watching the road ahead, he reached down to

the front passenger seat and felt the package he had left on the seat. He smiled; even though it was not a Friday, they could still make up for last week. He was away for the weekend on a fishing trip to Pigeon Cove, and they both worked late Monday and Tuesday, with an early start the next morning. Not so tonight.

He looked up at their building as he pulled into the lot. The light was on in one of their apartment windows. Fantastic: Gail said she might be home first. Ready, waiting and willing. He locked the car, walked across the lot in a dignified manner, then, package in hand, ran up the stairs to their apartment.

Gail was standing with her back to the door and swung round when it opened. 'So there you are,' she said. 'I thought you'd forgotten.'

'You thought I'd forgotten?' he replied.

He took off his coat and dropped it and the package on a chair. He walked over to Gail. She was wearing a cream dress. Coming to just below her knees, it accentuated every curve on her body. The colour showed up the rich tan on her legs and arms. He liked this: he was not sure whether it was natural, still showing six weeks after the last vacation; or artificial, spray or otherwise. Either way, he didn't care. He stepped over to her and put his arms around her narrow waist.

'Thought I'd forgotten?' he repeated. 'What do you think?' he added as his mouth brushed against hers.

She put her arms around his neck and opened her mouth slightly. Their lips, and then their tongues fought. He lowered his hands down to her behind and held it tightly, pulling her closer to him. Through his clothes she could feel him ready for her.

He reached further down and lifted her dress up. Gail gasped and began to nuzzle his face and chin as he felt for the elastic of her panties.

'Wait a second, buster,' she said, pulling away slightly. His hands returned to her back, letting the dress drop back into place.

'What's in there?' she asked, looking over at the package he dropped onto the chair.

He laughed, let her go, and reached over to the chair. Picked up the brown grocery bag and pulled out the contents.

Gail grinned and licked her lips as he pulled out a set of handcuffs, covered in black fur.

It was much later that evening. Both fully spent and dripping with sweat, they collapsed onto the bed. Gail sat up and ran both hands through her black hair, clearing it from her face.

He turned onto his back and ran a hand over his sweaty chest.

'Man,' he exclaimed, reaching over to the cigarette pack and lighter by the side of the bed. He lit up and offered one to Gail. Lit hers with the end of his.

Gail moved her head around as she reached up to massage her own neck.

'You okay baby?' he asked, reaching up and stroking her back.

She nodded, took a drag and rested the cigarette on the ashtray her side of the bed. Sat there a second or two, then swung over so she was sitting astride him.

‘But next time,’ she purred, leaning forward, ‘*you* can wear these.’ She shook the handcuffs which were still connected to the bed frame.

He nodded and laughed.

‘Now,’ she said as she climbed off him, ‘the first thing we need is a towel.’ She walked into the bathroom and picked up two hand towels. Threw one at him, and then walked naked out into the living room. He rubbed himself with the towel and then lay back again, looking up at the ceiling. Then he could hear Gail shout out from the living room.

He sat up and called out, ‘What is it?’

She returned to the bedroom holding her cell phone. ‘Goddam it. How could I be so...?’

‘Be so what?’

She sat down on the bed, staring at the phone.

‘I’d forgotten; I’d put my cell onto silent.’

He sat up a bit more. ‘Yeah; so what?’

Gail looked over at him, holding her phone out to him.

‘I’ve just checked my messages. Ryan called earlier. From home, asking where the hell I was. I’d forgotten we’d arranged to both get home early tonight, for a meal together.’

She tossed the phone onto the bed. She stared down at the bed, breathing heavily, trying to control her emotions.

Danny Clark leaned back against the bed, a serious expression on his face.

Chapter Forty

MATT ANGRILY SOUNDED his horn at the driver of the Wal-Mart rig as it finally switched lanes, allowing him to pass. The driver reciprocated by flashing his headlamps as Matt's Toyota disappeared into the distance. Now he was a mile past Braintree, as the Pilgrim's Highway merged into the I-93.

The Interstate traffic was heavier than that on the highway up from the Cape, and it became more difficult to overtake. It was made worse by the fact that he was now in the middle of Friday night rush hour, it was dark, and beginning to rain heavily.

Matt swore as he noticed the fuel gauge: the dial was half way between a quarter full and empty. He knew there was a gas station a little further up, just after the Neponset Avenue Bridge. Once he had filled up again and bought himself a candy bar and energy drink, he returned to the Expressway and headed back north. He was looking forward to being home, and sleeping in his own bed, but his first priority was to get hold of Nathan again. No, his destination was Medford, and Gail Smith's home. As soon as his parents' neighbour had said he saw Nathan get into a silver convertible, he knew where Nathan was and who had him. It all fitted into place: whatever Ruth was up to, Gail was involved as well. She must know where Ruth was. And that would explain why when they had spoken over the last couple of weeks, she never began the conversation with asking if there was any news about Ruth, as a concerned friend would do. Because she already knew! When she finally did ask, it was always as an afterthought. And Matt would take book on the fact that it was Gail who took the spare set of keys when she went up to the bathroom. And that proved that she and Ruth were in collusion; how else would she have known they keys were there? First, Ruth wanted the car keys, now she wanted their son. 'Over my dead body,' he muttered as he grasped the steering wheel harder and pressed his foot down harder on the gas pedal.

He had to brake sharply, skidding slightly; the traffic ahead had slowed down. He craned his head up to see what was the cause of the delay, but it seemed to be only volume of traffic and the rain. Irritated, he drummed his fingers on the wheel as he had to slow down to about twenty. After five minutes, the traffic speeded up again.

For the rest of the journey, the traffic was slow, stop-start, until he had gotten to the other side of Boston. Then it was even slower, as he had now joined the traffic leaving the city on a Friday night. He swung the car onto the exit ramp, and took the underpass onto Mystic Avenue, and made the rest of the journey through the residential streets.

It was almost ten thirty and the rain had turned to snow when he finally arrived at Gail and Ryan's building. The parking lot was fuller than normal, and there were only two spaces left. He pulled in between a dark coloured Ford and a silver Audi. Climbing out of his car, he looked up at Gail and Ryan's floor. There were lights on. He ran up to the lobby door and pressed the intercom. After a few seconds, he heard Ryan's voice.

'Ryan? It's Matt. Can you let me up?' His voice was breathless and he spoke impatiently.

‘Sure thing. Come up.’ Ryan sounded puzzled.

There was a buzz from the intercom and a click as the doors unlocked. Matt ran up the stairs. Ryan was waiting for him, standing in the open doorway.

‘Matt?’ Ryan asked, looking at his watch. ‘What’s up? What -?’

Matt pushed past him into the apartment. ‘Where are they?’ he demanded, looking around the room. Then he toured the place, checking the bedrooms, the kitchen, the bathrooms.

‘Matt?’ asked Ryan, closing the door. ‘Slow down, will you? Tell me what’s going on.’

‘Where’s Gail?’ Matt asked again, standing in the middle of the apartment, out of breath, his clothes wet from the snow outside.

‘I- I don’t… Why do you want Gail?’ stammered Ryan.

‘Because she has Nathan.’ Matt slumped onto an armchair. He rested his arms on his knees and looked up at Ryan. ‘She has Nathan and Ruth.’

‘Gail’s not here,’ Ryan said, sitting down opposite. ‘She’s on a weekend away; one of those baby shower affairs.’

Matt looked up at Ryan, sat back in the chair and closed his eyes.

‘Why do you think she has Nathan and Ruth?’ Ryan asked. ‘What’s going on?’

Matt opened his eyes and laughed bitterly. ‘What’s going on?’ he said. ‘I’ve no idea what’s going on. Ever since my wife...’ He paused. ‘Didn’t come home one night, all kinds of queer shit’s been going on. My car gets stolen a few days after the spare keys disappear from my bedroom closet. It reappears a few days later in Brooklyn -’

‘Brooklyn? Is that where you’ve come from?’

‘In a roundabout way. I was there this morning, Cape Cod this afternoon, here tonight.’

‘Let me get you a drink,’ said Ryan as he got up.

‘Just water please.’ Matt sat back in the chair again.

‘You sure? Okay.’ Ryan passed him a glass of water and sat back down again. ‘So your car was taken to Brooklyn?’

Matt took a mouthful and nodded. ‘The police told me that it had been found abandoned in a parking garage there. I picked it up from there this morning. From the police pound, I mean, not the garage.’ He sat back and closed his eyes again. ‘I went to the garage -’

He was interrupted by the sound of his cell phone ringing. ‘It’s my parents,’ he said. ‘I’d better take it.’

Ryan nodded and went to the bathroom while Matt spoke to his parents. Then into the kitchen to tidy up some cups. As he did so, he could hear Matt on the phone to his parents.

‘Any news? Okay, I’m at Gail’s now. No, Ryan’s here; she’s not. No, he’s not either. All right, I’ll call you in the morning. Call me first if anything…’

Ryan returned as Matt put his phone away. ‘You went to the parking garage, you were saying…’

‘Yeah. I went to the garage. I kind of bribed the superintendent there to let me see the CCTV footage of the day the car was left there.’ He looked up at Ryan. ‘Ryan, Ruth parked the car there.’

Chapter Forty-One

'IT WAS RUTH parking the car?' Ryan asked. 'Are you sure? Sorry – stupid question. But what does that have to do with Gail?'

'You know bits, I guess,' Matt sighed. 'But let me tell you the whole story. From the top.'

And so for the next hour, Matt related to Ryan the saga of the last couple of weeks, from Ruth's not returning home to his rush back up to Boston after Nathan's disappearance that day. Ryan sat quietly, nodding. Some of the story he knew, but from Gail's perspective. It was now almost midnight.

'I still don't get,' Ryan said, 'why you think Gail is mixed up in all of this. Sure, she and Ruth are best friends. Have been since – well long before she and I got together. From what you've said, Ruth's up to something. She's still alive, thank God, and may be in New York City. But you still don't know where in the city, and why. Now the same goes for Nathan, I'm sorry to say. Have you gotten the police involved?'

'Yes, for both of them. As soon as we found out about this woman in the silver convertible -'

'That's Gail's car, for sure,' said Ryan.

'I know,' Matt continued. 'As soon as I found out, I rushed straight back up here. My folks had already called the local sheriff who had begun a search of the locality. Then passed things to the state police. As far as Ruth goes, I called the BPD the day she vanished. The cop who I saw passed everything to their Missing Persons Unit. They're meant to be in touch with me if anything arises. But nothing has. Then she appeared on this CCTV in Brooklyn, withdrew cash at an ATM on East 53rd, then disappeared again.

'What I don't understand, Ryan, is if she thought things were over between us, then why not say something? Why just abandon our home, her child? What mother could do that?'

'Yeah, but Matt: don't you think it's a coincidence that Nathan's gone as well?'

'Oh, I know they're connected. Obviously wherever she went, she wants Nathan with her. But why not say something? If she was in some kind of trouble....' He broke off as his voice began to tremble.

Ryan rubbed his by now very stubbly chin. He checked his watch: now 12:15. He had this feeling there might be something in what Matt said. The bit about her taking the spare car keys when she went to the bathroom might be a bit tenuous; and Matt's theory about why she never asked about Ruth until the end of a conversation was pushing it – although Gail could be a bit narcissistic. He reached out and rested his hand on Matt's knee.

'Look, Matt. It's really late, and you're bushed. You can't do anything more now. You certainly can't drive anymore. Stop here on the couch tonight, and decide what to do in the morning. I'll give Gail a call first thing. Matt?'

Matt was already asleep.

Chapter Forty-Two

MATT WOKE WITH a start, nearly falling off the couch. Disorientated, and blinking, he looked around. Through the venetian blinds on the nearest window, he could see it was getting light. He rubbed his eyes and forehead, looking round again. This was not his house, but it looked familiar. Yes, it was Gail and Ryan's. Then he remembered why he was here, and his conversation with Ryan the night before.

A narrow shaft of light appeared against the darkened wall. Matt looked around at the source: a door was half- opened, and in the light from the room was the silhouette of a man's figure, wearing a tee shirt and boxer shorts. The figure reached down and felt about, then stepped into the room.

'Hey, Matt,' said Ryan. 'I heard you moving about.'

Matt rubbed his face. 'It took me a minute to figure out where I was.'

Ryan switched on a light and walked into the kitchen. 'What time it is?' he said, squinting at the clock on the microwave. 'Jesus, seven o'clock.' He walked round the room, opening the blinds. Weak daylight filled the room. 'Man, you look like shit,' Ryan said.

Matt rubbed his very stubbly chin. 'I feel like shit. Did I spend the night on there?'

'Don't you remember?' Ryan asked, as he prepared some coffee.

Matt rubbed the unkempt hair on the back of his head. 'Yeah. I do remember. I think.'

'Do you remember what you told me?'

'What I told you?'

'All that about Ruth and Nathan and how they disappeared, and how you think Gail has something to do with it.'

Matt nodded his head, rubbing his eyes. He took a mug of coffee from Ryan.

'Look,' said Ryan. 'It's a bit early right now, but after we've both showered – and boy, you need to shower – I'll give her a call and we'll get it sorted out. Okay?'

Matt opened his mouth to disagree, but Ryan cut in with another, 'Okay?'

'Okay.' Matt sat back down again and took a large mouthful of coffee.

Just before eight, they had both showered. Matt still had a days' growth on his face and yesterday's clothes on. Ryan looked immaculate as usual, closely shaved and smartly dressed in a black tee and grey sweatpants. He made more coffee.

'I'd got these special for this morning,' he said as he took a packet of croissants out of the refrigerator. 'Here: help yourself to a couple. Jelly's over there.'

As Matt sat at the breakfast bar eating, Ryan took out his cell phone and speed-dialled a number.

'Morning, sweetie. How are you?'

'.........'

'Great. How's the weekend going?'

'.........'

'And when are you back?'

'.........'

'Swell. Look, baby: Matt's here.'

'.........'

'He stopped over last night. Slept on the couch.'

'.........'

'Well, something's happened to Nathan.'

'..........'

'He disappeared from Matt's folks' place yesterday. Matt reckons you know something about it.'

'..........'

'Sure, I know that, but why don't you have a word with him. Put his mind -'

'..........'

'Okay, okay, baby. Tell you what: why don't you give him a call yourself when -'

'..........'

'Okay. Talk to you tonight. Love you.'

He waited a moment, then ended the call. Put the phone down on the counter. 'Sorry, Matt,' he said. 'She had to go. They were all about to go out for breakfast.'

'Where's she gone?' Matt asked.

'She's gone up to Cape Elizabeth. A girls' weekend. Retail therapy, that sort of thing. Gail and three or four others.'

'Do you know any of the others she went with?'

'Sure. Why?'

'Do you know any of their cell numbers?'

Ryan gave him a puzzled look. 'I – I guess so,' he replied slowly.

'Do me a favour – call one of them. Any one.'

Still with a puzzled expression, Ryan picked up his phone and trawled though his contacts list. Picked one, and dialled.

'Hello, Cindy. It's Ryan. Ryan Wilson.'

'..........'

'I'm good, thanks. Sorry to call you, but Gail must have her cell switched off. I just need to talk with her for a second.'

‘..........’

‘But I thought she was with you up at Cape Elizabeth…’

‘..........’

‘I’m sorry, Cindy. My mistake. Guess I misunderstood her.’

‘..........’

‘You too. Take care now.’

He hung up and looked over at Matt. ‘She’s not with Cindy. Not up at the Cape. Cindy is. But not Gail. Matt, what’s going on?’

‘You believe me now?’

‘But where the hell could she be?’

‘Get online. Look up your bank account. See if she’s used an ATM. That’s how I found Ruth had been to New York.’

Ryan swallowed. ‘Okay.’ He walked over to the desk where his PC was situated, and booted it up. Momentarily he got to his bank’s site, and checked his account. ‘My God,’ he muttered, sitting down at the screen.

‘What is it?’ Matt asked.

‘Two hundred bucks taken out. Yesterday.’

‘Can you tell where?’

Ryan clicked on a blue link. ‘It was at Banco Santander S.A., 45 -’

‘East 53rd Street.’ Matt finished his sentence.

Ryan looked up at him.

‘That was the same ATM location Ruth used,’ Matt said grimly. Believe me now?’

Ryan rested his elbows on the desk and rubbed his temples. ‘What do you want to do?’ he asked.

‘I’m going to New York. That’s where my family are.’

Ryan nodded, leaning back in his chair. ‘Matt, I’m

sorry…'

Matt rested his hand on Ryan's shoulder. 'Forget it. Thanks for the couch last night. And for breakfast.' He visited the bathroom and went to the front door, turning round as he held the handle. 'If Gail calls back, don't tell her -'

'I won't. Matt -'

Matt turned round again.

'Good luck.'

Matt nodded and closed Ryan's door behind him. He walked briskly downstairs and out to where he had left the Toyota the night before. Started the car up, and pulled into the street. He hit a red light at the first corner. Once it went green, he made a left and headed for the I-93. Three other vehicles made a left after him: a rusty green pick up truck, a yellow school bus, and a silver Audi.

Traffic on the interstate was relatively light that time on a Saturday morning and Matt was making good progress. As he headed west along the I-90, he felt his cell phone vibrate in his pocket. He was unable to reach the phone without losing some speed, so continued.

Just before he passed the town of Auburn, he pulled in to a gas station to fill up. He bought a sandwich and a coffee when he paid for the fuel. Walking back to the car, he reached down into his pocket and pulled out his phone. He had almost forgotten about the message that came through earlier. As he climbed into the car, he casually looked down at the screen, almost dropping his food when he saw where the message had come from.

It was Ruth's number.

Matt im so sorry please stay away. For nathans sake.

Chapter Forty-Three

MATT FELT DIZZY, faint. His eyes began to water. The characters on the screen of his phone – his wife's number and message – began to come off the screen and mingle in front of his eyes, like a DNA strand. He sat up in his seat, and looked around the gas station forecourt. As if Ruth was at another pump sending the message. He read it again. Why was she sorry? What did that mean? And the clincher: stay away for Nathan's sake. Did that mean he was in some kind of danger?

He looked around the forecourt again. A white RV had pulled into one of the adjacent pumps. A middle-aged man stepped out, selected self-serve and began to fill. He nonchalantly glanced over at Matt, then around the rest of the station. Matt returned his stare, and then looked back at the message.

He stabbed at the green call button. After a moment, it began to ring. His heart began to beat faster as he waited for it to be answered, but after four rings, it went to voicemail. As it had done every time he rang that number since that night.

'Focus, focus,' he muttered, and put the phone down on the passenger seat. It was time to continue his journey. He could figure out what Ruth meant in her message on his way to New York. If it was Ruth who sent it.

He fired up the engine and returned to the westbound I-90. As he continued on his journey to New York, he thought through exactly what he would do when he got there. It had to be more than mere coincidence that both Ruth and Gail had made cash withdrawals from the same ATM, although he was puzzled at what seemed to be an indiscretion. Surely they were aware that he and Ryan would be able to establish where the withdrawal took place? That must have been on Ruth's mind when she took the $500 before she left. So many questions: Matt was clear on only one thing, and that was that he had no idea what Ruth and Gail were up to. But now they had involved Nathan, the gloves were off.

As he saw the sign stating that New York City was 50 miles away, he considered what to do first when he arrived. He was not going to wrap everything up and be back in Boston in time for dinner, so he would need somewhere to stay. He thought about returning to the same hotel he had used in Brooklyn, but decided a base Midtown would be better. He still had the Holiday Inn number stored in his cell phone memory, so with the phone still resting on the passenger seat, he dialled. When he was answered, he put the phone on speaker. He was in luck: there was a Holiday Inn on West 57th. The 400 block. No parking facilities, but there was a 24 hour parking garage across the street, preferential terms for hotel guests. Perfect. Just a short walk from the ATM location. Not that they would be standing waiting there for him, but it was a start. He would figure out the next stage when he arrived. He asked the lady to make the booking for him – two nights – and hung up.

Saturday traffic was even heavier than the other day's; somehow he took a wrong turning and found himself heading on the 295 into Queens. Fortunately the slow traffic allowed him to take note of the direction signs better and make sure he was in the correct lane. A mile or two into the borough he was able to turn right onto the Long Island Expressway and made his way into Manhattan that way, passing through the Queens-Midtown Tunnel. After exiting the tunnel just past Second Avenue he headed west along 37th as far as 10th Avenue, whereupon he took a right into 10th for the next twenty blocks. As he reached 57th, he saw the parking garage entrance, and pulled in. He parked the car in a second floor section dedicated to hotel guests, then took the walkway across to reception. He checked in and went up to his third floor room. He took a shower, and checked the time. It was almost four, and beginning to get dark.

He sat on the bed and rang his parents. Unusually, his mother answered. Matt suspected that his father was avoiding the telephone, avoiding any potential bad news. His mother's voice was quiet and shaky.

'Matt, where are you calling from?'

'I'm back in New York. I arrived about an hour ago. Is there any news? Anything from the sheriff?'

'He called by about three to say no sightings yet, but he and the State guys were still looking. Matt, it is true what your father said about Ruth's friend Gail?'

'I don't know, Mom; I honestly don't know. All I know is that car your neighbour described is the same make and model, same colour as Gail's.'

There was a pause of a second or two, then his mother said, 'Why are you in New York then? Are you in the same place you stayed at before?'

'No, I'm in Manhattan. It's the Holiday Inn Midtown. It's on 57th. It would take too long to explain now, but I've got a lead that points to here.'

'So Nathan is there? With Ruth?'

'Possibly. The thing is, both Ruth and Gail had cash withdrawals from a bank ATM on East 53rd. On different days. So that's why I've come up here.'

'What about Gail's boyfriend? Brian, is it? Is he involved too? Oh my God.'

'Ryan, you mean? No, no; he's not. I went straight there from yours yesterday. Slept on his couch. She told him she was up in Cape Elizabeth for the weekend. He phoned one of her girlfriends to check; of course she wasn't. Then he checked their bank account and found the withdrawal here.'

'I see. Matt, have you called the police about this?'

'No, I haven't. Yet.'

'Matt, you must. You can't handle this yourself.'

Matt said nothing.

'Matt,' she repeated. 'Are you listening? You must call the police.'

'I know, Mom. I'll call that Lieutenant Weber from Boston PD. He'll know what to do. He can liaise with the police here.'

'All right.'

'How's Dad?'

'He's saying nothing. He's sick with worry, about you and Nathan. And Ruth, of course. That's why he's saying nothing. He won't even come to the phone. He's just sitting on the chair out back.' Her voice started to quake.

'Look, Mom, I'm going to get something to eat. I've only had a pastry at Gail and Ryan's and a sandwich on the way down here. Then I'll call Weber.'

'Weber?'

'The Boston Lieutenant. He gave me his cell number.'

'All right. Well, call us in the morning.'

'I will. Promise. You too if you hear anything.'

'Bye, Matt. Look after yourself.'

'I will. Night, Mom.'

After hanging up, he sat on the bed staring at the phone. One bar was showing on the battery indicator. Thank God he brought the charger. He plugged in the charger and picked up the room service menu. Then called and ordered a chicken burger and French fries, cheesecake and a cold beer. Really healthy stuff, he thought.

He was told the meal would be about twenty minutes, so he sat on the bed and turned on the television while he waited. He thought about Gail's boyfriend Ryan. Maybe it was his job: he was certainly earning more in one month than Matt was in six, probably. Matt couldn't help being a little envious. If he hadn't had the use of family money, he and Ruth would never have been able to afford the house in Beacon Hill. But today, that changed: Matt actually felt sorry for Ryan. He could see how devastated Ryan was when the realisation hit him that Gail had lied to him, and was doing something behind his back.

Then Matt realised something. Ryan said Gail had told him she was on a girls' weekend in Cape Elizabeth. A weekend! So she was planning on returning home Sunday, or maybe Monday. So – did that mean that whatever was going on with Ruth and Nathan would be over this weekend? Matt had a sick feeling in the pit of his stomach. This weekend….

His train of thought was broken by a knock on his door. The burger, fries and cheesecake. He checked the time: that was quick. Fortunately, as he had gotten hungry.

There was another double tap on the door. Matt took out a $5 bill from his pocket and walked over.

Not bothering to check the spy hole, he swung the door open.

It was not room service, but the last face he expected to see here.

'You!' Matt exclaimed.

Chapter Forty-Four

MATT STOOD IN the open doorway, his mouth open in surprise.

'Well, are you going to let me in?' asked Lieutenant Weber.

'Sure… Sure, come in.' Matt stepped aside to let the Lieutenant in.

'This is a surprise,' Matt said as he began to close the door. 'How -'

'Room service,' announced a voice behind Matt. He turned round and saw a little Italian-looking man wearing a white jacket and pushing a small metal trolley.

'Come in, come in,' said Matt holding the door open. He and Weber stepped out of the way as the waiter brought in a large tray holding two plates, one holding a thin slice of cheesecake, the other covered by a large aluminium cover, and an opened bottle of beer with an empty glass. He set the tray down on the dressing table and stood to go.

Matt signed the bill and returned it to the waiter with the $5 tip. 'Here you are,' he said. 'Thank you very much.'

The waiter nodded and, giving Weber a strange look, walked over to the door. 'Have a good evening, sir,' he said as he left.

Weber lifted up the plate warmer and looked at the burger and fries. He sniffed. 'You going to eat this shit?' he asked.

Matt looked down at the food. He had to agree with Weber: it could look more appetising. 'I was going to. Why?'

Weber shrugged. 'Was going to take you out for coffee, that's all. We could eat something as well, if you want. Unless you want to eat this.'

'All right,' said Matt. 'Let's go out. I need to talk with you, anyway.'

'I know,' said the Lieutenant enigmatically, as he led Matt out of the room.

'There's a place I know along here,' said Weber as he took Matt along West 57th. Matt looked around as they walked: Saturday night in Manhattan was already in full swing. The streets and sidewalks were full of people: the traffic along 57th was moving slowly; Matt turned and looked back to the hotel and could see the long row of red tail lights leading as far as he could make out; as far as the Hudson for all he knew. Horns blared in their vicinity and in the distance.

'It's not far,' Weber said, hooking his arm into Matt's. He had to almost shout on account of the street noise. 'Just past Carnegie Hall.'

They threaded their way through the crowds filing into Carnegie Hall. Matt glanced over at the billboard to see what everybody was lining up for. It was the Chicago Symphony Orchestra.

Weber pointed to a doorway just past the hall. 'In here,' he said. 'Up the stairs.' Matt looked up at the name above the door: *Noodle Town*. He could tell from the menu card in the doorway that it was a Chinese restaurant.

The narrowness of the stairway belied the size of the restaurant on the second floor. There must have been at least thirty tables on the premises, all occupied, with servers bustling to and fro. Weber was greeted by an Asian man in a dark suit. They spoke quietly and Weber led Matt to two stools at the bar. As they sat down, an Asian woman behind the bar passed over two cups of coffee. Matt took a sip, and then nodded at Weber. The coffee was surprisingly good.

'See?' Weber said, taking a large mouthful. 'You wouldn't think it from downstairs, but this is the best cup of coffee you can get Midtown. You want to eat here? My treat.'

'Sure,' said Matt. 'How do you know about this place?'

'Used to work the streets here,' replied Weber through a second mouth of coffee. 'Many years ago.'

'And how did you know I'd be staying down the road?'

Just as Weber opened his mouth to reply the dark suited man came over and asked Weber if he wanted to eat.

'My usual,' he said. 'Twice.'

The man bowed slightly and left.

'I recommend it,' Weber said. 'They also do the best Szechuan Chicken this side of Houston.'

'I'll take your word for it,' Matt said. 'Now, as I was asking...'

'How I knew you were in that hotel. Yes?'

'U-huh.'

'What's my job?'

'A cop. Why?'

'That's how I knew.'

'What – you're in the Sixth Sense Unit?'

Weber laughed. 'Very good. No. I've been keeping an eye on you. Following you, as much as I could, that is.'

'Following me. But I – I hadn't…'

'Well, you wouldn't, would you? That's what

surveillance is all about.'

'I see,' said Matt, not quite seeing.

'You've had a silver Audi on your tail for the last few days. Around Boston, that is. I spent the night outside that apartment block in West Medford last night.'

'Right. I see.'

'I must admit, I wasn't expecting you to be stopping over.'

'Well, neither was I. You see -'

'Your son?'

'Nathan? You know all about it? Do you know where he might be?'

Weber shook his head. 'No, sorry. I heard about it. I guessed that was why you were headed back here. But why here? Why New York City?'

Matt proceeded to tell Weber about Ruth and Gail's use of the ATM on 53rd Street. Weber scratched his chin thoughtfully.

'I see,' he said. 'Can I ask why you thought fit not to share this theory of yours – which isn't without merit – with us? With me?'

Matt paused as the Szechuan Chicken arrived. 'Yeah, I'm sorry about that. I had intended to. But I guess I got kind of caught up in this ATM transaction thing.'

'And you thought you'd play detective?'

Matt felt his face redden. He nodded.

'What about your son?' Weber asked. 'Were you going to tell us about him?'

'It had already been reported to the local police. The sheriff began a search, then escalated it to the State police.'

'Which is how I came to hear about it.'

'Can I ask you one thing?' said Matt.

'Go ahead,' mumbled Weber through a mouthful of chicken.

'You seem to be showing a lot of interest in me. You personally, I mean. I don't get how a detective investigating a disappearance in Boston can be working here in New York City.'

'That's a long story.'

'We've both come a long way.'

'I guess I'm trying to prove a point,' said Weber.

'Prove a point? How so?'

'Look, both my partner -'

'Detective….Mancini?'

'U-huh. Both she and my boss think you're implicated somehow in your wife's disappearance.'

'What? But I've no idea -'

'Neither have I. I'm ninety-nine percent certain you didn't. There's obviously no evidence, otherwise – well, you know…'

'I'd have been arrested?'

Weber nodded. 'Mancini: she's young, inexperienced, ambitious. O'Riordan, my Captain: he's just full of shit. More interested in politicking and clear up statistics than real policing. He was my partner back in the day, and he was an asshole even then.'

Matt took a mouthful of rice. 'I see.'

'I don't think you do. They are saying you're involved somehow; I say you're not. So I need to prove a point.'

'But how can you go to and from here and home? Don't you have your own cases to work on?'

'I'm not at work. I'm on leave.'

'You're doing this on your vacation time?'

'No. Sick leave.'

'Sick leave?'

'That's right. I had a queer turn the other day after chasing some guy through the mall at CambridgeSide. Caught the bastard, but collapsed afterward. They all thought I was having a heart attack and rushed me to hospital.'

'Jesus. I guess it wasn't a heart attack?'

'No. The doctor told me it was a kind of warning. You know, cut down on fatty foods – like this – and cut out the red wine. And lose some of this.' He patted his ample belly. 'And told me to rest for two weeks.'

'I see.'

'So, here I am. Resting.'

'With me?'

'Correct. And hoping that in my absence O'Riordan doesn't send someone out to arrest you. Assuming they find you.'

Matt nodded. 'I understand.'

'Now,' said Weber. 'Fill me in on everything. And I mean everything. Some bits I know anyway, but…'

Matt took another mouthful of egg fried rice. 'Okay. From the top, then.'

Matt then proceeded to tell Weber the whole story, right from the night Ruth failed to come home. Weber continued eating, sometimes nodding, sometimes asking Matt to repeat himself. Now and then, he would ask Matt to clarify something. He stopped eating when Aki Watanabe came up.

'You asked about her before,' he said.

'What's the police view?' Matt asked.

'The ME said it was an accident. She was filling her bath with water and an attachment of the shower fell off the wall. Hit her on the back of the head, rendered her unconscious. Her head and shoulders fell into the bath water and she drowned. But…'

'But?'

'But I noticed some bruising on the back of her neck. Here.' He reached round and touched the back of his own neck. But the ME said they weren't consistent with any force being exerted by a third party.'

'But you think differently?'

'I think there's a possibility she's wrong. A very small possibility. Not a probability.'

'And her boyfriend?'

'Danny Clark?'

'Yeah. I guess you've spoken to him?'

'We have, but he denies they were together. And we went through her condo with a fine toothed comb. No trace at all of him.'

'He could have killed her, and gone through the place.'

'Could have, but there's no evidence. And no motive.'

'Hm.' Matt finished his food and pushed the plate aside.

'Pissing you off isn't a cause for suspicion, I'm afraid. So carry on.'

Matt continued, only to be stopped when he got to the car accident.

'Hm,' Weber said slowly, 'I seem to remember reading about that. The DNA had been compromised.'

'Destroyed, according to the reports.'

'Yes, that's right. It happens sometimes if the fire causes heat over a certain temperature. Makes identification problematic.'

'Well, in this case they found part of her driver's licence which hadn't been burnt.'

‘Lucky licence,’ said Weber. ‘To survive when everything else gets vaporised. Anyway, carry on.’ He motioned over to a waiter for more coffee.

Matt carried on, up to his arrival in the City that day. ‘But what is weird,’ he said, getting out his phone, ‘is this text I got this morning.’ He retrieved the message, and showed Weber the screen.

Weber peered at the screen. Ruth’s name was right at the top of the screen. ‘Jesus!’ he gasped. ‘When did you get that?’ He tabbed the message down to get the date and time of receipt.

‘See for yourself,’ said Matt.

‘This makes quite a bit of difference,’ Weber said, passing the phone back. ‘One hell of a difference.’

‘Yeah, but who’s to say it was Ruth who sent it?’

‘True, but with this we can establish where it was sent.’

‘Where it was sent? To me.’

Weber sighed. ‘This is why you should have come to the police in the first place, rather than playing Sherlock Holmes yourself.’

‘Matt frowned. ‘I don’t understand.’

‘It’s possible to establish the geographical location of where the message was sent.’

Matt looked at him blankly; Weber spoke slowly.

‘Basically, the guys in the crime lab can tell us the address the message was sent from. Which could be the address where your wife and son are.’

Chapter Forty-Five

AT 8:50 THE next morning, Lieutenant Weber's silver Audi pulled up at one of the security booths guarding 1 Police Plaza. Matt was in the passenger seat. A uniformed officer stepped out of the booth and leaned over the car. Weber already had his badge and identification ready; he held it up to the officer who took it, studied it carefully, returned it, then stepped back into the booth to raise the barrier. Weber gave the officer a brief wave, then took the Audi over to a large parking lot adjacent to the main building.

'You been here before?' he asked Matt, as he looked around for a space.

Matt looked around out of his window, at the imposing brutalist structure, at the grounds and parking lots, and the large numbers of uniformed officers milling around. 'No. Seen it on TV, though.'

'Haven't we all,' Weber muttered as he reversed into a space. He activated the parking brake, and switched off the engine. 'Come on,' he said as he climbed out of the car.

They walked out of the parking lot and along a road way towards the Plaza building. As they neared it, Matt looked up at the building, squinting in the morning sunlight.

'Thirteen,' said Weber.

'Excuse me?'

'You were trying to count how many floors.'

'I wasn't, but thanks. Thirteen.'

'Thirteen above ground.'

'Right. How many below ground?'

'If I told you I'd have to kill you.'

Matt nodded. 'Best not tell me then.'

They walked in the main doors. Once they had passed through the metal detectors and X-Ray machines, Weber led Matt to a large reception area. Not dissimilar to Matt's office, there was a long counter behind which five uniformed officers were standing. One was unoccupied and was checking a computer screen; the other four were all individually engaged in conversation with other officers.

Weber stopped and turned to Matt. 'Give me your cell phone,' he said, holding out his hand.

Matt obliged. 'What now?' he asked.

'Up on the eighth,' replied Weber, 'is what the boys here call the Real Time Crime Center. It's one huge mother of a computer network which the NYPD use to assist officers in the field. I can get them, hopefully to triangulate – I think that's the word – where your wife's text message came from. No civilians allowed up there, I'm afraid; why don't you wait over there?' He pointed over to a waiting area with low soft chairs, a coffee machine and a table. On the wall was a sign stating that the restrooms were around the corner.

'Okay,' said Matt as he wandered off to wait.

'I'll meet you over there,' said Weber. 'Not sure how long I'll be, though. Could be a long wait.' He then walked over to the bank of six elevators.

Matt watched him step into one of the elevators and disappear from view as the doors slid shut. He sighed and slumped onto one of the chairs. He looked around. It was a busy place: figures in and out of uniform milling around. Two men, both wearing check shirts and jeans were sitting across the other side studying a map. One of them met Matt's gaze and stopped talking. Matt quickly looked away; maybe they were planning an operation.

He checked his watch. It was now nine thirty. He stood up and walked over to the coffee machine. 75c for a cup. He fed in three quarters and got a plastic cup filled with a watery brown liquid. He tasted it and pulled a face. Should have pressed the button for extra sugar. He wandered back to his seat, picking up a copy of the *New York Times* which was lying on the table. He sat down and opened it: it was last Friday's copy. He leaned back and tried to figure out what day it was. Yes, it was Sunday. He was surprised the Plaza was this busy this time on a Sunday.

The night before, after they had finished their meal, Matt and Weber stepped out into the street. The air was bitterly cold. Matt shivered and pulled his coat collar up.

'You be able to make your own way back to your hotel? Weber asked.

'Surely. Where are you staying?'

'My sister-in-law's place up in Harlem. Off 112th. We'll go down to Police Plaza in the morning. Should be quiet first thing. Especially on a Sunday.'

'Shall I meet you there?'

Weber shook his head. 'No point. You'd never get past the checkpoints. I have to come down past anyway, so be at Fifth and 57th eight thirty, okay?'

'Where's your car?' Matt asked.

'The same garage as yours,' replied Weber. As they got to Matt's hotel, Weber began to cross the street to the garage entrance. 'Don't be late,' he called out, weaving his way through a cluster of yellow cabs. Matt waved and stepped into the lobby.

Back in his room, he creased his nose up at the sight of the cold and now dried up burger and fries. He pushed it to one side and checked out the cheesecake. It still looked edible, though the beer was flat. He sat on the bed, ate the dessert, then made himself a cup of hot tea before leaving the tray outside his room and taking a bath.

After his bath, he laid down on the bed. Lying on the bed dressed only in a bath towel, he felt nervous. After all this time, there was a pretty good chance that tomorrow he was going to find out where Ruth was. And maybe get some answers.

After reading Friday's *New York Times* for the second time, Matt bought himself another plastic cup of plastic coffee. He noticed this time, however, he had the option of pressing a button for *Extra Strong* as well as *Sugar*. He pressed both, and this time the coffee was more palatable. He sat down again, peering over to the coffee table to see if there was anything else to read. Just as he had picked up a copy of *Time* magazine, he heard Weber's voice. He looked up.

'Here, catch this.' Weber tossed Matt's phone back.

Matt caught it and put it back in his pocket. 'Any luck?'

'Come on,' said Weber, heading off to the doors. 'We have our location.'

'We have?' Matt asked, as he scurried after the Lieutenant.

'Midtown,' Weber called back over his shoulder. 'East 57th.'

Chapter Forty-Six

'HOW COULD YOU tell that?' Matt asked as Weber took the Audi out of the parking lot and back out onto Pearl Street.

'To be honest, I don't know exactly,' replied Weber. 'I gave two of the guys up there your phone, told them which message it was, and left them to it. I think they link up with your service provider's network. I saw hundreds of damned figures and letters on one of their screens, and then it showed a map of Midtown Manhattan.'

'Right. I see. Impressive.'

'Ain't it just? I've no idea how it works; one of the guys working on it referred to it as GIS – or Geographical Information System – as he called it once. They use it to track down suspects; you know, the places where they are most likely to flee to.'

'Is that how you tracked me down last night?' asked Matt.

'Hell, no. I did that the old-fashioned way. Staked out where you were and followed you everywhere.'

'You didn't use GPS, then?'

'What? Listen, you've been watching way too much TV. What am I going to go? Slip by one evening and shove a transponder up your tailpipe? No, the City of Boston's budget doesn't stretch to that kind of expenditure. In any case, I'm on sick leave, aren't I?'

'So where exactly are we headed?' Matt asked looking out at the buildings and streets they passed. The Sunday Manhattan traffic was building up. The sky was an iron grey.

'They pinpointed the location as a building on Sutton Place. On Sutton and East 57th. Just by the East River.'

'East 57th? But that's just -'

'Up the road from where you're staying? Ironic, isn't it?'

'What do we do when we get there?' asked Matt.

'We do nothing. We just sit there and assess the situation. Or should I say *I* will assess the situation. If and when I think the time's right, I'll call for back up.'

'We can't just sit there!'

'Oh yes we can. For the moment. We need to get it right. We can't just go storming in there, on our own.'

'But there are two of us -'

'You are a civilian. You stay put, or I'll cuff you to the wheel here. When it's time to make a move, I'll put in a call. There's a big operation going down near Wall Street this morning – and I haven't told you that – so manpower is in short supply right now. Another reason to sit and wait.'

Matt made a tutting noise and looked out of his window.

'Look,' said Weber as he swung the Audi onto First Avenue. 'Think about it. If Nathan's been taken, he's most likely with his mother. So is he likely to come to any harm with her?'

'No,' said Matt, not entirely convinced. 'I guess not.'

'And don't forget: this location is where the message was sent from. There's no guarantees she's there now. She could have been walking past when she sent it.'

Matt said nothing; just nodded.

Weber took them further up First Avenue: past Bellevue Hospital, past 42nd Street and past the United Nations building. Made a right when he reached 54th; one block later they were in Sutton Place South. Weber pulled up outside an apartment bock.

'Is this it?' Matt asked.

Weber nodded across the street. 'It's that building over there,' he said. 'For now, we can get a clear view of the entrance. Tell me if you recognise anyone going in or out.'

Matt looked around the street. 'Quiet, isn't it?'

'That building over there,' said Weber pointing to the next block, 'was where they shot part of that movie *How to Marry a Millionaire*. You ever seen it?'

'Can't say I have.'

'That was where Marilyn Monroe's character lived.'

'And how do you know that? You a fan or something?'

'Not specially. Just know. Might have had to come up here when I was on the streets.'

There was a pause in conversation. They both watched a smartly dressed man lead an equally smartly dressed boy down the street. Both were dressed in dark suits, white shirts, shiny black shoes and bright orange ties.

'All dressed up,' Matt remarked.

'Probably off to church.'

'Oh, yes. Of course.'

Another pause.

'You're pretty close to your boy, aren't you?' Weber asked.

Matt looked over at the Lieutenant, puzzled. 'Isn't every father?'

'No. What about your own old man? You get on with him okay?'

'Yeah, I guess so. He's not very demonstrative, if that's what you're getting at. But yeah, we get on.'

'Always have?'

'Yeah. Why? Where are going with this?'

'Nowhere in particular. Just curious. On account of seeing that guy and his boy, I guess. Fathers and sons should always get on.'

Matt wriggled round in his seat. 'What about you? You got any kids?'

'Two. One of each. The boy – Sam Junior – is twenty now. His sister – Shanice -'

'An unusual name. Nice, though.'

'Thanks. It's an old African American name. She's eighteen now.'

'They live with you?'

Weber shook his head. 'They live with the first Mrs Weber in DC.'

'Right. I'm sorry. How often do you see them?'

'Two or three times a year. Maybe.'

'What about your father?'

'He died years ago. My mother passed away two years later.'

'Sorry to hear that. You got on?'

'Not really. Not sure if anybody did. He was an elder or something in the local church. Always quoting from the Bible at us. Keen on retribution and punishment.'

'He was a disciplinarian?'

'He was strict to the point of being cruel.'

'Shit. I'm sorry.'

Weber shook his head. 'Too long ago to be sorry.'

There was another pause.

'He used to beat me and my brother at the slightest opportunity. With his belt,with a paddle, with his fist.'

'Jesus.'

'I must have been six or seven when it started. Then when I was thirteen – maybe fourteen – and by that time taller than him, I hit him back.'

'Good on you.'

'I'd just had enough. I turned round, said "never touch me again", and hit him in the jaw. Clean knocked him across the room. It must have hurt him. My knuckles were sore and drew blood.'

'Jesus,' Matt said again. 'What happened then?'

'He stood up, wiped his mouth, and walked out the house. Was out for hours. He died a couple of years later, and hardly spoke to me after that night. I sat on the porch for a long time also.'

'How did you feel?'

'Mixed feelings, I guess. Hitting him, I never felt better.'

'It had to be done.'

'I know, but at the same time, I never felt worse. It was something I never should have done.'

'You were forced into it, though.'

'I know. But you want to know something: like I said, for the rest of his life, he hardly spoke to me. But the bastard never laid a finger on me again. Or my brother. Or my mother, for all I knew.'

Matt nodded silently, nodding.

'So,' said Weber. 'That's why I think fathers and sons should get on.' He could see Matt starting to well up. 'Don't worry, Matt. We'll get your son back.'

'I need the bathroom,' Matt said, looking around.

‘There’s a Walgreens over there on the next block. See? There’ll be a restroom there. I ain’t going anywhere.’

Matt crossed over the street and into the store. He located the restroom, and bought a couple of candy bars for himself and the Lieutenant. As he crossed over the road on the way back to the Audi, he heard a voice cry out.

‘Daddy!’

He spun round and saw on the corner of 58th, Gail carrying Nathan. Nathan was waving at him. Matt froze in the middle of the street and called out, ‘Nathan!’

Gail also froze momentarily, then, still carrying the boy, began to run back up 58th Street. Dropping the candy bars on the pavement, Matt ran after them.

‘Matt, wait!’ Weber called out as he leapt out of the car. ‘Wait!’

Half way up the street, Gail turned and entered a building by a side door. By that time, Matt was only twelve or fifteen feet behind. Weber was half a block back, still calling out for Matt to wait.

Gail had almost closed the door when Matt reached it; the opening was only six inches wide. He could see the expression on her face: anger and exertion as she tried to push the door with one hand. Matt leapt at the door, pushing it open.

‘Daddy,’ Nathan called again. Matt was inside the building. He could still hear Weber’s voice from outside. Then he felt in intense pain at the back of his head. He reached up to feel it, but by that time he was crashing to the ground.

Chapter Forty-Seven

'MATT? ARE YOU all right?'

Matt groaned. He tried to rub his head, but his arms wouldn't move.

As headaches went, this one was off the scale.

He squinted as he tried to get his bearings. He realised he was sitting on a chair, his arms tied with duck tape behind the chair. As he began to come to, he recognised two sensations. The smell was familiar; a perfume he recognised, although he couldn't remember the name. Then there was the voice.

It came again. 'Matt? Can you hear me?'

Still blinking, he looked up into Ruth's face.

For the last two weeks, ever since the night she failed to return home, he had visualised this moment, and gone over in his mind time and time again what he would say to her when – if – he saw her again.

Only one thing came into his mind now.

'Where's my son, you bitch?'

Ruth recoiled as he shouted at her. She looked around as the door opened. Gail walked in.

'He's come round,' Ruth said.

'So I see.' Gail walked over and looked down at him. 'Someone's going to have a sore head.'

'Where's Nathan?' Matt asked again.

'You tell him,' Gail said to Ruth as she walked back out of the room.

Matt craned his neck so he could take in a 360 degree view. He was in some kind of kitchen. Not a kitchen in somebody's home, rather one in a place of work. Larger, with less comfortable chairs. But there was no sign of the kitchen being in use: no pictures or notices pinned on the wall; no papers or magazines lying around.

'Can't we untie him?' Ruth asked as Gail stood in the doorway.

'I'll go check. Leave him there for now.'

'The police'll be here soon,' he called out after Gail.

'Yeah, right. In your dreams,' she called back.

'The guy with me was a cop, you idiot,' Matt shouted out.

'The police…?' Ruth said, looking at Gail.

'Wait one second.' With a less confident expression on her face, Gail left the room. Momentarily, she returned with Danny Clark.

'You!' said Matt as he saw Clark.

Clark smirked. 'Surprise, surprise.'

'I knew there was something about you. That you were mixed up in this,' Matt spat.

Clark smirked again. 'Untie him,' he said to Ruth. 'You,' he said to Gail as he passed her the gun, 'cover him. And her.'

He left the room. Matt could hear him in the corridor outside, unlocking some doors.

'This way.' Gail prodded Matt in the back with the gun.

'Where's Nathan?' he asked Ruth again.

'He's okay. He's in here.' Ruth opened a door and Matt saw Nathan playing on the floor with five garishly coloured plastic dinosaurs.

'Look, Nathan,' Ruth said. 'Daddy's come to join us.'

'Daddy!' Nathan leapt off the floor and into Matt's arms.

'Quick. This way.' Ruth hustled Matt and Nathan

along the corridor to where Danny Clark was waiting. Gail remained behind them with the gun. Once they had all passed through the door, Clark slammed it shut, locked it in two places, and pushed across two heavy bolts.

'There. That should do it,' he said to Gail.

'Go on. Forward.' Gail pressed the pistol hard into Matt's back. 'This leads to an adjoining building which we're also leasing. If the police arrive downstairs, they'll go to the building you came in. It will be some time before they figure out where we are.'

'What's going on?' Matt asked Ruth. 'You never show up at home, no word. Then this,' – he pointed over to Gail – 'abducts Nathan. Then, you send me that text message…'

'You sent him a text?' screamed Gail. 'Then that's how they know -'

'You stupid bitch,' Clark said, and slapped Ruth full in the face. She collapsed back against the wall, holding her cheek. Matt moved to intervene, but Gail had him at gunpoint.

'She's fucking ruined it now!' Clark yelled at Gail. He reached into one of his coat pockets, and pulled out a gun, almost identical to the one Gail was brandishing. 'Let's cut our losses, do them all, then get out. Now.'

'No,' said Gail firmly. 'We can still figure this through. If we bail out now, all the last year's been wasted.'

'The last year?' Matt said. 'What's he talking about?'

Nathan was beginning to get upset with all the shouting. He clung onto Ruth's leg.

'It's all right, baby,' she said softly, stroking his

hair. ‘Everything’s going to be okay. Go sit down over there. Look, one of your dinosaur books is over there.’

Through the closed windows they could hear the distant wailing of a police siren.

‘Listen,’ Clark said to Gail. ‘Can you hear that?’

Gail listened for a moment. ‘It’s nothing. It’s going in the other direction.’

Matt tried to take the initiative. ‘Who’s Ruth Dubois?’ he asked Ruth.

Open mouthed, all three of them stared at Matt.

‘How – how did you….?’ Ruth stammered.

‘Is that you?’ Matt asked. ‘And if it is, who was that poor devil in the car crash? And is Elisabeth Dubois your mother? The mother who died years ago?’

Ruth put her hand up to her mouth. ‘You’ve been to see...?’

‘Mummy,’ wailed Nathan. ‘What does Daddy mean?’

‘Shut that kid up,’ snapped Clark, walking over to the window. He cautiously peered out of the window, down at the street. Matt estimated they were on the fourth or fifth floors.

‘Can you see anything?’ Gail asked.

Nathan started crying again. ‘Shush, baby. Mummy’s here,’ Ruth soothed.

‘And Daddy,’ Matt snapped.

‘I told you: shut that kid up,’ said Clark, still looking out of the window. ‘Or I will.’

‘Can you see anything?’ Gail asked again, this time more urgently.

‘What? No, nothing.’ Clark walked away from the window as Nathan was still sobbing. ‘I told you to shut him up,’ he yelled, taking two strides over to

Nathan and slapping him round the face, knocking him to the ground.

Then Ruth erupted. Before Matt had the chance to react, she leapt over at Clark, almost crossing the room in one bound. 'You bastard!' she screamed, leaping onto his back. Wrapping her legs around him, she tore at his hair, raking his face with her nails. He staggered around, trying to get her off, dropping his gun in the process.

Gail remained frozen in shock, not knowing what to do. Her right hand was still pointing her revolver, but now she was covering a blank space. Ignoring her weapon, Matt dove down to Nathan, picking him up and cradling him.

'It's all right,' he whispered. 'Daddy's got you now.'

By now, Clark had shaken Ruth off. She lay in a crumpled heap. They both noticed the gun he had dropped lying on the floor. Both made for it, but before either of them could reach it, there was a loud *crack.* Silently, Ruth slid down onto the floor, and crumpled in a heap on the corner. Matt shielded Nathan from this sight, and looked up at Gail. She was standing on the same spot, her arm still outstretched, holding the gun, which was smoking slightly.

'Quick. Let's go,' Clark barked at Gail, who remained frozen to the spot. 'Gail!' he repeated. 'Let's go.'

Gail appeared to come out of her trance. Not even looking down at Matt and Nathan, she ran after Clark. Matt could see the door by which Clark was standing led to the fire escape.

Matt looked over at Ruth's still form, and stayed where he was, cradling his son in his arms.

Chapter Forty-Eight

MATT COULD HEAR shouting and commotion coming from the fire escape. Then a couple of shots being fired. He could hear footsteps coming up the iron stairs. He looked up and, flustered and out of breath, Gail came running back in. She was not holding her gun. She ran past Matt and Nathan and out into the corridor leading to the building next door. He could hear her pull open the bolts, then swearing as she realised she needed keys.

It turned out she did not need keys after all as there was a loud crash and the door flew off. Gail screamed. Still holding Nathan, Matt leaned over and looked up the corridor. The door had indeed been broken open, and Matt could see the large form of Lieutenant Weber in the doorway. Weber grabbed hold of Gail, and manhandled her against the wall, cuffing her hands behind her back. Her thin slight frame was no match for his burly figure as he almost threw her into the room.

'Matt, are you and the boy okay….Jesus Christ!' he exclaimed as he saw Ruth's body. He rushed over to her and knelt down beside her. Felt her pulse, then put his ear to her mouth. He pulled out his phone and speed dialled.

''This is Weber here. I need an ambulance like five minutes ago. Fifth Floor, 680 East 58th Street.'

'An ambulance?' Matt croaked. 'She's alive…?'

'Just,' said Weber. 'Touch and go.' He looked over at Gail, who was sitting on the floor, her hands cuffed behind her back. 'Was it just her?'

'No, there's another,' Matt said. 'Danny Clark. Remember him?'

'The son of a bitch,' said Weber. He walked over to Gail. 'Where'd he go? He won't get far downstairs. There's two squad cars down there.'

'Fuck you.' Gail turned herself round and faced the wall.

Weber turned round to Matt. 'He must have gone up. Gotten onto the roof maybe. You stay here with her. The ambulance and back-up will be here soon.' He coughed and took a deep breath.

'I'll go.' Matt stood up. He stood Nathan up and rubbed his head. 'You stay here with the Lieutenant, sport. Help him look after Mummy.'

'No way,' said Weber. 'No way you -'

'You go up there,' said Matt, 'and you really will have a heart attack. I owe you one. Look after my family.'

He ran out to the fire escape. Looked down. Weber was right: he could see two police cars, and there was an ambulance pulling in from Sutton Place South. He took a deep breath, took a hold of the handrails and began climbing up the fire escape.

There were just two more floors to the roof. On the intermediate floor there were no signs of entry, so Matt continued to the roof. Once on the roof himself, he looked around: he could see Roosevelt Island across the East River, the towers of Midtown Manhattan, and the Queensboro Bridge. He could make out the outline of a subway train crossing the bridge.

Then he saw Clark. He was on the roof also, further along, darting between elevator buildings and air conditioning equipment. As Matt began to make chase, Clark must have heard his feet on the gravel on the rooftop, and turned round. As he saw Matt following, he turned and fired a couple of shots. Matt ducked but Clark must have fired wildly as Matt did not even hear the shells ricochet.

He chased further along the roof. Although Clark was now out of sight, Matt still took the same route across the roof. As he got nearer the far end of the roof, he paused: Clark was nowhere in sight. He looked around, then suddenly Clark was upon him, leaping out from behind a wall. Matt assumed the gun was empty, otherwise Clark would have used it.

The force of the impact knocked Matt to the ground, with Clark on top. Clark grabbed the sides of Matt's head and began knocking it against the hard surface of the roof. On top of the previous bump, Matt felt himself losing consciousness again.

'I'll do the job properly this time, motherfucker,' Clark snarled.

Matt gave a push against Clark's right shoulder, and they rolled over. Now Matt was on top. Not sure what to do now, he tried to pin him down by holding his lower arm on Clark's throat. He lacked the force to do this for long, however, as Clark managed to push him off. While Matt was getting back up off the floor, Clark started to run towards the other end of the roof, where there was another fire escape. Matt made a dive at Clark's legs, but was just an inch or so too late to grab the legs. Instead, he succeeded in knocking Clark off balance.

All in one second, Clark wavered, tried and failed to correct his balance, and fell to his left, onto a dirty glass skylight. The glass panel on which he landed smashed and Clark's body disappeared into the panel frame. Clark managed to cling onto the frame. His body hung in the void. Matt looked down. The building they were on now had some kind of atrium. There was a sheer drop down to the ground, where there were numerous tables, chairs and tall artificial trees, almost reaching the skylight itself. The floor downstairs was deserted. Matt guessed it was an office cafeteria area, closed as it was Sunday.

'Help me up,' Clark called out, glancing between Matt and the drop below. Matt shuffled over to the frame.

'Help you up?' he spat. 'Why should I?'

'It – it was all Gail's idea,' he said. 'Selfish little cunt.'

'And Aki Watanabe?' Matt asked. 'Her as well?'

'That was Gail's idea as well. She's evil, man, evil. Help me up.'

Matt stood up at the frame, looking down at Clark and the floor below.

'You hurt my son,' he said calmly.

'What?' screamed Clark. One hand had slipped off; now he was hanging by the other. Panic stricken he looked desperately at the remaining hand, then up at Matt. He tried twisting his body in mid-air to try to get his hand onto the frame again. 'I can't hold on much longer. Please.'

'You hurt my son,' Matt said again.

Then, Clark's weight was too much for one hand. He lost his grip and, with a scream, plummeted down to the floor below.

Matt watched him fall, brushing against one of the trees and landing on one of the empty tables below. The table collapsed, knocking over two wooden chairs in the process. Table, chairs, and Danny Clark's body now lay on the floor below. As Matt leaned over and stared down at Clark's prone body, a dark shape grew from the head as he lay on the ground.

Matt stood up and turned away. As he turned round he saw a figure standing by the fire escape, watching.

It was Lieutenant Weber.

Chapter Forty-Nine

LIMPING SLIGHTLY, MATT slowly made his way over to the fire escape where Weber was waiting. The Lieutenant was leaning on the iron banister. He seemed out of breath. He said nothing as Matt approached, out of breath himself.

Matt opened his mouth to speak, but stopped as two other men appeared at the top of the fire escape. They joined Weber on the roof. One was in police uniform.

'What's happened up here, Sam?' the officer out of uniform asked. Matt glanced anxiously at Weber.

'The suspect attacked Mr Gibbons here,' Weber answered. 'Lost his balance and fell through the skylight. Mr Gibbons tried to save him, but…'

The officer nodded. 'Okay. I see.' He looked at Matt. 'Do you need medical attention?' he asked.

Matt looked down at the scratches on his hands. Shook his head. 'No, I'm okay.'

'Go to the hospital,' said Weber. 'Take your son. Get both of you checked out. Be there when your wife comes round.'

The NYPD officers stood aside as Matt climbed back down the fire escape, followed by Weber. Matt could hear Weber puffing as he followed him down. When they had gotten down to the fifth floor, Matt turned to speak to Weber, but the Lieutenant spoke first.

'Take Nathan downstairs. There's a second ambulance there. Go with him; both of you get checked out.'

‘But -’ Matt stuttered.

‘There’s nothing else to say. Get.’

Matt gave Weber a brief nod which the Lieutenant acknowledged, then limped over to Nathan, who was sitting with a female uniformed officer. Nathan ran over to him as Matt kneeled down to hug him.

‘Daddy,’ he said.

‘It’s okay,’ Matt whispered into his son’s hair. ‘Daddy’s here. It’s all over now. All over.’

Then he picked his son up and carried him downstairs. Outside, on 58th Street, an ambulance was waiting. The two paramedics helped Matt and Nathan climb into the back. Matt laid Nathan down on one of the gurneys and sat next to him, holding his hand and stroking his hair. The paramedics closed the doors and Matt felt the ambulance move away.

Chapter Fifty

AFTER 9/11, WHEN over 1,500 victims needed treatment – the largest disaster response in American history – a campaign was launched to construct a new, state-of-the-art facility.

The new Emergency Center at New York Downtown Hospital was officially opened five years later. It is the only emergency facility in Lower Manhattan, and is vital to the community's millions of residents, workers and tourists.

Matt sat back in the chair in the waiting room. He looked down at Nathan, who was asleep, resting his head in Matt's lap. Matt gently stroked his hair. He rubbed his eyes and yawned.

'You look like you could use a coffee,' said a familiar voice. Matt looked up at Lieutenant Weber.

'Oh, it's you,' he smiled. 'Yes please.'

'Soda for your boy?'

'No thanks. Let him sleep.'

'Okay.' Weber left, to return a couple of minutes with two paper cups.

'Any news on your wife?' he asked as he sat next to Matt.

'Still in surgery. Just waiting for news,' replied Matt as he took a cup from the Lieutenant.

'Okay.' Weber sipped his coffee and leaned forward in his chair. 'Gail Smith has made a confession,' he said.

Matt looked over. 'Really?'

'Yeah. She and that asshole Clark had been holding your wife under duress. A kind of duress.'

‘A kind of duress? You mean she didn’t leave voluntarily?’

‘No. Not really. Let’s start from the beginning.’ He sat back and took a deep breath. ‘Her real name was Ruth Dubois. At least till she married you. Though I wonder if her using a false surname when you guys married invalidates….’

‘Mm,’ said Matt. ‘Maybe it does.’

‘Anyhow, she was originally Ruth Dubois. Raised in Rochester with Ira and Elisabeth Dubois. She was still in High School when she met Gail Smith. They became friends. One Saturday night, the two of them were out. Ruth was driving. She was DUI. On the way home, they hit a guy. Killed the poor bastard outright. Buried the body.’

‘What? You’re kidding.’

‘No, not according to Smith. The body wasn’t found until a year or so later. Naturally it was decomposed. Now, in those days, forensic science was pretty much in its infancy, so the victim was never identified.’

‘But wasn’t he missed? Dental records?’

Weber shrugged. ‘I don’t know at this time. Remember, this is what she told the NYPD officers.’

Matt nodded, staring into space.

Weber continued. ‘Well, it seems they – your wife – got away with it. Then Gail and her sleazy boyfriend -’

‘Danny Clark?’

‘Right. Daniel Clark. They had the bright idea of blackmailing her. Said they would go to the police if she didn’t do things for them.’

‘What kind of things? What was she doing?’

‘Computer stuff. Apparently Ruth is quite a genius on a computer.’

'First I've heard of that. She's okay, better than me. But not what I'd call a genius.'

'Well, it appears she is. They had her hacking into personal and company bank accounts, getting personal details, and taking victims' identities. Then making withdrawals – phantom withdrawals I understand is the term – and using the stolen identities to launder the money. Of course, in those days online security was nowhere near as robust as it is now.'

'Jesus Christ.'

'All coming as a shock to you?'

'What do you think?'

'I get that, Matt. Well, after a few months of this, Ruth had had enough. She was apparently out walking one night, when she witnessed a bad automobile accident.'

'The car wreck?'

'That's it. She saw the car blow up. Incredibly, she climbed down to the highway, underneath the overpass where the car was burning and threw her drivers licence on some burning wreckage. Then, she ceased to be Ruth Dubois. Caught a Greyhound to Boston, got a job waiting at tables, and became Ruth Levene.'

'But she had a responsible job at Cambridge Pharmaceuticals. What about social security numbers and stuff?'

'By that time, Clark had moved to Boston himself. Weird coincidence or what? He happened to bump into Ruth there one day. By that time his relationship with Gail was on-off-on. And I think she was seeing someone else at the time. But they joined up again, and started over blackmailing her. Gail's new partner – Ryan somebody…'

'Ryan Wilson. I know him. They're still together.'

'Not now they're not. He was living in Boston already, so Gail moved there. To tighten their hold on her, he gave your wife a job – quite highly paid – at Cambridge Pharmaceuticals, where he, as you know, is an office manager. Provided her with false social security details. Once again, that type of thing was easier back then. Once she was settled they started up their old game again. And he could speak with the authority of a manager when he denied she worked there.'

'More hacking?'

'Yes. They started off with customers of Cambridge Pharmaceuticals, then expanded. Made millions, apparently.'

'She did all that? Ruth did that?'

'At first, no. She apparently told them to screw themselves and go to the police if they wanted. Then they began to make implied threats to you and to your son.'

'Oh, Jesus Christ.' Matt stopped stroking Nathan's hair and held onto his body.

'Which was why,' Weber went on, 'Ruth left. Wanted to make her way here to start afresh, maybe. Maybe call for the two of you later. Or return to Boston. But Gail caught up with her before she even left Boston. She and Clark decided to go to New York with her, away from you, to set up somewhere to do this online stuff. Somewhere the ISP address couldn't be traced.'

Matt shook his head. 'I – I'm not very IT minded.'

'Me neither. But the upshot is: she left you and your son here, to protect you.' Weber paused. 'A lot to take in?'

Matt looked over and said slowly, 'When…if she

recovers, what's she looking at? In terms of jail time?'

Weber shrugged his head. 'Too early to say. There's the DUI, the various frauds; we've no idea as to the extent of what happened.'

'Oh.' Matt looked down at Nathan and continued stroking his hair. Nathan stirred slightly.

'But,' Weber continued, 'at this time we only have Gail Smith's version of events. If Ruth denies what she told us, then – then we'll have to see. There are some mitigating circumstances.'

'What circumstances?' Matt asked.

'Well, the threats Clark and Smith made against you. And that text message she sent you. The one which led us to them.'

'Do you think she knew you could trace it? That she did it on purpose?'

Weber shrugged again. 'A good defence attorney would claim that.'

'What about that Japanese girl? The one I saw with Clark in that bar. Akira…'

'Akira Watanabe? Yes, well; she was his girlfriend. Or at least they were sleeping together. It's quite simple: she discovered what the three of them were doing. Challenged Clark – he must have been at her apartment at the time – and he killed her. The clever son of a bitch made it look like an accident. I guess he just held her head underwater in the bath until…. Or just hit her with the shower head.'

'You said there were marks on the back of her neck.'

'Yeah, I did. The initial theory was that they were caused by the impact of the shower head. I wasn't convinced.'

'Where he held her down?'

‘Possibly. She said Clark did it all on his own. Not sure about that. But we’ll see. After he or they killed Ms Watanabe, they removed all traces of him from the place. Nobody would know he’d even been there.’

‘The son of a bitch.’

‘Yeah.’ Weber put his hand on Matt’s shoulder. ‘You never did like him, did you?’

Matt shook his head.

‘No death penalty in Massachusetts, I’m afraid,’ said Weber.

Matt shrugged. ‘Doesn’t matter.’

‘What are you going to do now?’ Weber asked, standing up.

‘Not sure yet. Wait around here, I guess.’

‘It could be ages before there’s any news. You look dead beat. Why not book into a local hotel, get some rest, and come back in the morning? You can leave your number with them here.’

‘Yeah. I might just do that.’

‘Look, I need to go now.’

‘Back up to your sister-in-laws?’

‘Jeez, no. Back to Boston. But you have my number, don’t you? Just in case.’

‘Yeah. I do.’

‘See you then. Look after yourself.’

Weber stretched and began to saunter off.

‘Sam?’ Matt called out. Weber turned round. ‘Thanks. For everything.’

Weber winked. ‘You just stay out of trouble when you get back home.’

Matt smiled and nodded, and looked back down at his son. Nathan stirred again and muttered something unintelligible.

Matt looked around. Around at the medical staff and members of the public milling about. He could hear a female voice over the PA system, trying to page a doctor.

He took a deep breath. Weber was right: he should book him and Nathan into a hotel. Somewhere near here.

He looked down at Nathan and stroked his hair again.

He would get a hotel. But later.

Chapter Fifty-One

'YOU WANT EGGS?' Matt called out a few days later, his voice competing with the sound of Daffy Duck and Bugs Bunny on the television and the first batch of eggs cooking on the stove.

No answer. Matt shrugged and continued stirring the eggs.

'More Coco Snaps, Daddy,' called out a voice from the table behind him.

'Hold on a second,' said Matt, quickly turning some eggs over.

'I'll get them, Daddy,' came the reply.

'No, wait. I'll -' Matt moved the pan off the stove and turned round, just in time to see his five year old son lean over and knock the cereal box on the floor, spilling its contents over the floor.

'Oh, Nathan, no,' Matt wailed as he knelt down to pick up the box.

'Sorry, Daddy,' said Nathan quietly.

Leaning over, Matt reached under the sink and pulled out a small dustpan and brush. He swept up the mess and emptied the grains into a bin. Stood up and put the box back on the table.

'More Snaps, then?'

Nathan thought for a few seconds, then said, 'No. I don't think so.'

'Fine. Want some eggs then? Or just toast?'

'Just toast please, Daddy.'

'Okay. Let me just finish the eggs.'

Matt turned back to the pan of eggs.

'Just toast please, Daddy.'

'Yes, I heard, sport. Just hold a second.'

'And jelly.'

'Is it nice to be back at Bambinos?' Matt asked, through a mouthful of toast.

'U-huh.'

'Well, don't forget you won't be there tomorrow.'

'Won't I? Why not?'

'I told you. We're going away for the weekend.'

'We are? Where are we going?'

'Have you forgotten already? We're putting a few clothes and things in a bag, and first of all we're driving over to New York to see Mommy.'

'Ah, yes. I remember.'

'Maybe we'll stop off on the way and get her some flowers. To keep by her bed.'

'And some chocolate?'

'Maybe. As long as you don't eat it on the way. And as long as the doctors say it's okay for her to eat it.'

'Everybody eats chocolate, Daddy.'

'Hm. Then – once we've visited Mommy, we're going to drive over to see your grandma.'

'What about Grandpa? Won't we be seeing him?'

'No. Different grandma. Remember what I told you?'

'Er…'

'Grandma Estelle and Grandpa are my mommy and daddy. But Grandma Elisabeth is Mommy's mommy. Remember now?'

It came back. 'Yes, you told me yesterday.'

'Good.' Matt stood up. 'Now eat up your toast while I go upstairs for a minute.'

'So that means I have two grandmas?'

'That's right. You have two grandmas.'

'Cool,' Nathan said, taking a huge bite of toast.

'Back in a minute.' Matt turned and left Nathan alone in the kitchen finishing his breakfast. A quick bathroom visit, then time to take him to kindergarten. He paused on the stairs, smiling as he could hear Nathan in the kitchen, talking to himself.

'I have *two* grandmas. How cool is that?'

THE END

Also by Philip Cox

AFTER THE RAIN

Young, wealthy, handsome - Adam Williams is sitting in a bar in a small town in Florida.

Nobody has seen him since.

With the local police unable to trace Adam, his brother Craig and a workmate, Ben Rook, fly out to find him.

However, nothing could have prepared them for the bizarre cat-and-mouse game into which they are drawn as they seek to pick up Adam's trail and discover what happened to him that night.

Download from:

UK: **www.amazon.co.uk/dp/B005FZ0RAI**

US: **www.amazon.com/dp/B005FZ0RAI**

DARK EYES OF LONDON

When Tom Raymond receives a call from his ex-wife asking to meet him, he is both surprised and intrigued – maybe she wants a reconciliation?

However, his world is turned upside down when she falls under a tube train on her way to meet him.

Refusing to accept that Lisa jumped, Tom sets out to investigate what happened to her that evening.

Soon, he finds he must get to the truth before some very dangerous people get to him…

COMING 2013

1 NIGHT ONLY

Los Angeles, late September, and the hot Santa Ana winds are blowing, covering the city with a thin layer of dust from the Mojave and Sonoran deserts.

That night, there are three mysterious, unexplained deaths.

The official view is that they are all unrelated. The deceaseds had no connection, and all died in different parts of the city.

However, Police Detective Sam Leroy has other ideas, and begins to widen the investigation.

But he meets resistance from the most unexpected quarter, and when his life and that of his loved ones are threatened, he faces a choice: back off, or do what he knows he must do…

Read on for a sneak preview….

Chapter One

THE SANTA ANA winds are dry and warm - sometimes hot – winds that affect coastal Southern California and northern Baja California from September to March. They range from hot to cold, depending on the temperatures in the regions of origins, namely the Great Basin, which stretches from the Sierra Nevada range in the west to the Wasatch Range in Utah, and Northern Mexico up to Oregon, and the upper Mojave Desert.

The air from the Mojave Desert is relatively dense owing to its coolness and aridity, and tends to channel down the valleys and canyons in gusts which can attain hurricane force at times. As the air descends, it not only becomes drier, but warmer. The southern California coastal region gets some of its hottest weather of the year

Tonight was no exception. A warm and dry blast of air blew down the mountain passes. Warm and dry, and easily exceeding 40 mph, they brought with them a thin layer of reddish dust. They were hot too: the Santa Monica weather station's instruments were recording 98 degrees.

The man staggered along the empty road. Dressed only in torn white shorts, he weaved back and forth across the yellow centre line. He could make out some kind of reflection on the wet pavement below. He felt down and rubbed his leg. There were scratch marks down to his ankle from the tumble he had taken down the hillside from above. He stopped and looked round, disorientated, blinking.

Where was he?

Somewhere high up, he was sure; he could hear, or thought he could hear the muffled rumbling of traffic below.

But where exactly?

And how did he get here?

He stopped and looked around. He could make out lights above and below, but the road he was on was devoid of any buildings. It was only the light from the moon which gave him any form of illumination.

There was mist around: as the road disappeared round a bend ahead, and behind as it receded into the dark.

He felt cold, even though the strong winds blowing down the hillside were hot. He wiped the dust from his eyes, and continued along the road.

He needed to find shelter, some help.

After a few more yards' shuffling, he stopped again. A dog was barking. He looked around, trying to figure out where the sound was coming from. A dog would mean someone's house.

The barking seemed to be coming from below. Maybe the lights below were from a house. That meant a phone.

A phone. He could remember using a cell phone earlier that evening. Could remember putting the phone back onto the belt clip he used. Involuntarily, he felt down to his waist. All he could feel was the elastic of his torn, dirty shorts.

Where were his clothes? How did he end up here?

He started to walk again, this time towards where he thought the barking, which had now stopped, came from. He rubbed the side of his leg and looked at his hand. Blood. Then looked at his leg. The scratches were bleeding more; not profusely, but they would need attention.

He veered over to the right hand side of the road, so now he was walking partly on the pavement, partly on the bumpy verge.

He paused as he could make out a new source of light. They got closer. Two small separate lights, slightly diffused in the mist. Then the sound of a car engine.

By now he could make out the vehicle as it came round the bend. It was not coming at him very fast, no doubt because of the mist, which seemed to thicken as the road went downhill. He staggered over to the centre of the road as the car came round the bend. Feebly, he waved his arms in the air. The driver braked, and the car skidded slightly as it came to a halt around ten feet past the man. He ran up to the driver's door. A grey haired man was driving, with a woman of similar age sitting in front with him. The driver wound down his window.

'What in hell's going on?' the driver asked. 'I could have…' He stopped as he noticed the figure was wearing only shorts. 'Jesus H!' he exclaimed.

'Please, I need help…' The man leaned on the car roof and leaned over.

'Look, I'm sorry, I….'

'Can I borrow your cell phone? I need to make a call.'

The woman leaned forward and saw him. 'Tell him to go away, Gus.'

Gus looked over at her and back at the man. 'I – I, er…'

'Please, mister. Go away. You're scaring us,' the woman said.

'I just need a cell phone for a minute…'

'Sorry, pal,' said Gus as he wound up the window.

'We don't want any trouble.'

'But I just…'

Gus wound up the window and the car sped away into the darkness and into the mist.

He watched as the red tail lights faded away into the mist. After a few moments' pause, he continued to shuffle on. He cried out as he stepped on something sharp. He lifted up his leg and pulled out a sharp stone which had gotten embedded in the sole of his bare foot. Then moved on again.

Looking down, he could make out some lights. Maybe that was where the barking was coming from. This was the direction from which he could still hear the rumble of traffic.

He slowly stepped off the pavement and began to climb down the slope. It was steep in places but he was able to grab onto some bushes for support. As he climbed further down, the undergrowth became thicker. He tried to make out what the vegetation was. The smell seemed familiar: maybe buckbush. As he got further down, he realised he had lost sight of the lights. He panicked slightly as he lost his bearings. Looked around again. No sign of any lights now, but the ambient sound of the traffic below was still there.

He moved on again.

After twenty yards or so, the traffic noise was getting louder. Perhaps he should head for there; on a busy road he would stand a better chance of flagging someone down.

Then he missed his footing. Tried to grab a bush for support, but missed. Landing on his back, he slid down the slope. He cried out as his back was lacerated by the shrubs and rocks as he skimmed over them. He hit an obstruction, a tree stump maybe; rather than stopping his descent, it served to knock him sideways so now he was rolling down. He tried to put his hands in front of him to protect his face, but his momentum was too great. As he rolled down, one side of his head hit some hard ground. Just then, his fall stopped.

He lay there, dazed. He thought he had reached the end of the drop as he was now lying on level ground. He felt up to his temple: it was wet and sticky. His vision was blurred. He stood up and moved on. Suddenly under his feet he could feel not ground and brush, but a smooth surface. Not unlike the pavement above. Still disorientated he staggered forward.

His last sensations were a blinding white light, a loud, deep blare. Then, a microsecond of intense pain as something weighing 35000 lbs slammed into him.

Then nothing.

Thanks for reading *She's Not Coming Home.*

Hope you enjoyed it.

Now you have finished, PLEASE

- Tell a friend about *She's Not Coming Home*. If they don't have a Kindle, a PC, or I-devices, *She's Not Coming Home* is available in paperback, also available from amazon.

- Update Twitter or Facebook about this book

- Log onto amazon and post a review

Thanks

www.philipcox.moonfruit.com

Printed in Great Britain
by Amazon.co.uk, Ltd.,
Marston Gate.